HILDA

SADIE'S SPRING SURPRISE

Debbie Viggiano

ISBN: 9798425516985

www.debbieviggiano.com

Remembering Trudy Beagle
I hope you are enjoying Heaven's endless supply
of chew-chews

Chapter One

'He's gorgeous,' I murmured, nudging my bestie to pay attention. 'Look at those eyes. You could melt in them.'

'I prefer the blue pair over there,' said Charlotte, glancing after the guy who had briefly left us to confer. 'Do you think he's single? Sadie?' She tugged at my sleeve. 'Are you even listening?' Now she was nudging me.

I tore my eyes away from the dear little beagle sitting at my feet. He was gazing soulfully up at me, tail wagging like a conductor leading the orchestra through a particularly frenzied piece of music.

Charlotte and I were standing in the walled exercise area of a local animal sanctuary. Charlotte thought a cat would make a far less complicated companion than a dog, and she had a point. But cats – while lovely – were independent creatures. I wanted a mate. A buddy. One to take walks with. To get me out of the house. To hopefully engage with other dog owners. A pooch would force me to do these things, whereas a cat would enable me to carry on with what I'd been doing for far too long – mostly curling up in a ball and mimicking a hibernating creature. I'd spent most of last winter doing just that. Snuggling under the duvet in bed. Later, nestling on the sofa hugging a cosy throw while overdosing on Netflix.

My family had lost patience with this behaviour. Okay, we all had our own way of nursing a broken heart. But taking to our beds – or sofas – didn't meet with my family's approval. Well, in the beginning it had. But not now. Not all this time later.

Mum had recently told me to pull myself together. My sister had been equally firm, saying any lingering sorrow was indulgent self-pity. She had conveniently forgotten all about the time she'd found herself suddenly single. Flora had been shattered. But that was because she was the one who had always done the dumping and had never before experienced being on the receiving end. Her malaise had only lasted a fortnight but, boy, we'd all known about it. She'd been just like that old advert – make a drama out of a crisis. Whereas I'd simply retreated with my grief. Licked the metaphorical wounds in private. Okay, it had taken place over a longer period, but then I'd been engaged to be married. Whereas Flora, the younger sister, had still been playing the field. Still was.

My withdrawal from the world hadn't been a conscious decision. I'd simply been enveloped in sorrow ever since circumstances had dictated the cancellation of my November wedding. Like a Victorian maiden having the vapours, I'd instead begun a love affair with my bed, surfacing only for Christmas and then, as January rolled around, the absolute necessities in life. And whilst I didn't stay under the duvet for the entirety of the following year, let's just say that I welcomed the end of each day and fell into bed as if the mattress was a lover's pair of arms.

My best friend had often bullied me to join her for a drink at the local, and I'd obliged. And then Charlotte had suddenly found herself single too. Whilst she'd not been devastated about her breakup, she'd nonetheless been more than happy to pop in and share my throw while watching the telly. The pair of us had worked our way through many a bottle of wine and an awful lot of salt and vinegar crisps.

And then, just as the most recent hard winter had suddenly given way to a soft spring, it was as if the pale sunshine had finally signalled something within to unfurl.

Like the nodding daffodils and snowdrops now bursting forth in the various gardens of Little Waterlow, it was as if my very essence had stirred and said, "Okay, enough. Time to put out some fresh shoots and start feeling your way out of a dark place."

My father, milder mannered than Mum and Flora, had suggested I rescue a dog. Dad's words had floated around in my head, then landed in my frozen heart. A thaw had begun to take place.

I'd gone online. Done a bit of research. Checked out what breed would make the best companion in my compact home – for that, read "miniscule". Clover Cottage was a two-up-two-down affair like most of the properties that edged the narrow lanes of my rural hometown.

Mum had suggested getting a pug on the grounds of them having regal faces. She was a terrible snob. I suspect my

3

mother had only approved of my ex-fiancé because he'd had a double-barrelled name. As if that made him vaguely royal, or something.

'What about a Labrador?' Flora had suggested. 'They're meant to be super intelligent and easy to train.'

And now, on this first Saturday in March, I was at a rescue centre where a lovely Labrador had wagged her tail at me, hope in her eyes. Feeling like a traitor, I'd put my head down and walked on by. Realistically the Lab would have taken up half my front room, never mind the handkerchief-sized rear garden.

My heart had been squeezing ever since stepping over the threshold of this place. Let's face it, one's first reaction in a building like this one is to declare, "I'll have them all." Fighting emotion, I'd spotted a small tri-coloured dog who'd tried to lick the palm of my hand through the metal bars of his pen. His little face had melted my heart faster than ice-cream in a heatwave.

'Heads up,' said Charlotte, talking sideways out of her mouth. 'He's coming back.'

'Oh for goodness' sake,' I tutted. 'We've come here to check out pooches for me, not men for you. Put your tongue in. You look like one of these rescue dogs, panting away.'

'I can't help it if a handsome stranger is having a major effect on me. It's probably my hormones sending out SOS signals to my biological clock. Reminding me that I'm thirty next birthday and that there's still no man on the horizon.' Charlotte's mouth drooped. 'Time is marching on and I want to settle down and–'

'How are you both getting along?' asked the man, giving us both the benefit of an admittedly attractive smile. He reminded me of Leonardo DiCaprio in his heyday. Not my cup of tea, but most definitely Charlotte's. But then, to be fair, she liked most men. They were all in with a chance so long as they met two requirements – they had to have their own teeth and hair. There had been one disastrous long-ago date where she'd been in a passionate clinch with a guy, reached up to tangle her fingers in his hair and promptly pulled off his toupee. Cue much screaming from both sides. And no, there hadn't been any further dates. Charlotte was now licking her lips, like a dog anticipating treats.

'Oh we're getting along just fine,' she said cosily. 'This is Sadie Harding. She's my bestie.'

The man's smile widened as he tried not to laugh. 'That's great, but I was actually enquiring about how your friend might be bonding with our resident beagle.'

'Silly me,' Charlotte demurred, batting her eyelashes flirtatiously. With her long dark hair, huge brown eyes, and trademark red lipstick, she was a natural head turner. She pointed to the badge on his sweater. 'So, you're Luke.'

'I am.'

'What a lovely name,' she twinkled. 'In fact, it's one of my favourites.'

Standard Charlotte patter.

Luke twinkled back before turning his attention to me. 'What do you think?'

'He's adorable,' I beamed, stooping to scratch the dog's head. 'What's his name?'

'Ah.' Luke looked rueful. 'That's a bit of a story. When he was brought in for re-homing, we were told his name was, um' – he lowered his voice to a whisper – 'er, Dickhead.'

My smile wobbled, and Charlotte snorted.

'So we renamed him,' Luke hastily continued.

'Dick?' Charlotte suggested.

'No.' Luke shook his head.

I mentally heaved a sigh of relief. This little beagle didn't look like a Dick. And I don't mean that facetiously.

Luke gave me a reassuring look. 'He's now called Willy.'

'Willy?' I said, aghast. 'But he doesn't look like a Willy.'

'Certainly none that I've ever seen,' Charlotte murmured.

I had visions of taking this little beagle home. Letting him off-lead to run in the local woods. Yodelling, "Willy! Will-eeeeee!" and feeling a tad self-conscious. Not to mention if his recall was lousy and me resorting to asking dog walkers, "Have you seen my Willy?" No. That name would have to go.

'Oh dear. He now answers to it,' said Luke apologetically.

'I'll change it to William,' I said. 'It's not so different. I'm sure he'll catch on.'

'Does that mean you want him?' asked Luke, looking delighted.

'Yes,' I said impulsively. 'Subject to you telling me his history,' I added. I didn't want Luke thinking I hadn't properly thought this decision through.

'There's not much to tell about Willy... I mean, William. He was brought in approximately a month ago by a distraught woman who couldn't stop crying. She said the dog's name was a joke that had stuck. She cited her reasons for rehoming him as not having the time to give him proper walks and attention.'

'I suppose she was crying because she was upset to let him go,' I said, scratching William's ear.

Luke pulled a face. 'I'm not sure. She was sobbing hard, but it was like... angry crying rather than, you know, tears of despair. She certainly didn't give William a backward glance when she left.'

'How old is he?'

'Coming up to twelve months.'

'He's a pedigree,' said Charlotte. 'Does he have any papers?'

'No, unfortunately not.' Luke shook his head. 'We did ask the original owner, but she said she'd lost them. She was very hard to extract information from. Her whole attitude was one of dumping the dog and scuttling off. I suppose everyone handles rehoming a beloved pet differently.'

'Perhaps I could have her details and follow up with a phone call?' I suggested. 'After all, I'd love to know more about William's background.'

'I'm afraid I can't pass on that information. It's

confidential.' Luke noted my disappointment. 'It's a two-way thing,' he hastily assured. 'Likewise, we don't tell former owners where their pet has gone. It's our policy. Fresh starts for all parties.'

'Right,' I said, blowing out my cheeks. 'Well, are you able to share what you've learnt about William while he's been staying here?'

'Absolutely,' Luke smiled, happy to be back on familiar territory. 'He's an absolute poppet. Very sweet-natured. Extremely sociable with the other dogs when they're let out to exercise. He likes a fuss and loves his grub.'

'Perfect,' I said, feeling reassured.

'I wonder why he wasn't snapped up immediately by someone else?' Charlotte frowned.

Luke's mouth quirked. 'Because he's a beagle.'

'What's wrong with beagles?' I said, faintly alarmed.

'They have an extremely low boredom threshold. Do you work?'

'Yes, but from home. I'm a potter. Sometimes I do events and am out of the house all day, but it's irregular.'

'My advice would be to have a dog sitter if an event takes you out of the house all day. Left to their own devices, beagles can trash a home in minutes.'

'By trash, what exactly do you mean?' I asked nervously.

'Oh, you know. Chewing legs off chairs. Chomping on sofas. Ripping cushions apart. Busting open bins. That sort of thing. They're completely food-obsessed, so don't leave your lunch on the table while you go to the cupboard for

8

condiments, or your meal will be stolen. Gone in a nanosecond.'

'We'll do some training classes,' I said firmly.

'The breed is also deemed untrainable,' said Luke cheerfully. 'Are you sure you still want him?'

I looked down at William's appealing little face. He'd been sitting at my feet for the last ten minutes and not moved a muscle. He couldn't be that much of a reprobate.

'Yes, please. I have a feeling this little fella is going to change my life.'

Little did I know how much.

Chapter Two

Two weeks later William's training was still very much a case in progress.

The intention to lay down clear boundaries had disappeared on the first night. My bedroom – intended to be a dog-free zone – was now William's sleeping quarters too.

On his first night at Clover Cottage, William had howled until two in the morning. Finally exhausted – me, not the dog – I'd brought his basket upstairs and placed it at the foot of the bed. As I'd finally started to drift off, a solid lump had landed on the quilt then flopped down against my leg, sighing contentedly. I'd been too knackered to protest. It seemed William was also training me. "If you want sleep, comply!". Round One to William Beagle.

On the upside, he seemed to be housetrained. There hadn't been any accidents. When he wanted to relieve himself, he tapped the back door with his paw, whereupon I opened it and he'd attend to his morning ablutions. A further tap on the door would let me know when he was ready to come back in. The dog training book I'd purchased had *sort of* paid off. William could now sit, stay, and come to heel providing there was a chewy reward. But without a biscuit, there wasn't a hope in hell of him obliging.

Conversation with other dog walkers hadn't been quite the positive experience I'd hoped for on account of William launching into high-pitched baying every time we encountered someone coming in the opposite direction. Socialising with other dogs was something to be worked on.

Meanwhile, Charlotte was keeping me company on some of my dog walks. Before leaving the rescue centre, she'd slipped Luke her phone number with a jolly, "Call me if there's anything else that comes to mind about William." He'd responded with, "If I remember any other details, I'll be sure to get my wife to call you." Charlotte had visibly deflated.

The doorbell rang, and William instantly began baying. Grabbing hold of his collar, I opened the door to find Charlotte standing on the step.

'Hello,' I said, moving out of the way to let her in, and hanging on tightly to William's collar. 'I wasn't expecting to see you this morning.'

'I'm meant to be getting to grips with a new piece of furniture, but instead found myself going out the front door in search of a serious sugar fix.'

Charlotte had her own small business, mainly the upcycling of furniture. Sometimes she came to commercial events with me. Many a time my pots had made an arresting sight on her revamped dressers and shelving units.

'I picked up something for you too.' She rummaged in her tote and produced a couple of paper bags. 'Chloe was getting rid of yesterday's unsold cake. Freebies! So I took advantage. It's not stale. She simply wanted to clear the cake stands for some freshly baked goodies.'

'Lovely,' I said, shutting the door behind her and letting go of William.

'Has he been for walkies yet?'

'No, I was just going to have a coffee before taking him out.' I went through to the kitchen, Charlotte trailing after me. 'Want one too?'

'Oooh, yes please.' She flopped down on a chair at the table and William immediately stood up on his hind legs, trying to sniff the goodies. 'No, darling.' She tapped him lightly on the nose. 'Cake isn't good for doggies.' William let out a yip to say he didn't agree. Charlotte looked at me enquiringly. 'Met any lush men while out walking?'

'Nope,' I shook my head, waiting for the kettle to whine to the boil. 'What about you?'

'I caught the eye of a guy at a house clearance place.'

'Oh yes?' I said, pouring water into mugs.

'But he wasn't really my type.'

'Too many tattoos?'

'Nah, too many facial studs. It would be like trying to snog a porcupine.'

'Right,' I said, setting the coffees down along with a couple of side plates.

She sighed. 'It's a shame Luke turned out to be married. I really fancied him.'

'Plenty more fish, as they say.'

I pulled out a chair and sat down while Charlotte put the

cake on the plates.

'But that's the thing, Sadie. There really aren't.'

'What do you mean?'

'Well, look at this place.' She flung her arms wide, presumably to encompass our tiny village. 'Little Waterlow isn't exactly heaving with heartthrobs.'

'What about Jack Barrowman's son? He's single.'

'Ernie? Do me a favour,' she snorted. 'He spends ninety percent of his time with his dad's dairy herd. He was queuing behind me at the post office the other day. I knew it was him before the door even swung open.'

'Ah, don't tell me. A waft of *Eau de Moo.*'

'You've got it.'

'Perhaps he's immune to the smell.'

'Yeah, but I'm not. Anyway, never mind my empty love life. How's yours?'

I gave her an eyeroll as I bit into the cake. 'You know perfectly well' – I reprimanded, licking buttercream off my fingers – 'that it's as arid as yours.'

'Is William still sharing the bed?'

'Yes, and I wish I'd put my foot down from Day One. His snoring is as bad as a man's. And he farts,' I added, as William placed his paws against my leg, making a small trump in the process. 'I had no idea beagles were so windy.' I flapped the air as William fixed me with a beseeching pair of eyes. *Please share the cake. I haven't been fed for over an hour.* 'Down!' I said sternly. William obeyed, but instead homed in on Charlotte.

'Oh, yuck. Your dog is dribbling. Anyway' – she waved William away – 'you seem a lot more cheerful since your four-legged friend came to live at Clover Cottage.'

'Do I?' I mused. 'Yes, now that you mention it, I do feel happier.'

William was now gazing intently at the cake plates, as if willing them to slide off the table and fall at his feet.

'I haven't heard you mention you-know-who in over a week,' said Charlotte approvingly.

My mouth drooped slightly as a picture of my ex-fiancé came to mind. Irritably I pushed the image away. That chapter of my life had long closed but – just like this glorious cake – it was something I couldn't always stay away from.

Chapter Three

I first met Felix Barrington-Jones a little over three years ago in London.

I'd been invited up to the Smoke via a gallery's newsletter advising of an exhibition of contemporary ceramics. It was a bit of a trek, but I'd gone along seeking fresh inspiration. I'd also wanted to check out what was popular and what wasn't.

I'd admired various award-winning hand-built pieces and related groups of vessels, each object informing the next. I'd also raised eyebrows at the work of one sculptor who'd used clay to express her responses to the environment. The results were risk-taking, to put it mildly. As I'd stared at a black block covered in indecipherable graphic line work, I'd privately wondered if anybody would be mad enough to part with the five thousand pounds asking price. *The Emperor's New Clothes* had sprung to mind.

The gallery had been very elegant. All stark white walls and ash flooring. I'd accepted a glass of champagne from a passing waiter and moved around, pausing next to another strange piece entitled *Farmer's Field*. As my own stomping ground was rural and surrounded by rolling farmland, woodland, and endless meandering hedgerows, I'd stared in bemusement at the artist's representation. Another black block, but this time with a tree etched into the clay's centre – and when I say "tree" I use that in the loosest sense of the word. The depiction of twigs was more like the work of a five-year-old. And the artist wanted *how much*?

'What do you think?' said a man's voice.

I'd looked up and found myself gazing into the turned-down eyes of a guy who wouldn't have looked out of place in a rugby team. Mike Tindall sprang to mind. Not my usual type. I'd sipped my drink thoughtfully.

'Er, well, it's certainly very cutting edge,' I said diplomatically.

'It's definitely that,' he agreed. 'The stoneware is slab-built with a tin glaze interior. The exterior is decorated with monochrome slip and careful *sgraffito* markings.'

He was knowledgeable. Too knowledgeable. Oh, help.

'Are you the artist?'

'No,' he grinned. 'My sister is, but you should have seen your face! You think it's a load of rubbish, right?'

I'd opened my mouth to say something tactful about the piece, but he'd waved a dismissive hand.

'It's okay, you can be honest. I take the rise out of Arabella all the time. She spends hours in her studio, hand-building as a making process, all the while spouting arty crap. "Today I'm embracing textured and carved surfaces that possess a raw, tactile quality." Or, "I'm aiming at achieving earthenware blacks and greys through raku, wood and charcoal saggar firing and the work will be both organic and elemental in nature, sitting in harmonious dialogue with one another." I mean' – he'd snorted down his nose – 'is she even talking English?'

I'd grinned, deciding that I quite liked his frankness, even if his words might be anathema to some creative types.

'I was going to say that the wood kiln had produced perfect dark greys and matt glazes providing a wide range of textures and densities of surface and body, reflecting the varied geology of the land.'

He'd paled. 'Christ, you sound like Arabella. Are you exhibiting here too?'

I'd laughed and drained my glass.

'No. But I *am* an artist, although my work is… more traditional.'

'I like traditional,' he nodded. 'And – if I may be so bold – I also like tall, slim redheads with slate grey eyes.' Okay, a smooth talker, but the words had been delivered with an impish grin, as if he were mocking his own chat-up line thus allowing him to get away with it. 'Do you fancy escaping this place and having something to eat? I can promise some fine dining involving plain porcelain plates that won't have you searching to find expression – consciously or unconsciously – nor have you complaining about the china missing a deep essence that fails to connect one human being with another.'

I'd giggled. The man was no pin up, but he'd made up for it with oodles of confidence, a direct manner, and – I would later find out – buckets of charm.

I'd inclined my head to one side, as if considering his

17

invitation. Then, using the same playfully deprecating tone as him had said, 'That sounds most delightful. I accept.'

And that was how it began.

Chapter Four

'So is William helping you forget about you-know-who?' said Charlotte.

We were bowling along a muddy bridle path that cut straight through a field. In a few more weeks it would likely be full of grazing sheep. Currently the pasture was being rested. Even so, the local farmer wouldn't appreciate William cavorting – and possibly pooping – in his many acres, so for now my beagle was on an extendable lead.

'Sadie?' Charlotte prompted.

'Yes,' I said, deliberately vague. 'I heard you the first time.'

'And?'

'And… yeah. I guess so. Having a dog is keeping me nicely preoccupied, especially when I'm in my garden studio. William is great company. Doesn't mind me wittering on when I'm working on commissions. That reminds me. There's a big arts and crafts exhibition in May. Fancy teaming up?'

'Where?'

'Sevenoaks.'

'Why not. There's less of the mud-and-welly-brigade

over there. The occupants are' – she wrinkled her nose in consideration – 'more of the brown-brogues-and-shoe-polish category. You never know, we might even meet some dashing executive types. Wouldn't that be nice,' she beamed. 'A couple of guys who dabble in the money markets and want to wine and dine us at The Ivy before saying that our personalities are so sparkling and our looks so stunning that they can't imagine getting through the rest of their lives without us by their sides – cue the moment they go down on one knee and propose.'

'Those types usually bray instead of laugh and are prone to boring the pants off women.'

'Hey, as nobody else is getting my pants off, I'll take that,' Charlotte quipped.

I tutted. 'Right, I'll fill out the forms and copy you in on the dates.'

'Meanwhile, keep your eyes peeled for sexy male dog walkers striding manfully through Little Waterlow's countryside.'

'What, you mean a vision in green Barbour coats and sensible hiking boots?'

'Well we're not much better,' Charlotte countered. 'Look at the pair of us. You're in Primark joggers and a hoodie that looks like it should be consigned to William's basket, and I'm in ancient jeans that are distressed purely because of their age and nothing to do with fashion.'

'But we scrub up nicely,' I pointed out.

'I think I've forgotten what we look like wearing make-up, it's been so long.'

I shrugged. Personally, I found it pointless glamming up when, most days, the only seen neighbour was the nosy cow on the other side of the garden fence. I'm talking about the one whose vocabulary was limited to *moo*, not pensioners Fred and Mabel Plaistow next door.

We climbed over a stile and entered a cluster of woodland that joined up with Trosley Country Park. Moments later we were on a long meandering trail overhung by a thick umbrella of branches. This route was a favourite with dog walkers due to it providing shade in summer and shelter from the elements in winter.

'Why don't you let William off the lead for a little while?' Charlotte suggested.

'Not yet.' I shook my head. 'It's early days. Apart from anything else, what if he buggered off? Or caught a squirrel or a rabbit? Luke said beagles like to hunt.'

'Wow, talk of the devil,' Charlotte muttered, nudging me.

I looked ahead and, sure enough, it was the guy from the rehoming centre. Luke wasn't alone either. A woman had her arm linked through his. It was body language that spoke of companionship, but also proprietorship.

'Hey,' Charlotte dimpled, as Luke approached.

'Hello,' he smiled. 'Your faces are familiar but, forgive me, I can't recall your names.' He stooped to make a fuss of William. 'But I remember this little fella,' he laughed. William planted two muddy paws on Luke's thighs in his quest for a muzzle rub.

'Down,' I instructed. William took no notice.

'I see the dog training is coming along nicely,' he bantered.

'He's still learning,' Charlotte beamed, totally blanking the woman by Luke's side. 'And it's Charlotte,' she reminded him. 'And this is Sadie.'

'Lovely to see you both again,' he smiled. 'And this is my wife, Rachel.'

'Hello,' I said pleasantly. Rachel and Charlotte ignored each other.

'Can you recommend any decent dog training classes?' said Charlotte. 'Sadie here would love to take William to doggy school, but she's a bit shy, aren't you, hm?' Charlotte was now addressing me as if I were a simpleton. 'She wants me to come along with her.'

'That's very thoughtful and, as it happens, I do. I co-run a weekly class with my mate Carl.'

'Do you indeed?' Charlotte purred.

Rachel's mouth was disappearing into a thin line. She wasn't stupid.

'We're not exactly the Dog Whisperer, but overall, we get some decent results.'

'When and where do the classes take place?' I asked, determined to show that I did have a brain cell or three in my head and was perfectly capable of thinking and speaking for myself.

'Sunday mornings in the local park. Between nine and

ten.'

'Wonderful,' said Charlotte, fluttering her eyelashes. She'd be wobbling her bosoms next. 'Consider it a date.'

Rachel was starting to look like she was chewing a wasp.

'We'll look forward to it,' I said politely. 'Enjoy the rest of your walk.'

I took Charlotte by the elbow and propelled her forward.

'Bye Lukie,' she called over her shoulder.

'For heaven's sake,' I hissed, not quite trusting that we were out of earshot. 'Why are you flirting with a married man?'

'I was not,' Charlotte protested.

'I don't think his wife would agree. Your face was an open book.'

'Really?' said Charlotte, looking delighted. 'What did it say?'

'That you wanted to pull him into the undergrowth, wrestle him to the ground and glue your lips to his.'

'Keep going,' she chuckled.

'Not funny,' I chided. 'He's taken.'

'Yes, I did spot the battle-axe on his arm.'

'She looked cross because you were being overly cosy with her husband,' I pointed out.

'Just being friendly,' Charlotte demurred. We were now mixing with a small throng of people also walking along the trail. Fellow dog walkers. Joggers. Families out for a stroll. 'I don't mean to be horrible, but how does a woman like that

23

end up bagging a guy like him? It's not fair.'

'There's nothing wrong with Rachel's looks.'

'If you like French Bulldogs,' Charlotte muttered.

An old boy creaked past with his ancient Spaniel. He'd overheard our conversation and paused to give Charlotte a consoling pat on the arm.

'If I were fifty years younger, darlin', I'd be more than happy to whisk you down the nearest aisle.'

'And if I were fifty years older, I'd probably accept,' she said gamely, making the old boy chuckle as he tottered off.

'Bluebell Café coming up,' I pointed out. 'Fancy stopping for a sausage sandwich?'

'Why not,' Charlotte sighed. 'It's the only sausage that's currently going to provide some excitement.'

Chapter Five

'Whose turn to pay?' said Charlotte, plonking her bottom down on a wooden bench seat.

'Yours,' I replied.

'Oh, bum holes,' she groaned. 'My overdraft is getting so ridiculous the bank will soon be taking out their own overdraft to cover it.'

'I'll get it,' I sighed.

I loved Charlotte to bits, but she was chaotic with money. When she had it, she was generous and splurged. Not just on herself, but family and friends too. Many a time I'd been on the receiving end of a gorgeous pashmina or pretty lipstick because, "It was buy two and get the third free, so I bought twenty of everything. Look at all these freebies!" Her personal overdraft was a bone of contention between her and her bank manager. Sometimes she bailed herself out of financial crisis by plundering her business account – which, in turn, upset the bookkeeper.

'Thanks, sweetie,' she said sheepishly. 'The next one is definitely on me. I just need to shift that vast revamped bookcase sitting in my workshop, and then the cash will start to flow again.'

'Here, hold William while I sort out our grub.' I passed her the lead.

I was only gone for five minutes, but a lot can happen when your attention is diverted by two cappuccinos and several bangers squashed between granary slices. As I headed back to the trestle table, I saw that Charlotte was no longer alone. Luke was sitting alongside her. Charlotte was obviously pulling out all the stops entertaining him because he was laughing his head off. Body language on both sides signalled mutual attraction. Both were leaning into each other. There was no sign of Rachel. The pair of them were so invested in each other that neither had spotted William's extendable lead stretched to breaking point and my beagle attempting to mount an unattended golden retriever. I blanched. I thought he'd been sorted out in that department. Surely castrated male dogs didn't have urges. Did they? But William's thrusting hips told me otherwise. Oh for...

'Hello, again,' I said, dumping the tray down harder than necessary. Frothy milk slopped into saucers.

Neither Luke nor Charlotte immediately acknowledged me but, at the sound of my voice, William's head whipped round. He was visibly torn between continuing to hump the Retriever or get down to the more serious business of sharing sausages. The latter won. Unfortunately, William didn't have the brains to retrace his steps. Instead, he took a circuitous short cut around a guy's legs – presumably the Retriever's returning owner. The man, preoccupied with a mug of tea and a plate of chips, tripped over William's lead, and promptly went flying.

As chips rained down like confetti, William dithered. Sausage sandwich or French fries? The Retriever, not to be outdone, was first to fall upon the chips. William let out a yip of outrage that his beau had taken advantage of a head start. However, the Retriever wasn't up for sharing and warned William off with some baritone growls.

'Whose bloody dog is this?' said the man, staggering to his feet, only to be felled again as his dog furiously barrelled into William who was attempting to hoover up chips faster than a Dyson.

'For God's sake, Charlotte,' I snapped, as mayhem broke out on Table Seven.

'Wha–?'

She looked up at me in confusion. Her pupils were dilated to the size of dustbin lids.

'Hopefully see you on Sunday,' said Luke, before slipping away.

'Where's William's lead?' I demanded.

'Tied to a table leg. Blimey, what's all that racket? Sounds like someone's dog is completely out of control.' Her gaze fell upon the sandwiches. 'Oooh, yummy, I'm starving.'

Ignoring her, I ducked down, quickly unfastened the lead, then followed it around Table Six, through a gap, over to Table Seven and to the grassy patch where the felled man was muttering oaths. As he once again attempted to get to his feet, I caught sight of his face. A young Channing Tatum sprang to mind. He would have been good-looking if his hair hadn't been covered in mayo and his hazel eyes weren't blazing with anger.

'Is this your dog?' he demanded, sitting up and trying to loosen the lead wound around one ankle.

'Yes,' I said breathlessly. 'I'm so very sorry,' I grovelled, attempting to reel William in like a fisherman wrestling with a particularly large sturgeon.

William was having none of it and was now intent on licking the mayonnaise off the man. His tail was wagging furiously, and he was making happy snuffling noises. The man finally disentangled himself and stood up. He was about to launch into an angry tirade when William paused and let out a strangled yelp. The guy gave William an incredulous look, then scooped him into his arms. Holding him tightly, he turned his attention back to me. The fury in his eyes stopped me in my tracks.

'You have a ton of explaining to do, lady,' he growled.

'I know, I know,' I conceded, discreetly letting the lead wind out again. Best not to get any closer. 'I apologise and obviously I'll fully reimburse you for–'

'Never mind the food,' the man glowered. 'Where did you get this dog?'

I felt momentarily thrown. 'Who wants to know?' I quavered.

I wasn't getting a great vibe here.

'Me, obviously.'

'Why?'

This conversation wasn't going the way I'd expected.

'Why? I'll tell you *why*, lady. Because this is *my* dog.'

'I beg your pardon?' I bristled. The man was obviously a nutcase. William was starting to wriggle and wanted to be put down.

'You heard,' he said, voice rising.

Heads were turning. It was one thing to watch a bit of theatre involving a strapping six-footer being knocked over by a small beagle. It was another to see him squaring up to a female over doggy ownership.

I straightened my spine. 'I insist you put William down.'

'William?' For a moment the man looked non-plussed. 'Close, but his name is actually Will. And yours is Thief!'

Chapter Six

'How DARE you,' I spluttered. 'I have proof of ownership, so return William to me immediately.'

'Oh yeah?' he hissed. 'Show me.'

'I don't have the paperwork on me.'

'Convenient.'

'But there's a man here who will vouch for me.'

'Where?'

I cast around frantically for Luke, but there was no sign of him. Charlotte was now gazing my way, frowning. She took a massive bite of her sausage sandwich, rubbed the crumbs from her hands and stood up. Moments later she was by my side.

'Woss goin' on?' she said, sounding like a character out of EastEnders and spraying crumbs everywhere in the process.

'This *idiot*—' I began.

'Excuse me?' said the man. Someone tittered while others began to look away, hastily stuffing food in their mouths, necking their drinks, getting up and moving away, no longer interested because – when it came to the crunch – nobody wanted to get involved. '*You're* the idiot because you're a dognapper and might end up behind bars.'

'Just one frigging flaming moment, Mister.' Charlotte's hand shot up like a traffic cop's. It was covered in brown sauce and William's eyes lit up like a pinball machine. 'My friend bought this dog in good faith.'

'I most certainly did' – I nodded emphatically, grateful for Charlotte's intervention – 'and I paid a lot of money for him too. Seventy-five pounds.'

'Seventy-five?' The man gave a snort of derision. 'Stick a zero on that figure, because that's what I paid for Will.'

'Seven hundred and fifty?' I gasped. Who the heck paid that sort of money for a mutt?

'Will is a pedigree,' explained the man, as if reading my mind.

'No more arguing,' snapped Charlotte. 'Return William to Sadie right now or I'm calling the police.'

All around us people were scrambling to their feet, desperate to get away and avoid making witness statements. Wow. What a load of saps.

'Where's Luke?' I demanded.

'How should I know?' Charlotte shrugged.

'Because the pair of you were very cosy while his wife was off the scene. He can't be far away, surely.'

'We weren't cosy,' Charlotte protested.

The man looked at Charlotte. 'So let me get this straight. One of you steals husbands and the other steals dogs.'

Charlotte turned crimson. 'My love life is no business of yours.'

'Thank God.'

31

'And for your information, the gentleman in question was waiting for his wife. She was using the loo.'

'Okay, so you might now be in the clear, but your friend is still a thief.'

'I am *not* a thief,' I exhorted. 'Now return William to me.'

'No. I'm taking Will home.' He unclipped the extendable lead and it snapped back into the handle I was still holding. 'You can call the police, the Pope, and your local MP for all I care because they will all be redirected to one person – my solicitor. And I can promise you that my lawyer will have the matter zipped up faster than that broken fastener on your dognapping hoodie. Come on, Sylvie,' he said to the Retriever.

The man started to walk away, William tucked under one arm and Sylvie the Retriever walking obediently to heel while off-lead.

'Stop right there!' I commanded.

Two words floated back. 'Buzz off.'

'FREEZE!' yelled Charlotte, pointing her mobile at the man's back.

He paused and turned.

'What are you going to do?' he ridiculed. 'Shoot me with your phone?'

'Don't trigger me,' growled Charlotte. She lunged towards an adjacent empty table and snatched up an abandoned fork. Suddenly she was prodding the air with it. 'Put the dog down, and you won't get hurt.'

The guy raised his eyebrows. 'You're threatening me with a utensil?'

'We both are,' I quavered, grabbing a second fork from the same table. I copied Charlotte and stabbed the air, except my hand was wobbling violently and my legs were starting to feel a bit rubbery. I had a nasty feeling that the police would take a dim view of this behaviour on top of a dognapping accusation. How had a peaceful woodland walk descended into this standoff?

'Oh look, there's Luke,' squealed Charlotte. 'Luke! LUKE!' she fog-horned. 'Over here.'

Rachel was back by her husband's side and looking none too pleased that Charlotte was once again after her husband. At the sight of two women brandishing forks, Luke raised an eyebrow and came over.

'Ladies?' he enquired.

'Tell this man' – Charlotte stabbed her fork back and forth – 'that William belongs to Sadie.'

'I can confirm that Charlotte is speaking the truth,' said Luke. 'Sadie visited my rescue shelter where William was staying, and she is now the registered owner. There was no microchip to say that William belonged to anybody else.'

'Yeah, you should have got him microchipped,' said Charlotte, her fork waggling going into overdrive.

The man gave Charlotte a withering look. 'Chips run the risk of travelling in a dog. They're also incredibly painful to the animal. Will had a collar and tag id.'

'Which regrettably' – Luke pointed out – 'can easily be

removed. However, I did meet the former owner.'

'The former owner is *me*' – the man asserted – 'and I've never met you in my life.'

'That's because you're not the person who brought this dog in to be rehomed,' Luke countered. 'It was a woman.'

The man's eyes narrowed and for a moment he was silent. When he next spoke, the words came out as little more than a whisper. 'What did she look like?'

'Sir, we rehome pets every day of the week, and William was with us for a while. I can't remember every person who comes into the shelter.'

'You must have documentation.'

'Yes, but that's private and confid–'

'Don't spout that nonsense to me. My dog was stolen, and a court of law will insist you show all documentation in your possession.'

'Okay, okay.' Luke put up his hands in a placatory gesture. 'It was a woman. She was distraught. Lots of tears. We initially thought she was upset about saying good-bye to the dog, although oddly she didn't seem that fond of him.'

The man made a hissing sound. 'Was she petite? Blonde hair?'

'Er, yes, as it happens. Do you know her?'

The man's mouth twisted. 'Gaynor. My ex-girlfriend. I broke up with her. It didn't go well. I told her to pack her bags and left her to it for an hour. When I returned, she'd gone, but so had my dog. There was a note pinned to the fridge. She said that Will had escaped, and she'd been unable to catch him. I put out Missing Dog posters immediately and posted Will's picture to social media. However' – the man nodded his head at Luke – 'it would seem that Gaynor lied and took revenge by dropping my beagle at your rehoming centre.'

Luke looked pained. 'The dog brought to us wasn't called Will. His name was, um, something quite different.'

'Yeah, rude, I'll bet,' said the man. 'Ah, I can tell from your expression I'm right. What was it? Wanker?'

Charlotte sniggered. 'Appropriate,' she muttered.

'Dickhead,' said Luke reluctantly.

'What a bitch,' said the man softly.

'Well I'm glad we've sorted that out,' I piped up. 'I'm sorry your girlfriend did that to you. It was beyond mean. But William belongs to me now, and I'd like you to hand him over.'

'But he *doesn't* belong to you,' the man countered.

'If neither of you can agree' – Luke asserted – 'then you'll have to go through the legal system to determine ownership.' I looked at Luke in horror. 'I'm really sorry, Sadie, but this gentleman might well have a valid claim.'

'What?' I quavered. Suddenly I couldn't bear the thought of losing William. He might take up half the bed, parp all night, snore like a farrowing pig, chew trainers, destroy slippers, and steal food at every opportunity, but I couldn't imagine life without him.

'We had a case of this once before at the centre,' said Luke. 'Despite a dog being a much-loved family member, a

35

court will dispassionately regard the pet as a chattel. A bit like a car or a piece of furniture. The judge will decide who owns that chattel.'

I gulped. This man claimed to have paid seven hundred and fifty pounds. How did that compare to seventy-five quid? I had a feeling it didn't.

Chapter Seven

'Right, I'm going now,' said the man. 'And Will is coming with me.'

'B–But,' I stammered. 'Please. I'm begging you.' My eyes brimmed. 'Don't take my dog. He means the world to me.'

'You're a horrible, *horrible* person,' Charlotte spat.

'Have you any idea what I've been through?' the man countered. 'I've lain awake night after night worrying about my dog. Wondering whether he's ended up being used as bait in illegal dog fights. Oh yes' – he clocked my expression – 'they still go on. I've tortured myself imagining him injured by a car and laying helpless in a ditch where nobody could find him. It's been a horrendous time. Now he's back and I won't be letting him out of my sight ever again.'

'But William was Sadie's *medi*cine,' said Charlotte, dramatically changing tack. 'Her *therapy*.'

Oh Lord. She was making me out to be some sort of headcase.

'Then I suggest Sadie goes back to your mate's rehoming centre and gets herself another four-legged counsellor.'

Luke gave me an apologetic look. 'I'm sorry for your loss' – his tone was soothing and reminded me of a vicar – 'but this gentleman is right. We have plenty of other dogs desperate to find their forever home. Why don't you pop along later?'

'I… er… maybe,' I said, putting down the fork and swiping a hand across my eyes. A headache threatened. I looked at the man. 'Um, if for any reason you change your mind about William, would you be kind enough to get in touch?'

'I won't be changing my mind.' His tone was emphatic.

I reached into my pocket and extracted one of my business cards which had my home address on it. 'Take this. Just in case.' I walked over and handed him the card which he reluctantly took. 'Bye, William. Be a good boy.' I gave my beagle – correction *his* beagle – a final rub around the ears. William wriggled frantically to get to me, but the man hung on tight. My eyes brimmed and I quickly turned away. I just wanted to go home now. Before I had a very public meltdown.

'Come on, sweetie,' said Charlotte, draping an arm around my juddering shoulders. 'Let's get back to Clover Cottage.' She gave Luke a rueful look. 'Guess I won't be seeing you on Sunday after all.'

Rachel, who hadn't said a word until now, suddenly spoke up.

'And why would you have been seeing my husband anyway?' she asked, giving Charlotte a frosty look.

'Dog training,' said Charlotte sweetly.

'Can we go, please,' I muttered. We'd already been involved in one head-to-head about ownership. I wasn't prepared for Charlotte and Rachel to roll up their sleeves and start squaring up over Luke.

'Hey,' said the man, as we began to walk away.

I turned back. 'Yes?' For a moment I thought he was going to change his mind. He must have caught the look in my eyes because his expression visibly softened.

'Look, I'd pretty much given up on ever finding Will, which is why I recently rescued Sylvie, here. Maybe we can both take a deep breath and sleep on this?'

'You mean you might let me have him back?'

'I was thinking more along the lines of you visiting Will. Taking him for a walk, or something,' he shrugged. 'I'm not a completely mercenary git.' He'd glanced at Charlotte as he'd said that. 'Here.' He reached into a denim pocket with his free hand and passed me his own business card. It said *Jack Farrell, landscape gardener and tree surgeon* and had an email address underneath. 'Have a think about it anyway.'

I took the card, tears now pouring down my face. 'Thank you.'

'Come on, lovie,' said Charlotte gently, leading me away. 'Let's get you home and have a nice cup of tea with a big dollop of brandy in it.'

Great. At this rate Jack Farrell would be thinking I was not only a nutter but also an alkie. I didn't dare turn back to look at William but, as Charlotte propelled me away, I could hear the little beagle letting out a series of shrill yelps and whines, as if to say, "Come back, Mum!".

My heart squeezed as I kept on walking.

Chapter Eight

By the time we were back at Clover Cottage, I was crying a storm. Signs of William were everywhere, from the hair on the sofa and my chewed-up slippers, to his basket and favourite doggy toy. But there was no beagle.

'I feel like I've been bereaved,' I bawled.

'I know,' Charlotte soothed. 'There, there. Hush now.'

She pushed me down on the sofa and bustled off to the kitchen. Cupboards were now opening and closing. The kettle was boiling. There came the sound of a glass bottle clinking against china. I could smell the alcohol from here. Two minutes later she was back, pressing a mug into my hands. A cautious sip confirmed the drink was more like tea-in-the-brandy than brandy-in-the-tea.

'Sip,' she ordered, as I continued to sob.

I couldn't remember the last time I'd wept so hard. Well... yes, I could. Over Felix. Obviously. Lethargy was stealing over me. I recognised the feeling. Hello darkness, my old friend. Oh yes, I'd spent a lot of time listening to songs full of mournful words. Self-indulgent? Probably. Everybody handled things differently. Some took shitty stuff on the chin. Others were felled by the first blow and toppled like skittles.

I didn't want to get sucked back into that place again. Suddenly I felt so, so tired.

'Sadie?' Charlotte was peering at me anxiously. She wasn't sitting down and joining me.

'Do you need to go?'

'Not particularly, but your eyes are closing and there's no point in me hanging around if you're going to crash out. My life is so exciting that I could be doing plenty of other exhilarating things while you're snoozing. You know' – she attempted banter – 'getting to grips with my laundry. Addressing last week's ironing pile. Changing my bed sheets. Life in the fast lane, as always.'

I dredged up a smile. 'Go. I think a nap might help. Just for an hour or so. I'm sure I'll feel much better afterwards. And maybe I should go back to the rehoming centre.' My mouth instantly became an upside-down smile. 'Find a new friend.' Even though the little voice in my head told me that William was irreplaceable.

'Definitely something to think about.' Charlotte patted my hand while giving an encouraging smile. 'And I'll come with you.'

'You don't have to.'

'But I'd like to,' she nodded emphatically. Ah yes. The Luke factor.

'Okay. Onward and upward, eh?'

'That's it,' Charlotte nodded. 'And if you fancy, we can go out for dinner later. Visit The Angel and get smashed.'

'You *are* trying to turn me into an alkie,' I tutted,

draining my tea. It wasn't hot due to all the brandy.

'Okay, forget the booze. What about comfort food instead? Cathy's locally sourced bangers with mash and green beans, all swimming in a thick pool of rich gravy. Apple crumble and oodles of custard to follow. How does that sound?'

'Like it will play havoc with my waistline, but I really couldn't care less.'

'Attagirl,' Charlotte grinned. 'I'll drive just in case you want to change your mind about getting stuck into the wine.'

'I won't.' Using alcohol as a prop was a slippery slope. I'd found that out after my wedding had been cancelled.

'Shall we say seven'ish?'

'Okay. Glad rags or just rags?'

Charlotte wrinkled her nose. 'It's The Angel, sweetie, not The Ivy.'

I smiled. As Charlotte quietly stole away, my eyelids closed, and Morpheus almost immediately led me down the corridors of sleep. At the end was a bright light. Well, look at that! A restaurant. And this one *was* The Ivy. It was where Felix had taken me directly after we'd first met at the gallery where I'd perused his sister's appalling sculptures with inflated price tags.

I'd never been to the Covent Garden restaurant before and was thankful to have taken care with my appearance earlier that morning before leaving home. I'd left Clover Cottage with my dark red hair blow-dried into a sleek curtain falling over my shoulders, and followed through with an elegant wraparound dress accessorised with a smart jacket and high heels.

At Ebbsfleet International, I'd caught the train to London with the intention of looking like a city-slicker, even if my heart had reminded me I was a hick from the sticks.

There had been no trace of the potter that day. No tresses piled up in a messy bun. No biro poking out of hair like a Chinese chopstick. No oversized denim dungarees, and no scruffy trainers covered in splatters.

A ceramics studio can be a dirty, messy place, no matter what precautions are taken. There was always tell-tale clay under my fingernails despite keeping them short and scrubbing them clean. I'd made sure that, on that particular morning, they'd been coated in a layer of sugar-pink polish to hide all traces. My handbag had also contained a tube of moisturising cream. Clay dried out the skin, and a good cuticle cream was essential if you regularly worked on a pottery wheel.

When I'd stepped off the train at King's Cross St Pancras and headed for the underground, I'd been confident of looking like *Girl About Town*. I was glad I'd made the effort to project such an image, especially when Felix had later led me out of the gallery and opened the passenger door to his snazzy sportscar.

Surprisingly the traffic hadn't been horrendous. Felix had found a place to park one minute away from the restaurant. He hadn't mentioned he was taking me to The Ivy, and I'd attempted nonchalance when he'd led me by the hand and greeted the bar manager like an old pal. Over a late lunch, I'd learnt that Felix's family always celebrated *occasions* here.

I'd hoped that this impromptu date might lead to another and had even had a little daydream about "us" becoming an item. I'd known instinctively that should that be the case, my mother – who had more than a touch of Hyacinth Bucket about her – would squeal with delight. Just as Felix's mother would surely squeal with horror.

Chapter Nine

As on all first dates – which I now look back upon perceiving that one to be – it was about getting to know each other.

There were the usual questions. "What do you do?" and "Where do you work?". This bit was always a bit of a trial. It could go two ways. Either you were genuinely fascinated about the person you were talking to, or you had to pretend, until excuses could politely be made before taking one's leave. Except Felix and I were genuinely interested in wanting to find out more about each other.

Thankfully, the polite chit-chat flowed. The questions about each other's work took place over a delicious starter of cream of cauliflower soup with crumbled Stilton for me, while Felix made short work of a duck liver parfait with a pear and ginger compote, tamarind glaze and sourdough toast. He'd also ordered a bottle of Cabernet Sauvignon which I'd belatedly realised seemed to be me mainly hoovering up on account of Felix later driving.

I'd been both surprised and delighted to discover that the gallery – which had long been a vital force in the art world – belonged to Felix's father. However, Mr Barrington-Jones Senior had passed over much of the running to Mr

Barrington-Jones Junior. I'd also learnt that both father and son had fingers in the antiques market too, with a shop in Soho's Dering Street.

Over our mains – Chicken Saltimbocca Risotto with prosciutto crudo for the two of us – Felix had asked how old I was. Back then I'd been twenty-six to his distinguished thirty-two. Not a huge age gap but nonetheless enough to have me quietly wondering if he'd ever been married. I'd already discreetly checked out his left hand before leaving the gallery and been partially reassured by the lack of a wedding band. Nonetheless, there was always the possibility of "baggage". An ex-wife. Children. Monthly maintenance payments. Nothing wrong with that, of course, but not something a fresh-faced twenty-six-year-old was looking for in any potential new love interest. After Felix had told me his age, I'd felt a need to be cautious and discreetly reined in the earlier exuberance. No girl ever wanted to find herself playing second fiddle to a man who might say, "Sorry, Sadie. Our weekend together is cancelled. I have a chance to see my boys. Quality time and all that. And no, I won't be introducing you. They're both too young and have had enough confusion in their short lives. You know how it is." Followed by a deprecative shrug.

No, I didn't know how it was, but I'd heard enough from a mate who'd fallen in love with a divorced guy and tried to befriend his surly children only to suffer salt in her tea, drawing pins under the duvet, and even a crude voodoo doll in which needles had been stuck. She'd endured it for six months before admitting defeat and walking away.

But by the time we'd moved on to dessert – white chocolate mousse with pistachio and raspberries for me and an unpasteurised soft camembert with rye crackers, apple, and celery for him – I'd happily discovered that Felix didn't possess a Decree Absolute and had no offspring. In short, the man was – as my mother would have gleefully squealed – "a catch".

As I'd scraped up the last bit of white chocolate from the pudding plate, only to remind myself that noisy spoons on china probably wasn't done in a place like this, I'd idly wondered if there was a catch with "the catch". Why wasn't Felix married? Or, at the very least, co-habiting with a significant other? By the time we'd got to the coffee stage, I'd been so bold as to ask the question.

'I'm rarely short of company,' he'd said honestly. 'But the simple answer is, up until now, I've never met the right girl.' The words "up until now" hadn't been lost on me. Was he hinting that I might be that girl? He'd followed those words up with a look that had made me flush with delight. Intense. Direct. There had definitely been a few smoulders being volleyed my way, and mellow from so much wine – I'd brazenly lobbed a few back.

'And you?' he'd asked. 'Are you dating?'

'No,' I'd replied. 'The relationship I was in ended rather abruptly at the start of the year.'

He'd grinned. 'Who dumped who?'

I'd been honest. 'Him. I'd wanted to get on the property

47

ladder and thought Michael might like to join me. We'd been together long enough. Unfortunately, he wasn't as committed as I'd previously been led to believe.'

I'd shrugged as if to say *you win some, you lose some.*

Michael had been in my life since starting university. Distance had intermittently sent the relationship floundering. His family were from Southampton. We'd drifted apart for a while, then back together again, seemingly unable to be without each other. Then, after we'd both graduated, Michael's parents had moved to Scotland. He'd gone with them. And that, I'd thought, was that. But, like a boomerang, he'd returned to London a few months later. I'd been in digs by this point, but he'd sought me out. Once again, we'd picked up where we'd left off.

At this point I'd been working at an auction house learning the ropes around post-war, contemporary, impressionist, and modern art. The salary had reflected my age and experience. Affording rent had been tricky. Consequently, I'd joined forces with three other girls. In the beginning, flat sharing had been fun. Twelve months later the novelty had well and truly worn off. Suddenly it was no longer highly comical to have a bath with tights dripping from the overhead makeshift washing line. Nor was it amusing to have clothes borrowed that either never got returned or were given back covered in make-up. The overflowing ashtrays and endless chaotic mess, once considered charming, had become plain annoying.

The final straw came when I'd blown money I could ill

afford on fillet steaks, garden vegetables and baby potatoes followed by a summer pudding for Michael and myself. I'd come in from work only to find that someone – I never did find out who – had scoffed the frigging lot.

From that point on I'd hankered for my own place. Somewhere to retreat. Somewhere that was just mine. Where I could open the wardrobe and find the crisp white shirt bought from Next was not only still hanging within but remained pristine.

When Mum had told me about a tiny, just-about-affordable cottage for sale in my home village, I'd leapt at the chance of buying it. The commute to London was a little lengthy, but not impossible. I'd told Michael about it with shining eyes. "What do you think?" I'd asked, assuming he'd be excited. Except he wasn't. "I think, Sadie, that we're not on the same page and that we haven't been for a while."

I'd been flabbergasted. But our split hadn't traumatised me. We'd had too many lengthy separations in between. Strangely, the final break had felt quite liberating. The only thing I'd initially missed was having a regular bed-companion. After all, I'd been a normal red-blooded girl. But I'd told myself that I wouldn't be alone for ever and it was far better to buy Clover Cottage as a singleton, and at least there would be no arguments with a man about his seventy-five-inch flatscreen hanging off my tiny lounge wall.

By the time I'd finished decorating and furnishing – the latter at a vast discount thanks to having now met Charlotte with her upcycling business – I'd also had something of an enterprise epiphany. I'd been regularly dabbling with clay for some time, but only at classes. However, I'd considered my talent enough to be put to the test. Part-time in the beginning. Evenings and weekends. That sort of thing. Giving up the day job wasn't initially an option with a mortgage to pay.

My father had been delighted and encouraged me by rolling up his sleeves and erecting a basic garden building – one up from a shed – that didn't need planning permission. It had sported windows for both light and, more importantly, ventilation from any potentially dangerous fumes, and enough space for a workbench and wheel.

An electrician had been summoned to safely install a kiln, but the drainage system had proved a problem and I still didn't have a water supply to the studio. It was easy enough to carry water back and forth and at least I didn't have to worry about washing clay down a domestic sink and developing blockages.

Things had taken off at such a pace that after six months I'd abandoned the day job and exhibited more and more frequently with Charlotte, who was by now a firm friend.

As I'd sat in The Ivy with Felix, all this information had been shared. By this point we were gazing into each other's eyes.

'So you're not only young, free and single, but also wonderfully ambitious,' he'd crooned, chin in the palm of his hand, elbows on table. I'd mirrored his body language and our faces had been mere inches apart.

'Absolutely,' I'd murmured back.

'Me too,' he'd smiled. 'Do you have to be anywhere, or would you like to come back to my place to continue this fascinating conversation?'

'Is that a euphemism for inviting me to see your etchings?' I'd said playfully.

Okay, I'd been a bit pissed.

'It is,' he'd nodded.

I'd blinked. Wow, he didn't mess about, did he! I should have had warning bells going off left, right and centre. But if they did, I was too smitten to hear.

Felix had paid the bill and lead me back to his car. He'd driven to Soho with one hand resting on my knee. I'd found his touch thrilling. Once inside his loft-apartment I'd admired the feature high ceiling, exposed pipes, beams, and brick walls for... ooh... a good three seconds.

Then his mouth had come down on mine.

Chapter Ten

'SADIE HARDING!'

I shot upright, heart pounding. What time was it? A bleary-eyed glance at the clock on the mantel informed me I'd been asleep on the sofa for hours. The letterbox clattered and a familiar voice fog-horned through the gap.

'Are you AWAKE?' Charlotte boomed. 'For heaven's SAKE. Let me IN. It's FREEZING out here.'

'Coming,' I called, waiting for my galloping heart to settle. Hauling myself off the sofa, I promptly trod on one of William's squeaky toys and nearly went into orbit. Talk about a doubly rude awakening.

'Blimey, look at you,' said Charlotte, as I opened the door.

'Is that another way of saying I look a tad dishevelled?'

'Your left cheek is sporting an awful lot of cushion creases and you have bed hair.'

'Channelling the sex kitten look again, eh?'

Charlotte stepped into the tiny hallway. Some leaves blew in as I shut the door behind her. We were two-thirds of the way through March and the evenings were currently a nippy seven degrees or so.

'Have you been in the Land of Nod ever since I left?' she

asked, following me back into the lounge.

'Seems that way.' I stooped to pick up William's squeaky toy and chucked it into the empty dog basket. 'I think that earlier cup of tea with a "dash" of brandy was, unintentionally on your part, rocket fuel.' I grinned as I straightened cushions and folded up the throw Charlotte had thoughtfully placed over me earlier. 'Give me two ticks and I'll splash some water over my face and put a brush through my hair.'

'That's it. Pull out all the stops.'

'Very funny.' I rolled my eyes but noted Charlotte had glammed up considerably. Interesting. 'What's with the eye-shadow and posh top?'

'Nothing,' she said innocently. 'But you might want to exchange that sock-grey t-shirt and scruffy hoodie for something a little more… you know.'

'What?'

'Smart.'

'Oh. Why?'

She blew out her cheeks in exasperation. 'Sadie, I'm your best mate and I'm going to say this straight. You're a gorgeous looking woman who almost deliberately seems to make herself look as awful as possible.'

'No, I don't,' I protested, but I knew my words were a lie.

I didn't want to be – as Charlotte put it – *gorgeous*. Or even a teeny bit attractive. I was quite happy with my crumpled clothes with accessorised cheek, thanks to that sofa cushion. Charlotte was dressed and made up to attract male attention – should there be any – whereas I wanted to avoid it at all costs.

'Okay, keep the jeans' – she sighed – 'but team them with that lovely satin-grey top I've always coveted. You know the one?'

'I think so,' I said. I knew perfectly well which one she was talking about.

'And wear your grey suede boots.'

'Right.'

I hadn't worn either the top or the boots post-Felix. In fact, I deliberately avoided wearing anything that Felix used to admire me in. A part of my brain – the sabotaging bit – had floated the idea of bagging up all my "Felix clothes" and donating them to a charity shop. The saner and more sensible part had scalded me for even having such a ridiculous thought. Nonetheless there was a considerable section within my wardrobe that hadn't been worn since that cancelled wedding.

'I'll be back in a minute,' I said, swinging out of the lounge.

'It's Saturday night. Is lipstick too much to hope for?' Charlotte called after me as I scampered up the stairs.

I pulled an ancient sweater from a drawer and found my old black boots. That would have to do. A quick peek in the bedroom mirror revealed a pasty-faced female with dull grey eyes.

Sighing, I brushed my teeth, rubbed a cold flannel over

my face, pinched my cheeks for colour and – as a sop to Charlotte – slicked on a rose-pink lip gloss. My hair hung limply. No time to wash it. I twisted it into a messy up-do, then threaded some dangly earrings through my ear lobes in a nod to glamour.

Charlotte was waiting for me in the hall. As I came down the stairs, she ran an appraising eye over me.

'Oh well. The earrings are an improvement if nothing else.'

'Thank you.'

'Come on. Let's go and get stuck into village life at The Angel. I heard earlier that Cathy has booked a band for tonight.'

'Really?' I said, hesitating. 'I thought we were going out for pub grub and Prosecco.'

'We are,' said Charlotte, propelling me through the door before I could change my mind.

'But we won't be able to hear ourselves talk,' I protested.

'Then we'll shout.'

Terrific. Whenever landlady Cathy had a band playing, she always cleared an area for those who wanted to dance. And by that I don't mean *Strictly* show-offs, or clubbers giving London a miss to do some smooth moves at our local. No, I'm talking about people like Ted, the village's new postman. Once he'd downed a few pints, he thought he was John Travolta in *Saturday Night Fever*, but looked more like someone's dad doing disco moves. My elderly neighbours would likely be there too. Cathy could always count on Fred and Mabel Plaistow giving a creaky waltz to a cover of *Uptown Girl.*

Oh yes, if you wanted a fun night out in Little Waterlow, this was about as exciting as it got.

Chapter Eleven

When we arrived at The Angel, the band had yet to turn up. A makeshift "stage" had been made by pushing tables and chairs together, clearing some floor space.

'All right, girls?' Cathy greeted us. She plucked two menus from the bar's counter before leading us into the restaurant area. It was a vast room but managed to maintain a sense of cosiness thanks to its low knotted beams and a huge woodburning stove that held centre stage on the far wall. 'Nice to see you getting out, Sadie,' she said, giving me a warm smile, although I caught the pity in her eyes.

Cathy was one of Little Waterlow's biggest gossips. Whenever someone's personal life took a disastrous turn, The Angel's landlady was always the one with her finger on the pulse of a breaking story. And she was always the first to cover one hand over her mouth and stage whisper, "Far be it for me to gossip, but have you heard…?"

'I'll put you in the corner so you can hear yourselves talking. The band is due any moment.'

'Please don't tell me you rebooked that "Tribute to Abba" group,' said Charlotte.

Cathy gave a snort of laughter. 'No, I didn't.' She

paused, eyes momentarily far away no doubt remembering the group's unfortunate caterwauling. 'You might not be able to judge a book by its cover, but you can when it comes to a tribute band.'

'What do tonight's group call themselves?' I asked.

'The Beagles.'

'Oh no,' Charlotte groaned. 'Am I going to listen to a terrible version of *Let It Be?*'

'Ha! No. They're not taking off The Beatles or even The Eagles. They're an indie band and all material sung tonight is their own. The lead singer let me listen to some sample tracks before Frank and I booked them. They're all right. And so's the lead singer,' she chuckled, giving a lewd wink. 'Right, girls, while you're looking at the menus, what drinks can I get you?'

As soon as we were sipping our Proseccos, Charlotte steered the conversation to returning to the rehoming centre on Sunday morning.

'I know you're sad about William, but I honestly think the best thing to do is move on and get another poor unwanted doggy.'

I noted her description. Not: Totally unmanageable lunatic that traumatises the postman and carts you when on the lead. Or: Ancient dog requiring so much veterinary care that the former owners were bankrupted. Rather, words that painted the picture of a pitiful abandoned mutt.

'I'll think about it.' I wasn't making any promises.

Charlotte wasn't prepared to give up on the subject.

'Well, let's go anyway. You don't need to go home with a pooch. Just, you know. Have a look. See if a pair of big brown eyes reel you in.'

'For someone who isn't getting a dog herself, you seem awfully keen to get me back there.'

Charlotte gave a nonchalant shrug. 'I'm simply looking out for you. Doing what I think is in your best interests.'

'Hm.' I sipped and regarded her pensively over the rim of my glass.

'What's that supposed to mean?' she said, her face a picture of innocence.

'Call me a cynic, but I can't help feeling that you're keen to accompany me so you can see Luke again.'

'You're definitely a cynic,' said Charlotte, her mouth pursing. But she'd also gone a bit pink, which was nothing to do with the Prosecco or the heat blasting out of the woodburning stove.

'Sweetie,' I said, my tone sympathetic. 'He's married.'

Charlotte's shoulders drooped. 'But maybe he's not happy?'

'In which case he can leave his wife. Luke is a big boy and quite able to make his own decisions.'

'But maybe he's too nice to do that to her.'

'We saw them together at the woods. He didn't seem miserable to me.'

'Did you see the way Rachel was holding Luke's arm?' Charlotte flashed an indignant look. 'Like a policeman making an arrest. She had him in a vice-like grip.'

'It looked like some romantic arm-linking to me,' I countered.

'There was nothing loved-up about Luke's body language. He looked unhappy.'

'And you think you're the one to restore his *joie de vivre*?'

'Well why not? There's nothing wrong with me. I'm a nice person.'

'Yes, you are,' I reasoned. 'But I suspect his wife is a nice person too. He made a point of mentioning her when I was making friends with William. A gentle way of saying he was taken. Remember?'

'I can't say I do,' said Charlotte, avoiding my eye. A dead giveaway that she did.

'It would be different if Luke had told you his wife was giving him the runaround. That she was a serial flirt. Or constantly having a fling. But he made no mention, so there isn't really any motive for him to have a wandering eye or ask for your phone number.'

'Maybe he will tomorrow. Perhaps Luke will reveal some secrets. Like… the fact that Rachel doesn't put out. That they go to bed night after night and just lay there. Her plugged into her phone listening to pan pipes while Luke stares into the darkness and plots how to set himself free and elope with the gorgeous brunette who haunts his dreams and consumes his every waking thought.'

'Who are you planning to elope with?' said Cathy, returning with her pad and pen.

'No one,' said Charlotte quickly.

'I won't tell anyone,' said Cathy cosily. 'Just make sure that, whoever he is, you bring him to my pub. I like this place to have plenty of bums on seats. Now, what's it going to be, ladies?'

'I'll have the chicken kiev,' said Charlotte.

'Ham, egg and chips, please,' I said.

'Excellent choices,' said Cathy, scribbling down the order. 'Any more drinks?'

'We're good, thanks,' I said.

'Phew,' said Charlotte, as Cathy walked away. 'You have to be so careful what you say around here.' She glanced about furtively. The restaurant was rapidly filling up. 'Anyway, where were we?'

'I was putting the kybosh on your romantic hopes and dreams regarding Luke.' I gave her an old-fashioned look. 'Have you forgotten how things panned out with Hugo?'

'Oh him,' said Charlotte dismissively.

'Yes, him. And don't look at me like that. There was a time when you swanned around in a dreamy haze for weeks on end. Pouncing on your mobile and then biting everyone's head off if it wasn't Hugo calling. And look how you treated poor Ted.'

'What's our postie got to do with Hugo?' Charlotte frowned.

'On Valentine's Day, when Ted delivered a brown envelope from the taxman instead of a pink one from Hugo, you told Ted to sod off.'

'I wasn't myself.' Charlotte shook her head. 'Back then I was very stressed.'

'Yes. You were. And you don't want to go down that path again. Stay away from Luke. He's taken.'

'Oh all right, all *right*. How was I to know that Hugo had spun me a completely fictional story about his private life? I had no idea Caroline even existed until she turned up at our stall and appropriated the village tannoy.'

'Yes, that was a bit embarrassing,' I nodded.

Caroline had brought Little Waterlow's annual fete to a standstill calling upon members of the public to take a look at "Charlotte the Harlot" over on Stall Two who, in addition to stripping old furniture, liked stripping off for men who didn't belong to her.

'It's not my fault Hugo knew every smarmy chat-up line in the book and I fell for his lies. The git.'

'He was,' I agreed. 'But this time you *know* the man in question is married. There's no excuse.'

Charlotte sighed theatrically. 'One day my prince will come. And I don't mean that rudely,' she sniggered.

I grinned at her, and we clinked our glasses together.

'Heads up. Here comes our grub,' I said, nodding at Cathy coming our way. She was bearing plates full of heavenly smelling food.

'Never mind the food for a minute,' said Charlotte. 'There's the band.' She stabbed a finger in the direction of the bar. 'Check out the guitarist. I'm sure I know him. Oh, my goodness. We both do. It's *him*.'

'Who?' I peered myopically past Charlotte. Then blanched.

It was Jack Farrell. The man who had taken my dog and claimed William Beagle as his own.

Chapter Twelve

I sat, momentarily transfixed, as the band set up.

Jack was dressed in ripped jeans and a torso-hugging t-shirt that outlined well-defined pecs and showed off strong arm muscles. I felt my lip curling like William's used to whenever he caught a glimpse of next door's cat in my garden.

'I thought he was a tree surgeon,' I hissed to Charlotte.

'That's what his business card said.'

'So what's he doing with a guitar slung around his neck in this pub?'

'Well clearly he's a musician too,' Charlotte tutted.

I regarded Jack through narrowed eyes. He was fiddling about with an amp. Now he was talking to a guy on keyboards. A note was being played. Jack and another guitarist adjusted strings. Another man – who reminded me of a vast shaggy bear – was easing himself down on a stool by an electric drum kit.

'Thank gawd for that,' said Charlotte, nodding at the drummer. 'Silicone pads. That will dramatically reduce the noise, so we won't leave here with thumping headaches.' She caught my expression. 'Why are you giving Jack daggers?'

'Because if he's here at The Angel, who is looking after William?'

'I'm sure William can look after himself. He isn't a child, Sadie. A dog doesn't require a babysitter.'

'William has a low boredom threshold. That man' – I stabbed an accusing finger in Jack's direction – 'is going to be here all night.'

'Hardly. Cathy locks the doors at ten o'clock.'

'You know what I mean. He's in here while William is home alone.'

'Sadie, William is a beagle. Not Macaulay Culkin defending the house from bungling burglars.'

'How do you know burglars won't come a-calling while that man' – *that man* again, Sadie? – 'is in here twanging his guitar and pretending he's a rock star.'

'Aren't you being a little bit over the top?'

'No. William used to howl if I even went to the supermarket for an hour. I know that as a fact, because Fred and Mabel Plaistow came round to see me, complaining they hadn't been able to hear Phil and Holly talking on the telly. They suggested I shop on a Thursday morning when it was Dermot O'Leary and Alison Hammond's turn, because they weren't such fun to listen to.'

Keen not to upset the Plaistows, I'd gone a step further by switching my weekly shop to online ordering. I'd then topped up the larder with any forgotten items by taking William on lead to the corner shop. The *corner shop* was, in fact, a twenty-minute walk from Clover Cottage, but

65

William had loved trotting along at my heel and had also enjoyed being fussed by passers-by whilst briefly tied to the dog hook.

'Jack Farrell is bang out of order,' I continued, getting worked up.

'William isn't alone,' Charlotte soothed. 'Sylvie is with him.' I looked at her blankly. 'Jack's golden retriever,' she reminded.

'That's a fat lot of good to William,' I spat. 'What's Sylvie going to do if William gets bored?'

'Well I don't know,' Charlotte shrugged. 'Perhaps she'll let him slip her one. After all, William tried shagging her at Trosley.' She caught the flash of horror on my face. 'Joke, Sadie. For goodness' sake, stop fretting. Sylvie seemed like a well-trained dog and I'm sure she's being an excellent companion.'

'Yes,' I nodded, my head now going up and down at high-speed. 'Perhaps Sylvie will whip out a pack of playing cards and entertain William with a game of *Snap*. Or maybe she'll get the Scrabble board out of the sideboard and coach him in high-scoring words like *meaty chunks*.'

'Now you're being ridiculous,' Charlotte sighed. 'Listen, we came out tonight to enjoy ourselves, not get het up about–' She broke off as I leapt to my feet. 'Where are you going?' she said in alarm.

'To have a quiet word,' I replied, all the while glaring at Jack Farrell. 'Or even several noisy ones.'

Chapter Thirteen

I'd only taken three steps towards The Beagles – ha, what was *that* name all about, woof flipping woof – when the band launched into their first number of the night.

'Back so soon?' said Charlotte, raising an eyebrow.

'I'll talk to Jack Farrell in the interval, whenever that may be.'

I reluctantly sat down again.

'Finish your meal. And stop stabbing your food,' Charlotte chided, as I savagely speared several chips and busted the yolk on the fried egg. 'Have you got PMT?'

'Yeah, *and* GPS,' I growled. 'Meaning that right now I'm a bitch *and* I'll find him later.'

'Everything all right, ladies?' said Cathy coming over. She paused to look at me. Frowned. 'Is the grub not up to standard?'

'Y-Yes, it's smashing,' I stuttered, hastily ditching the bad mood, and wiping the last of the ham around my plate. I popped it into my mouth, then kissed my fingers with appreciation. 'That was delicious.' The last thing I wanted was to get on the wrong side of The Angel's landlady.

'Sure? You looked like you were murdering that egg.

Was something not to your liking? I'd rather you tell me now so I can pass on any negative feedback to Cook.'

'It was the band,' said Charlotte helpfully.

'Eh?' said Cathy, looking even more put out. 'What's wrong with them?'

I kicked Charlotte under the table. 'Nothing,' I assured. 'Their music sounds great.' It did, as it happened, although I hadn't wanted to admit it. But right now, needs must, and all that.

'It's the lead singer,' confided Charlotte. 'He isn't on Sadie's Christmas card list.'

'Why, what's he done?' Cathy raised her eyebrows.

'We, er, had a small misunderstanding.'

'He took her dog,' said Charlotte helpfully. 'William Beagle.'

'He *stole* William Beagle,' Cathy gasped. 'I saw you with your pooch the other day. The two of you were walking over the common. You were chatting away to him, and he was looking up at you in absolute adoration. I said to my Frank, "See Sadie's darling beagle? Isn't he a sweetheart!" And Frank peered at the two of you and then had a proper gooey expression on his moosh. And you know what my Frank is like. It can take a heatwave to melt his heart. And you say this guy took him? How dare he. He can stop his crooning right now and get out of my pub.'

Cathy made to turn, but I grabbed her arm. 'It's fine. Really.'

'How can it be fine?' Cathy was looking more and more

68

perplexed, as well she might.

'Look, it's a bit of a story. Yes, Jack Farrell did take my dog, but not in the way you're thinking.'

'Right,' said Cathy, looking uncertain. 'So I can leave him to carry on warbling?'

'Yes,' I said, sighing with relief. 'And, um' – I put my knife and fork together – 'Charlotte and I would love to see the dessert menu.' Distraction was necessary.

'Okay.' She swept up our plates and glasses with practiced hands, balancing everything in a seemingly precarious stack, but we knew nothing would tumble. 'Back in a jiffy.'

'What did you say that for?' I hissed, when Cathy was out of earshot.

'To save you the trouble of murdering Jack Farrell,' Charlotte grinned. 'Cathy would have done a far more thorough job and there wouldn't have been blood on your hands.'

'Very funny. And I'll have you know–'

'What?'

'Oh help. Jack Farrell is looking this way.'

Charlotte turned to peer. 'You're right. He's recognised you. And he doesn't look too thrilled to see you. That makes two of you.'

Chapter Fourteen

The Beagles proceeded to play for an hour.

During that time, they performed mainly ballads which almost brought the usual hive of activity in Cathy's pub to a standstill. Conversation at the bar ceased to the occasional whisper. Likewise, diners stopped chatting about their awful week at work or the unpredictable weather and instead stared at Jack who, eyes closed, head thrown back, delivered lyrics about losing one's heart to love, also recovering from unrequited love and, ultimately, experiencing the euphoria of falling in love.

Every now and again Cathy's old-fashioned till made a ding as she took money from a punter, or a waitress clattered plates while quickly clearing a table, but it seemed as if everyone paused to listen to a man who sounded like Ed Sheeran but looked like a god.

'I know you don't like him, Sadie, but you have to agree the guy can sing,' Charlotte whispered. She was resting her chin in the palms of her hands, elbows on table, and looking at Jack with a dreamy expression.

'If you like that sort of thing,' I grunted.

'Don't be like that.'

'What am I supposed to be like then?' I hissed. 'Get up

and dance the flaming Tango?'

'No need,' she giggled. 'Fred and Mable are looking all set to strut their stuff.'

I sighed. My neighbours were indeed here, along with many other locals, several of whom – moved by the music – were squeezing themselves into the small dance area by the band. Fred and Mabel – usually on walking sticks – were now doing some rickety moves from their ballroom dancing days. Local florist Daisy and her artist husband Seth Kingston were having a smooch. Daisy and Seth had recently finished knocking two cottages into one and the newly named Apple Tree Cottage looked stunning. Daisy's floral assistant and bestie, Becky, was also out for the evening and up for a slow dance. She was gazing raptly into hubby Alfie's eyes. I looked away, not wanting to be reminded about love and other people's joy at finding it.

'This evening is about to get even more cosy,' murmured Charlotte.

I gave her a sharp look. 'Who have you spotted?'

'Over there.'

I followed her gaze and inwardly groaned. Coming through the pub's door was my sister, Flora. Even worse, behind her were my parents. We all saw each other at the same time and, dutifully, I lifted my arm in a wave, pasting on a forced smile.

Now don't get me wrong. I love my family. But they have some serious foibles. Flora, younger than me, has flawless skin and gorgeous waist-length blonde hair –

admittedly helped by a hairdresser. She's the sort of female who puts her make-up on just to take the rubbish out... not that she does the bins very often. My sis still lives at home and whilst she laments about not being on the property ladder, she isn't exactly working her socks off saving for a deposit. She prefers to spend her money on clothes, cosmetics and a London social life that is a serious drain on her bank balance due to her endless pursuit of snaring a rich banker looking for a dolly-bird wife. What she was doing in The Angel on a Saturday night was a mystery.

Flora had asked me several times if she could move into Clover Cottage, and each time I'd said no. Whenever this happened, she'd sulk for weeks and there would be a protracted period of her not speaking to me. Mum had once called me harsh, but I'd pointed out that Flora was the epitome of my previous messy flatmates all rolled into one. I'd bought Clover Cottage to escape all that. Mum sympathised to a point, but she had her own agenda with her youngest daughter – that of wanting to reclaim her house as a tidy one, not to mention escaping all the exhausting drama when Flora spent weeks targeting Mr Suitable, only to discover he was Mr Shit. The last one who'd failed to be "the one" was a stinking rich CEO of an international energy corporation and nothing but a playboy.

As my sister walked past the band, it seemed as though every man within the pub followed her with their eyes and sighed. Flora knew she was a head turner and played to the crowd. Like most beautiful young women, she was something of a narcissist. She had an Instagram account with thousands of followers. Her posts were entirely of herself striking a pose in various skimpy outfits, enhanced bee-stung lips always doing the same pout but in different coloured lipsticks.

As Flora clocked Jack Farrell, her body language instantly changed. The walk became an undulating sway. As she headed towards our table, her hair seemed to flow out behind her. I looked at the band to see what effect she was having on them. All four members appeared to be looking at Flora's pert little backside showcased perfectly by her on-trend designer jeans. God, men were pathetic.

Mum and Dad were now bringing up the rear. Not only did my mother look like a fifty-year-old version of Hyacinth Bucket but she seemed to positively cultivate the character as a role model. She had taken a lot of laughing off when I'd been with Felix. Mum had wanted to be fully involved in the wedding plans and, as mother of the bride, she'd had every right to be. But Tara Barrington-Jones had insisted on the nuptials taking place in London. Mum had been terribly excited by this. It was all her social-climbing dreams come true. However, I had seen Tara's chosen venue for what it was. A building that held a small number of people with the wedding breakfast later taking place in Tara's elegant orangery where the bride's family wouldn't be a social embarrassment. From there, Felix and I would leave for the airport to go on honeymoon. I'd only later found out – we're talking long afterwards – that Tara had planned to talk to her son and new daughter-in-law about a "formal blessing" within a vast chandeliered marquee in her manicured grounds with a guest list full of society names that would have made my mother's eyes bulge. Except my family's names hadn't been on that second guest list. Not that it mattered anymore.

I watched Mum now as she threaded her way through the tables, coming over to Charlotte and me. She was wearing a hat worthy of the Queen Mother and her smart buttoned-up coat covered a floral dress fit for any high-tea event. The only thing missing was a pair of white gloves.

Dad brought up the rear. He looked a little hen-pecked, as always. His grey hair was cut short with a neat side parting and this evening he was wearing smart trousers with an open-necked white shirt. I was amazed Mum hadn't forced him to wear a tie. And then I caught his expression. Defiance. Okay, he'd put his foot down. It wasn't often he asserted himself but when he did Mum knew it was time to back off. As a self-employed electrician, it pained my mother that Dad drove a van but if anybody asked what vehicle the family had she truthfully told them it was a Mercedes, omitting that it was a commercial vehicle.

'What are you doing here?' was Flora's opening gambit.

'I could say the same of you,' I said, standing up to greet her and my parents. She gave me an air-kiss and treated Charlotte to a lukewarm smile. In Flora's book, anyone who upcycled other people's junk needed their head examining. Who wanted a distressed sideboard from Charlotte's workshop when you could buy one from John Lewis at three times the price?

'There was nobody to hang out with this evening,' Flora continued. 'Minty is holidaying in the Caribbean with her family.'

'Ah,' I said, as if this was perfectly understandable. Flora had lots of acquaintances with names like Minty and Jonty, but they abandoned her the minute their wealthy families suggested skiing a few mountains in Switzerland or grabbing some winter sunshine in the Bahamas.

'I also heard there was a hot guy playing in this band tonight,' Flora shrugged, nicking some chairs from the table next to us and squashing them around ours.

Hot guy? I was just about to splutter a retort when Mum bore down on me.

'Darling,' she beamed, enveloping me in a cloud of Chanel. 'How unexpected and delightful.' I was immediately released so she could address Charlotte. 'My *dear*, how charming to see you.' Mum tucked her handbag over her left forearm so she could formally shake Charlotte's hand.

'And you, Cynthia,' said Charlotte, gamely playing along. She was used to my mother. 'Hello, Bill.' She stood up to greet my father and they pecked each other on the cheek. No delusions there.

'Hello, sweetheart,' said Dad, kissing my cheek. 'You're looking a bit peaky, love. Everything okay?'

'Yes and no. I'll tell you all about it when this racket' – I couldn't resist sniping about The Beagles – 'has finished.'

'Okay. I suppose I'd better get some drinks in. Oh look.

Cathy's coming over. What would you all like?' He looked expectantly around our newly-expanded table.

'I'll have a gin and tonic,' said Flora, settling in her seat. 'And afterwards' – she turned to me and laughed throatily – 'I'll ask Cathy to give me an introduction to that heavenly looking guitarist.'

Chapter Fifteen

By the time I'd had the opportunity to bring my family up to date on my beloved beagle's departure to the lead singer of the band, Flora's eyes were on stalks.

'The Beagles have your beagle?'

'Well, one of them does. Jack Farrell. Although he insists William should never have been put in the rehoming centre in the first place. Apparently, his girlfriend – correction, ex-girlfriend – objected to their relationship ending and took revenge.'

'She *stole* William?' said Mum.

'Well, dognapped him, I suppose. But she didn't keep him. Instead, he was dumped at the centre. Then I came along and unwittingly thought I'd found my fur-ever four-legged best friend only to have him whipped away again.'

'I'm so sorry, darling,' said Dad. 'What will you do, get another dog?'

'I'm trying to persuade Sadie to return to the rehoming centre tomorrow morning,' said Charlotte.

'Good idea,' said Dad. 'It will keep you centred, sweetheart.' He picked up his pint, took a sip, then regarded me over the rim. I knew what he really meant. Not "centred" after losing William, but "centred" after the cancelled wedding fiasco. The last thing my parents wanted was a daughter returning to that other type of dog – sometimes known as the *black dog*. Depression.

'How's your beautiful garden, Bill?' asked Charlotte, diplomatically steering the conversation away from my life that was now minus both a fiancé and a dog.

'Oh, it's marvellous,' Mum gushed, butting in before Dad could speak. 'In fact, it's so good, I was thinking about opening it to the public.'

'It's a thirty-by-thirty plot, Cynthia,' said Dad mildly. 'Hardly Kew Gardens.'

'Mrs Quinten-Smith would be delighted for me to do such an event,' Mum protested. 'She's raising money for her distressed gentlefolk charity.'

I flinched at Mum's description of the charity she was involved in. My mind started to dart along a forbidden path, and I frantically reeled it back in again.

Mrs Quinten-Smith was the wife of a retired Queen's Bench Division Judge and one to whom my mother constantly tried to ingratiate herself. I took a sip of my drink and zoned out of the conversation. Flora leant in. The gesture was that of having a cosy tête-à-tête, but her body language said otherwise.

'So he's single,' she purred. I looked at her in confusion and she rolled her eyes. 'Him.' She gave a discreet nod at Jack Farrell. 'Mr Gorgeous, over there.'

I shrugged. 'I suppose. You can't seriously be interested

in the likes of him?' I felt a surge of irritation. 'He took my dog. Have a bit of loyalty, eh!'

'No, Sadie.' Flora tutted. 'Because William was never yours in the first place.'

'A receipt from the rehoming centre says otherwise.'

'Except I'll bet Mr Sexy has a receipt too, and probably for a far greater amount than yours.'

My mouth turned down. 'That's basically what Jack said.'

'Jack,' murmured Flora reverently. 'What a lovely name. It suits him, don't you think?'

I rolled my eyes. 'I don't think Jack is your type.'

'Says who?'

'Me. He's a landscape gardener – not the Chairman of some city corporation. Not your usual target.'

'Target? I object to your choice of language.'

I ignored my sister and swept on. 'And his business can't be doing that well if he's topping up his income in pubs and making that din.'

'Perhaps he simply likes making music,' Flora pondered, a smile playing about her lips. 'I'm certainly happy for him to do that with me.' She winked lasciviously.

'So you're after a roll in the hay with a local bit of rough?' I sneered.

'You should try it yourself sometime,' said Flora archly. 'When was the last time you got your leg over?'

'I beg your pardon?' I spluttered.

'Exactly. You can't even remember. You need to loosen

up, Sadie. Let go of all your frustrations and misery. A bunk up would do you the world of good.'

'Right,' I nodded furiously. 'Is that the sort of advice you give to all your girlfriends?'

'No, only my sister, because my girlfriends do precisely that. If a relationship ends, they swiftly move on. It's all very well feeling upset about life dealing you a dud card, but at some point, you need to get over it and stop being a diva. Everyone is bored to tears by it.'

I was so angry that for a moment I couldn't speak. A diva? Was that what everyone thought? That I was some sort of drama queen? I boggled into my glass of Prosecco. Watched the bubbles pop. Wondered how Flora would have dealt with things had she been in my situation.

'Everything all right, girls?' said Dad, sensing tension and looking our way.

'Never better,' I said stiffly, before turning back to Flora. 'Well thanks for that little pep talk, sis,' I said through gritted teeth.

'My pleasure.'

'Nothing like being reminded that it isn't the done thing to feel ever so slightly deflated about life.'

'That's the spirit.' Flora ignored my sarcasm. 'Be more buoyant.'

'I can't be like a sodding helium balloon all the time.'

'Sadie, you've haven't been like a helium balloon *any* of the time. Now for God's sake, lighten up. Finish your drink and then you can get in the next round.'

Chapter Sixteen

By the time everyone was on their third drink, The Beagles were wrapping up their gig. As Jack's voice hauntingly held the last note of the band's final song, thunderous applause broke out, as did a rash of goosebumps over my arms.

'Flipping brilliant,' yelled Charlotte, clapping like mad.

Jack caught my eye just as the others started unplugging electrical instruments and overseeing trailing cables.

'Heads up,' hissed Flora. 'I think he's coming over.'

Sure enough, Jack was threading his way through the tables.

'Good,' I muttered, straightening my spine. 'It saves me the trouble of going to him. I have a bone to pick.'

'Presumably not of the Bonio kind,' said Charlotte, butting into the conversation. 'Sadie is still up in arms about Jack having her dog and—'

'Evening,' said Jack, nicking an empty chair from the table alongside and parking it next to Flora. She immediately pushed her arms together so that her boobs swelled like two cakes rising in an oven.

'Hello,' she giggled. The hair flicking instantly went into overdrive. 'Is it me you're lookin' for?' she warbled. 'One of your songs sounded a bit like his.' Jack regarded Flora blankly. 'Lionel Richie,' she put in helpfully. 'I love his music but – dare I say it – I think your band is *waaaaay* more talented.'

'Er, thank you,' said Jack.

'Do you have an agent?' Flora persisted.

'No. We're not in the music business for–'

'Oh, but you really *should* have representation,' Flora insisted. 'You could be huge.' She licked her lips provocatively. 'I could make you big.' She momentarily dropped her gaze to Jack's crotch. 'In fact, enormous.' She looked up at him again.

'Are you a scout or something?' Jack frowned.

'No, but I have a friend who's in the industry,' she improvised. 'My pal has contacts. It's great to have talent,' she said airily. 'But ultimately it always boils down to who you know and' – she dropped her voice to a confidential whisper – 'my friend is like *this* with Simon Cowell.' She crossed two fingers by way of demonstration.

'Are you talking about your mate Ally?' said Charlotte, trying not to laugh.

'Her name is Allegra,' said Flora haughtily.

'Yes, I know who you mean. She went on *The X Factor*. Hardly Simon's bestie.'

'She made it through to round two,' said Flora, shooting Charlotte a venomous look.

'Only because her singing was so dire it provided audience entertainment,' Charlotte hooted.

'Ignore her,' said Flora to Jack, before turning her attention to me. 'Sadie, are you going to properly introduce us?' Her eyelashes were now fluttering like butterfly wings in a hurricane.

'Jack, this is Flora. My sister,' I added sourly.

'Younger sister,' Flora quickly replied. 'Currently footloose and fancy-free.'

I shot her a warning look before continuing with the introductions. 'You know Charlotte, of course, and next to her are my parents, Bill and Cynthia.'

'Delighted,' smiled my mother, giving a regal wave.

'Nice to meet you, lad,' said my father, picking up his pint glass and sipping. 'Can we get you a drink?'

'Thanks, Bill, but I'll pass. I just came over to say hello to Sadie.'

'Whatever for?' said Flora, looking put out.

'To be friendly.'

'Well there was really no need,' I said tersely. I wasn't looking to be buddies with this man. He'd ruined my life. And while that might sound a bit dramatic, it had taken a long time to move on from Felix Barrington-Jones. As far as I was concerned, my few weeks of finding delight and happiness – albeit with a dog – had been cruelly sabotaged. 'Where's William?' I demanded.

Jack looked taken aback. 'At home.'

'Why?'

'What do you mean *why*? Where else would he be?'

'He hates being left alone.'

'You think I should have brought him here?'

'Yes.' My chin jutted. 'Why not?'

'I'm not sure Cathy would have appreciated Will howling along to the music. He's not a lover.'

'I bet you're a great lover, Jack,' said Flora, crowbarring her way back into the conversation. 'Of music,' she laughed throatily. 'What did you think I meant, you naughty boy.' She slapped his hand playfully. 'Any time you want a female band member, I'm your girl. I've been told I have a voice like Bonnie Tyler.'

'Yeah,' Charlotte agreed. 'I've heard you sing but your voice sounded like a deflating balloon. More a case of *Total Eclipse of the Fart.*'

Ignoring Charlotte and Flora's sparring, I glared at Jack. 'It was irresponsible accepting this gig. You should be at home with William.'

'He has Sylvie for company.'

'He doesn't *know* Sylvie,' I protested.

'I think you're forgetting about that little episode at Trosley.'

'Even more reason not to leave them alone together,' I said furiously. 'In a few weeks' time there will be a litter of puppies to rehome. There's quite enough unwanted dogs in the world.'

'Sylvie has been spayed,' said Jack evenly.

'And your point is?'

'That I'm a responsible dog owner. Sorry, what point are *you* trying to make? That Will should have come along tonight and propped up the bar, a pint of shandy in one paw while the other delved into a packet of cheese 'n' onion? He's a dog, Sadie. He's safe at home, and perfectly happy in his crate.'

'A *crate?*' I gasped. 'You mean, you've caged him, like an animal?'

'He *is* an animal,' Jack pointed out.

'That's where you're wrong,' I protested. 'William is practically human, and he was treated accordingly in my home.'

'Yes, I'm aware he's picked up a load of bad habits after living with you,' Jack nodded. 'The first thing he did once home was clamber up on the sofa. Then, when I turfed him off, he went upstairs and lolled all over the bed. And when I shooed him off, he went back downstairs, located the kitchen, upended the bin, and began scoffing all the vegetable peelings.'

'He was probably hungry. I hope you're giving him three meals a day.'

'Three meals? No wonder he's put on so much weight.'

'My poor dog,' I whimpered.

Jack stood up. 'Right, well I thought I'd come over and be sociable, but it seems to have backfired, so I'd better go and help the boys load up the van.'

'Yes, good idea. Get back to William. I never left him alone for more than an hour.'

Flora got to her feet too. 'Let me help you carry your guitar, Jack. You must be exhausted after all that strumming.'

'There's really no need,' said Jack, looking faintly alarmed.

'But I insist,' Flora asserted. I recognised that tone. Pure steel. If Flora wanted her way over something, Flora got it. 'See you later everyone.' She gave Mum and Dad a meaningful look. 'Don't wait up,' she mouthed. 'I have my key.'

And then, giving Jack a little prod, she weaved her way through the tables behind him. A moment later and the two of them were gone.

'Wow,' spluttered Charlotte, staring after her. 'How the hell did she do that?'

'It's called *tenacity*. She rides roughshod over everyone. My sister is like the proverbial greyhound after a rabbit. Keeps going until the person she's pursuing is exhausted and caves. The word "no" isn't in her vocabulary.'

'Perhaps I should try and be more like Flora.'

'Please don't,' I murmured.

Watching Flora in action had "triggered" me. Back in time. Back to another place. And the memory wasn't a pleasant one.

Chapter Seventeen

The first six months of dating Felix had been blissful, so much so that he'd asked me to move in with him.

'But I haven't even met your mother and father,' I'd laughed.

'What business is it of my family's if I ask a woman to move in with me?' he'd protested.

'Well… you know… it just seems a bit strange living under your roof without having been introduced.'

'Maybe I don't want you to meet them.'

I'd mock-frowned and laughed uncertainly. 'Why? Are they terrifying?'

'My mother is,' he'd calmly replied, and in that moment, I'd known he wasn't joking. 'She's quite keen for me to' – he'd hesitated for a moment, as if unsure whether to spill the beans – 'go down on one knee to her best friend's daughter, Henrietta Cavendish.'

'O-Oh,' I'd stuttered, thoroughly taken aback. 'And, er, why haven't you obliged?'

'Because the only horses I'm into are the ones of the four-legged variety. There's nothing wrong with Henny if you like a girl that looks like a Grand National winner.

Indeed, she has an amazing body. Unfortunately, she also has a face like Red Rum and teeth like a donkey. And as for her laugh – let's not even go there.'

'Er, right.' My heart had been clattering rather unpleasantly at this point. 'Can I ask you a question, Felix?'

'Fire away.'

'Does your mother know you're dating me?'

'No.'

'Do I detect' – I'd gulped loudly, like a cartoon character – 'that I'm not the sort of female who will meet with her approval.'

'You detect correctly.'

'Ah. I see. Can I ask what the eligible Henrietta has that I don't?'

'I'd need to call upon that great British expression to sum up your question. Henny is someone who was born with a silver spoon in her mouth. From the moment she was delivered into Chelsea and Westminster Hospital's maternity ward, Henny has been groomed for marriage. Finishing schools are almost an estranged concept to people nowadays. Many have disappeared. Others have modified and adapted. But Henny's parents made sure she went to London's finest. Henny's family are minor aristocracy, and my mother would like a daughter-in-law that assures the merging of such a family.'

'Right.' I'd gaped at Felix. In other words, Henrietta had breeding. 'Are you related to royalty?'

He'd laughed. 'Only if you go back a zillion generations,

but my mother has delusions.'

'She sounds like my mum,' I'd said lightly, attempting to laugh off Felix's mental picture thus far of Tara Barrington-Jones.

Here we were, two individuals with mothers who alluded to grandeur, except I suspected my dear mum was way down the scale in any posturing. Whilst Dad was a take-me-or-leave-me type of person, Mum's aspirations to social climbing were borne from insecurity.

My mother came from a humble working-class family where money was scarce. Instead of poring over homework and school studies at evenings and weekends, she'd taken waitressing jobs in the evenings and stacked shelves at weekends to help my grandparents put food on the table. There had been no truck, back then, with employment rules, or health and safety regulations. Mum had been a grafter. Strong and capable. And if the local corner shop needed someone to help in the stockroom for cash in hand, or the chippie needed help serving a queue that spilt out of the shop and halfway down the street, then so be it.

Mum had left school with no qualifications, and dyslexia had played havoc with her spelling and written English skills. She'd taken solace in what she *could* change about herself, and bought magazines like *Tatler* and *The Lady*. If she had spare time, you'd have found her at the ancient family sewing machine, copying the latest fashions. Her acute lack of confidence had her seeking role models. The royal family were favourites. Before long, she'd settled down at her sewing machine to copy designs not dissimilar to Norman Hartnell, Alexander McQueen, and Christian Dior. She meant well, and her all-consuming desire to climb the social ladder was harmless. Nonetheless, I'd swerved off introducing Felix to her at this point in our relationship. Not because I was ashamed of my mother. More because I wasn't yet sure what Felix's reaction to Mum's pretentiousness might be. I was fairly sure he wouldn't ridicule her. But I wanted to protect Mum, just in case.

'So, are you feeling brave?' he'd winked, picking up the phone. 'I'll give Mother a call. We can pop round there now. Have a cup of tea. You can admire her dainty porcelain cups and saucers while we make amiable small talk about the British weather.'

I hadn't been sure if he'd been joking or not.

'How charming,' I'd said instead, pasting on a smile. 'Okay, let's do this. I'll bet your mum is absolutely lovely.'

Felix hadn't replied. Instead, he'd grimaced, and I'd been filled with a sense of foreboding.

Chapter Eighteen

When we'd rocked up at the parental home, my voice had shrivelled and died.

As I'd gazed at the narrow three-storey white townhouse in Kensington's Philbeach Gardens, I'd been momentarily gobsmacked.

In this quiet crescent close to the High Street, the house's architecture was from a bygone era. The first floor showcased a chic wrought iron balcony where one might wish to relax, streetside, and partake the London air. It suddenly struck me just how wealthy Felix's family were.

'Have your parents lived here long?' I'd twittered nervously.

Felix had shrugged. 'It belonged to Dad's side of the family before he and Mother married.'

I'd craned my neck upwards. 'There must be a lot of bedrooms.'

'Eight.'

'*Eight?*' I'd squeaked. 'I thought you had just the one sister. Are there other siblings you haven't told me about?'

'No. I know Dad was meant to have been a bit of a naughty boy in the past, but as far as I'm aware, it's just

Arabella and me. My mother is always entertaining. There's usually guests in some of the spare bedrooms. Thankfully there's six bathrooms, so you're never left hopping from one leg to another if someone is hogging the loo.'

'This place is massive,' I'd said crassly.

The home in which I'd been raised had six rooms, never mind six *bath*rooms. Mum and Dad's house contained a small kitchen, snug lounge, three bedrooms – one for my parents, one for Flora, and one for me – and a single bathroom that everyone seemed to want at the same time.

'It's even bigger than it looks,' Felix had added. 'There's a two-bedroomed basement flat that you can't see from this side of the street.' I'd boggled. Who lived in it? Staff? As if reading my thoughts, Felix had continued, 'My grandparents moved downstairs after giving up the house, but they passed away some time ago. Dad has since turned it into a large man-cave. There's a gym, somewhere to play snooker, and a cinema room. Arabella appropriated the remaining area as a working studio.'

'Amazing,' I'd warbled, wondering what Arabella would have thought of my own far more basic working space in Clover Cottage's garden.

'Come on.' Felix had taken my hand and led me along a terracotta tiled path, then up three stone steps that stopped short at a solid, black-painted door with the shiniest brass knocker I'd ever seen.

An elegant middle-aged woman had greeted Felix effusively.

'Darling! Your timing is impeccable. We're just about to sit down to dinner.'

Her cocktail dress and carefully applied make-up had signalled that she didn't mean eating a meal while sitting on the sofa in front of Coronation Street.

Felix had pulled a face as she'd released him.

'Are we talking bangers-and-mash in the kitchen, or a dozen handpicked guests in the formal dining room?'

'When did we ever eat *bangers*' – she'd mocked – 'let alone in the kitchen?'

Felix had looked resigned. 'I see. So who are tonight's guests?'

Taking him by the elbow and ignoring me, she'd drawn him inside.

'Why don't you come through and find out.'

So far I'd remained standing on the doorstep like a spare part, but it was at this point that Felix had gently removed his mother's hand and turned her round to face me.

'I've brought a guest along.' Felix's mother had looked at me, feigning surprise, as if seeing me for the first time. 'Mother, I'd like you to meet Sadie Harding. Sadie' – he'd smiled at me – 'my mother, Tara.'

Tara's smile had been glacial. Nervously I'd rubbed my palms against my jeans, unsure whether to shake her hand – which seemed awfully formal – or peck her on the cheek, which is what everyone in my family did whether meeting someone for the first or thousandth time. In the end I'd done neither because Tara's smile had quickly been replaced by a look of confusion.

'And you are?'

'Er, Sadie,' I'd repeated, my smile faltering.

'Yes, I heard that bit,' Tara had replied. 'What I meant was… who *are* you?'

There had been a nasty pause during which my heart had begun to beat out of time to the blood pumping through my veins. For a second or two, I'd experienced a horrible sensation of arrhythmia.

'O-Oh,' I'd stammered, hoping her son might come to the rescue regarding this rather important revelation. But he hadn't. 'I'm Felix's girlfriend.'

There had been a pause. Only a small one. But it had been long enough to translate as an awkward moment. To let me know without any doubt that this was not only a surprise, but also a shock – and an unpleasant one at that.

Chapter Nineteen

After the hideously uncomfortable introduction, Tara hadn't lingered.

We'd been ushered down the hallway straight into – as Felix called it – the formal dining room where a vast highly polished mahogany oval had been laid up with shiny silver cutlery and thick crystal glasses. All the chairs had been occupied by men and women seemingly dressed for the opera, not dinner – and certainly not *bangers and mash*.

I'd inwardly cringed as Tara had led us into the room where a maid – yes, a maid! – had added two more place settings. The guests had duly shuffled up to make room for Felix and myself. Two more chairs had appeared, as if by magic. The maid had obeyed Tara's sudden revised seating plan putting Felix alongside a horse-faced young woman at one end of the table, while I'd been positioned right at the far end.

I'd discreetly studied the horsy looking woman on Felix's left. She'd looked to be about the same age as him, give or take a year, and I'd instantly deduced her to be Henrietta Cavendish. On his right had been another woman. Older. I'd have hazarded thirty-eight if asked. Long brown hair aside, she was the image of my boyfriend. I hadn't needed any introduction to work out that this was Arabella, Felix's sister.

My boyfriend had already told me that Arabella was single but husband hunting. The septum of her aquiline nose was a dead giveaway that she had a completely different relationship going on with *Charlie*, which couldn't have helped when looking for a suitor.

Both women had counteracted their plain looks with lavish evening dresses and some seriously sparkly jewellery that had shrieked *Van Cleef & Arpels* from the family vault, rather than bling from Primark. Never had I felt so completely out of place in my jeans and t-shirt with an overlaying checked shirt to hide a hole under one arm.

A further study of the guests had revealed everyone else to be somewhere between fifty and sixty. The men had been ruddy faced. The women, po-faced. And Tara, of course, had been one of them.

On my right had been a heavily made-up woman with three chins and a well-upholstered bosom that constantly got in the way of the maid serving. To my left had been a man who'd reminded me of David Attenborough. He'd also been wearing two huge hearing aids that, like his dinner jacket, looked distinctly vintage. Next to him had been a florid-cheeked gentleman wearing a scarlet cummerbund that matched a drooping bowtie. His likeness to Felix had been obvious and I'd deduced him to be Mr Barrington-Jones Senior. He'd caught me looking and had given the friendliest smile thus far.

'My dear! I do believe we haven't been introduced.' He'd leant across Hearing Aids and taken my hand in his. For one ludicrous moment I'd thought he'd been about to kiss my knuckles. Instead, he'd caught my fingers in his and given my hand something between a squeeze and a handshake. He'd had a twinkle in his eye that might have been used – in his youth – to charm the ladies.

'Hello,' I'd quavered. 'I'm Sadie Harding and a friend of Felix's.'

I hadn't dared use the *girlfriend* word again, especially with Tara looking my way and radiating disapproval.

'A friend of my boy's, eh? Any friend of Felix's is a friend of mine too. I'm his father, Freddie.'

'Lovely to meet you, Freddie.' I'd managed to crank up a grateful smile. 'Sorry to gatecrash your dinner party. I seem to be horribly underdressed.'

'Nonsense,' Freddie had assured, before turning to Hearing Aids. 'We don't mind Sadie being underdressed, do we, Albert?'

'What's that?' the old boy had boomed, fiddling with the volume control. 'Sadie wants to get undressed?'

Whereupon everyone's discreet murmuring had ground to a halt and the guests had stared at the denim-clad woman who apparently wanted to strip.

Someone had tittered, and I'd caught Arabella giving me a cool look. Tara's mouth had pursed like a dog's backside, and I'd wondered how on earth I was going to get through the evening.

'What do you do, Sadie?' Henrietta had kindly asked.

'I'm a potter,' I'd smiled, appreciative of her coming to the rescue.

'Oh, like Felix's sister!' she'd exclaimed, indicating the woman sitting next to her. 'Arabella often exhibits fabulous statement abstracts,' she'd said loyally. Arabella had smirked at the lavish compliment before homing in on me.

'What pieces do you produce?'

'Mostly traditional,' I'd answered eagerly, glad to have something in common with one member of Felix's family. 'Most of the exhibitions I do are local.'

'Ah,' Arabella had said, managing to load the word with derision. 'Don't tell me. Kitsch bowls on a makeshift table at a leaky-roofed village hall.'

I'd flushed with embarrassment. She hadn't been far wrong. Some venues were distinctly naff with harsh fluorescent lighting and that old-building smell of rotting cabbage. Other sites, like the Christmas special at Paddock Wood's Hop Farm, were absolute visual works of art in themselves, from both the organiser and those exhibiting.

I'd hastily got off the subject of my little business and instead asked Henrietta what she did.

She'd looked perplexed. 'Do?' Her expression had then cleared. 'Oh, I see. Gosh, all my work is voluntary. You know, visiting hospitals. Distributing toys to sick children. Popping in on local hospices. Raising money for various charities.'

Rouged Lady had discreetly nudged me. 'Henny doesn't

need to work,' she'd whispered. 'She's a trust fund baby.'

I'd been glad when the maid had returned, interrupting conversation, but then regarded my plate in dismay. The food might have been presented on the best porcelain, but the chef hadn't graduated from any renowned culinary school. The soup had been semi-warm and full of raw potato. Mains had been no better with meat so chewy my jaw had ached. Albert, faring no better, had removed his teeth and popped them next to his wine glass.

'Sorry' – he'd informed no one in particular – 'but my gums are better than dentures when it comes to a tough steak.'

Freddie had kindly tried to include me in further conversation, but it wasn't easy talking across Albert who misheard everything. Rouged Lady had then addressed me.

'I suppose you're here for the charity?'

I'd turned red with indignation.

'I've never taken charity from anyone in my life,' I'd gasped.

Rude!

'*Charity*,' she'd repeated. 'Tara's latest project. Distressed gentlefolk.' She'd leant in. 'One of them is sitting right next to you.'

'Oh, I see.' I'd flushed to my roots.

'Tara likes to appear magnanimous,' she'd confided. 'But she has an ulterior motive. Albert is a squillionaire and also a relation of Camilla Parker-Bowles. It helps enormously having decent contacts when looking for patrons and planning a society ball.'

'Quite,' I'd agreed, feeling more and more out of my depth.

'Albert wouldn't be sitting around this table otherwise,' Rouged Lady had informed, as we'd watched him pop his teeth back in. 'So how do you know Felix?'

I'd caught Tara eavesdropping as Rouged Lady had asked this question.

'I'm his girlfriend,' I'd said bravely.

'Really?' Rouged Lady had frowned. 'I thought he was stepping out with Henrietta?'

I'd gulped. 'Er, no. I think you're misinformed.' Tara's spine had stiffened. 'Felix and I are going steady. In fact' – I'd warbled – 'he's asked me to move in with him.'

Rouged Lady's eyebrows had shot up into her dyed hairline and Tara had looked livid. She'd also instantly reacted.

'Henny, I'm so pleased you're partnering Felix at the ball next month. It's going to be a spectacular occasion.'

'I can't wait, Tara,' Henrietta had simpered, before looking adoringly at Felix.

'Er, I think you'll find' – I'd dared to assert – 'that it will be me on Felix's arm.'

Murmured conversation had instantly halted with a collective holding of breath as all eyes swivelled to look at the person who'd dared to contradict Tara. She'd bestowed me with another chilly smile, then proceeded to publicly put me in my place.

'I'm very sorry, Sarah–'

'Sadie,' I'd corrected.

'–but the ball is by invitation only.'

Chapter Twenty

'Nonsense, Tara,' Freddie had boomed. 'Of course Sadie can come to the ball.'

In that moment I'd known exactly how Cinderella must have felt.

'It will mess up the numbers,' Tara had quickly retorted, glaring at her husband.

'Sadie can be *my* plus one,' said Albert gallantly.

'No need,' Freddie had said. 'I have the perfect solution. The lovely Henrietta can partner Albert for the night, and then Sadie can be Felix's guest.'

Albert had given Henrietta a lecherous wink. 'That's settled then.'

Felix had made our excuses just before the coffee and cheeseboard had been served. To say I'd been glad was an understatement.

'So what did you think of my family?' he'd said, as we'd roared off in his convertible.

'Terrifying,' I'd answered honestly.

'Dad isn't.'

'No,' I'd agreed. 'But – and I don't want to offend you Felix – your mother is something else. She so obviously doesn't approve of me.'

'Don't take any notice of Mother,' he'd said dismissively. '*I* approve of you, and that's all that matters. Now, are you moving into my place, or not?'

I had subsequently "sort of" moved in with Felix. "Sort of" in the sense that I'd already had a good proportion of my clothes in his loft apartment and stayed every weekend and a night or two during the week, but had sensibly retained the bulk of my belongings at Clover Cottage. It was a place to escape to when Tara was due to visit, and of course my studio was at the cottage too.

Felix had gone on to meet my parents. Flora had been out when we'd visited Mum and Dad. I'd been faintly embarrassed as we'd sat down to, yes, bangers and mash in the kitchen, while my mother had fussed about with linen napkins rather than a torn off sheet of kitchen roll, but I'd quietly reminded myself that at least my mother wouldn't dream of publicly humiliating a guest.

In the interim I'd attempted to learn more about Tara's charity and tried to ingratiate myself by offering to be a part-time volunteer – talking to lonely old folks over the phone, taking them out for a coffee, or even fundraising. Monetary donations were used to help them in some way, from paying an electricity bill that a pensioner couldn't quite cover, or providing a run of *meals on wheels*. Tara dismissed every one of my offers of help. In the end I gave up trying to make a friend of her.

Felix had, thus far, been a charming and attentive

boyfriend and I was, by now, completely in love with him. His mother aside, our relationship was perfect with romance, laughter, and lots of activity between the sheets.

The date of the ball eventually rolled around. It was understandably a glitzy affair, well attended, and fulfilled every single one of Tara's profile-raising plans. It was also the night that I detected, for the first time, a shift in Felix's attention.

At first, I'd not been able to put my finger on it and work out what it was. He'd made conversation with me, introduced me to Lady This and Lord That, and mostly been by my side. But his attention had been elsewhere.

As I'd chatted to people, enjoying glass after glass of champagne, I'd tried to convince myself it was simply my imagination, and I'd almost succeeded. But then, while listening to a man drone on about the net worth of his company, I'd spotted Felix's gaze wander. My eyes had tracked his, moving to the far corner of the ballroom where I'd caught a glimpse of a woman who'd exuded sexiness. She'd been wearing a sheath of a dress with a plunging back. Her bare skin had been semi-covered by long blonde hair that had fallen in a waterfall of waves and stopped short at the cleft of her buttocks. I'd never clocked Felix looking at another woman until this point. It hadn't initially rattled me because, frankly, half the men in the room had been distracted by the blonde's figure. I'd even hidden a smile in the palm of my hand. Men! What were they like! Except my man had continued to be distracted.

Henrietta had then come over and buttonholed me, asking if I'd consider donating one of my ceramic pots to a charity raffle she was organising. In that moment, Felix had excused himself. He'd done so with charm and politeness, but a sixth sense had told me he was on a mission.

'See you in a bit, darling.'

As he'd set off, he'd reminded me of a bloodhound on a scent. Tail up, nose down.

Henrietta had watched him go too. Then she'd turned to me and asked a question that had made my heart skip a beat.

'Have you caught him out yet?'

'I… pardon?'

'You know. With another woman.'

'W-What?' I'd blanched.

She'd shrugged. 'Tara was hoping that Felix and I would one day get together, but I knew I'd never hold him. Women like me – Plain Janes – take it on the chin. But you're something else, Sadie. You're in another league. I didn't think he'd muck you about.'

'He's not,' I'd protested. 'I mean, he isn't.'

'Then it looks like he's about to,' she'd calmly stated. 'Excuse me, Sadie. It's time for the raffle and Tara wants me to assist.'

Henrietta had glided off leaving me feeling not so much rattled as completely shaken up. I'd stood there, alone, watching Felix say something to the blonde woman. She'd looked up at him in delight, and in that moment, I'd caught sight of her profile. I'd been horrified to discover that not only did I know her, but I knew her ways. In a flash I'd realised that it shouldn't have been a surprise to see her here. This type of function was right up her street, as were the guests. They attracted her like a moth to a flame in her quest to secure a rich husband. Earlier, when Henrietta had told me all about the must-have Stella McCartney dress she'd bought, I'd privately blanched at the cost, but such a conversation would never have unnerved *this* particular female – the one now gazing in rapture at Felix. She'd have bashed her credit card to buy the same, ensuring she'd always look the part, for her social climbing was aggressive and relentless. I'd had no doubt that she'd already worked half the room, and been amazed that our paths hadn't already crossed. And then, feeling sick to the stomach, I'd looked on as Felix had disappeared from the ballroom with the woman on his arm.

My sister, Flora.

Chapter Twenty-One

'Are you all right, Sadie?' Charlotte asked.

I yanked my mind out of the past and back to the present in the pub, shocked at my physical reaction to the sight of Flora leaving with Jack Farrell. Even though the guy was nothing to do with me, my body was remembering that other time – the moment my sister had left a glitzy ballroom on the arm of my boyfriend.

'Sadie?' Charlotte prompted.

'Sorry, I was miles away. Yes, I'm fine. Never better.'

'Okay. Sarcastic.'

'Oh dear. I didn't mean for your Saturday night to become as much fun as a wet firework. I just wish I had William to go home to.'

'Even more reason to go to back to the rehoming centre tomorrow.'

'Maybe. I don't think I could bring myself to look at another dog though. Somehow, it seems disloyal to William. Perhaps I'll think about having a cat instead.'

'That's a good idea,' said Mum, who'd been earwigging. 'Since you no longer have a dog, you don't have to worry about having a little pussy.'

Charlotte's mouth twitched, and I gave her a warning look.

'Come on, Cynthia, love,' said my father to Mum. 'We'd best be getting back.' He looked at Charlotte and me. 'Can we give you a lift, girls?'

'Thanks for the offer, Dad, but Charlotte's car is outside.'

'My last two drinks have been lemonade,' she assured. 'So I'm not over the limit.'

'Come for Sunday dinner tomorrow, darling,' said Mum to me. 'Charlotte, you're welcome too.'

'That's very kind of you, Cynthia, but I'll have to pass. I'll be in my workshop most of tomorrow catching up with work.'

'On a Sunday?'

'Yep,' said Charlotte cheerfully. 'The joys of being self-employed.'

'I'd love to come,' I said to Mum.

'Excellent. And if you change your mind, dear' – Mum touched Charlotte's arm – 'it won't be a problem because I cook as if feeding the five thousand. Bill always moans because we end up having re-heated leftovers for two days afterwards.'

'True,' Dad nodded. 'Come on then, love.' He got to his feet and passed Mum the handbag she'd failed to pick up. 'See you later, girls.'

Cheeks were pecked, and I watched them go with a great deal more fondness than when I'd watched Flora's departure with Jack.

'Let's go and settle our bill with Cathy,' said Charlotte.

We wandered over to the bar and waited for the landlady to total up our meal tab.

'I'll pick you up in the morning,' I volunteered. 'Shall we say about ten?'

'Fine by me. It's not like I have a heavy night planned. More's the pity,' she said gloomily. 'Things have got to change, Sadie. I'm going to put on my thinking hat and come up with a grand plan to get us out of Little Waterlow and into the bright lights. Away from the local yokels. It's time we met some men with a bit of refinement.'

'You sound like Flora,' I tutted.

'God, I'm not that bad,' she retorted. 'I'm not after meeting Lord Poncey-Bigwig or Sir Rodney Whopping-Bank-Balance.' She rolled her eyes. 'It would simply be nice to meet someone who wears leather shoes as opposed to hiking boots or wellies and has a wardrobe that sports a few suits rather than joggers or jeans. Not too much to ask surely?'

'I guess not.'

'All right my lovelies?' said Cathy, coming over. 'Here's your bill.'

'Thanks,' said Charlotte. 'We'll split it straight down the middle.'

'Right you are.' Cathy entered the amount into the terminal and waited for it to connect. 'What did you think of the band tonight?'

'Good,' said Charlotte, holding her card against the

machine.

'Weren't they just!' Cathy grinned. 'And if I wasn't a happily married woman – not to mention a couple of decades younger – I'd be hitching up my hemline when walking past that lead singer.' She laughed uproariously. 'That other guitarist was nice looking too. Did you notice him?' Her eyes gleamed as she ripped off the receipt and gave it to Charlotte.

'I did,' Charlotte nodded. 'To be fair, they were both pretty easy on the eye.'

'I might book them again. They went down a storm with the punters, and that's what matters. Looks like your sister had her eye on Jack,' said Cathy conversationally. 'I saw her following him out. Didn't think he'd be good enough for her,' she sniffed, indicating that she knew what Flora was like. In other words, shallow.

'I think Flora was just after a bit of sport,' said Charlotte good-naturedly. 'Something decorous to entertain her in bed later.'

'I certainly wouldn't kick Jack out from under my duvet,' Cathy sighed, pushing the terminal towards me. 'Oooh, hark at me,' she giggled, as I tapped my card. 'Don't tell my Frank what I just said.' She tore off the receipt and handed it to me. 'See you again soon, ladies. Enjoy the rest of your evening.'

'We will,' Charlotte trilled.

As we headed out to the car park, I wondered what progress Flora had made with Jack. Had he introduced her to Sylvie? Had she made a fuss of William? Had she tossed back

110

her mane of hair and given Jack a come-hither look before reaching for the top button on his shirt. "I've seen the dogs. Now I want to see you."

Were they already thrashing around on his sleigh bed? Flora's hair spilling seductively across black satin sheets. No doubt she'd spit out Jack Farrell the minute he'd pleasured her. Or until something better came along. A banker. Or a trader. A man with a bank balance that ended in loads of zeroes. She'd been incredulous at me landing a man like Felix. And, it had to be said, very envious.

Don't go there, Sadie.

Instead, once back at Clover Cottage and after I'd waved off Charlotte, instead of sinking down on the sofa and letting a late-night movie wash over me, I found myself changing into some old work clothes. Five minutes later I was in my garden studio under the stars, preparing some clay. Or *wedging* to give it the correct name. As I kneaded it like dough, ridding the material of air bubbles and transforming it into a workable consistency, I let the task in hand blot everything from my mind.

Chapter Twenty-Two

I was awoken on Sunday morning by the doorbell giving a series of urgent rings.

'Sadie!' squawked a voice through the letterbox. 'Are you awake, or have you died?'

Squinting at the bedside clock but too bleary-eyed to make out the time, I flung back the duvet and hastened across the bedroom to the sash window. Creaking it up, I stuck my head through the gap. Charlotte was standing on the doorstep.

'What are you doing here?' I frowned. 'It's meant to be me picking you up, not the other way around.'

She peered up at in me in surprise. 'Well you never turned up, did you!' she retorted. 'Blimey, look at the state of you.'

'Sorry, sorry. I've clearly overslept. Two ticks and I'll be down. Give me a moment to use the loo otherwise my bladder will explode.'

'I don't think your mum would approve of such an unrefined description about weeing,' Charlotte pointed out.

'Ah, but my mum isn't here,' I grinned. 'Two seconds.'

I drew down the sash and hastened off to the bathroom,

quickly did the necessary and then splashed cold water over my face before giving my teeth a record-breaking brush. My dentist wouldn't have approved but at least I was now minty-fresh and didn't have dog-breath like William's.

At the thought of William, my mouth drooped, but I quickly reminded myself that an unwanted kitty was just waiting to be spoilt with love and affection. And on the plus side, a cat wouldn't raid the bin or hump sofa cushions. Feeling slightly more chipper, I opened the door to Charlotte.

'Rough night?' she said, peering at my face.

'Funny,' I responded, rolling my eyes.

'Just saying it how it is.' She flashed me an apologetic look. 'You'd better get some caffeine in your veins before we head off to the rehoming centre. Tell you what, as you're still looking a bit bombed, go and sit down and I'll make the coffee.'

'Thank you,' I said, following her into the kitchen. 'I might need a couple of pieces of toast smothered in chocolate spread too. Sugar gives you energy, right?'

'And diabetes too, I believe. What about an egg on toast instead?'

I looked at Charlotte in horror. 'That would involve cooking.'

'And God forbid you do any of that,' said Charlotte caustically. 'Do you ever make yourself a decent meal, Sadie?'

'Not very often,' I admitted. 'There never seems to be any point. Do you regularly cook for yourself?'

'Sure,' Charlotte nodded. 'Tell you what, I'll make it for you.'

'Oooh, aren't you lovely,' I said, sitting down gratefully and leaving Charlotte to peer within the fridge, then raid the cupboards for a frying pan and some oil. 'One day you'll make someone a wonderful wife.'

'Yeah, if I ever find a man,' Charlotte pointed out. 'So why are you sporting bags under your eyes a decade before your time?'

'Oh, you know,' I said vaguely.

'No, I don't.' She deftly cracked eggs into the pan. 'That's why I'm asking.'

'I decided to do some work in the studio.'

'After getting home last night?'

I shrugged. 'The house seemed so quiet without William, and I didn't fancy my own company in front of Netflix. So I took myself off to the studio.'

Charlotte shook her head and tutted. 'What's wrong with snuggling down under the duvet with a good book?'

'It didn't appeal. There was no beagle bouncing onto the bed before nestling down alongside me.'

'Never mind William,' she huffed, lathering butter on toast. 'You need a *man* bouncing those mattress springs.'

'Well there isn't one.'

'Tell me about it,' Charlotte sighed. She stuck a spatula under the eggs and flipped them onto the toast. 'Damn. I've broken one. The yolk is running everywhere.'

'That's okay. It will still taste good.'

I picked up my knife and fork and eagerly tucked in. It had been a long time since Cathy's dinner at The Angel.

'Coffee,' said Charlotte, placing a mug by my plate.

'Ta,' I said, wiping egg yolk off my chin.

'And now' – Charlotte pulled out a chair and sat down opposite – 'while you're filling your stomach, I'm going to fill you in.'

'On?'

'The dating game.'

'Oh, please, no.'

'Yes.' She produced her mobile from her handbag. 'There's a new dating app.'

'*Another* dating app?'

'Well, I suppose it's a bit like social media. One platform is never enough.'

'But surely you will simply find all the same old *same old* on the new app?'

'Possibly,' Charlotte agreed. 'But it's fun looking.' She gave a toothy grin. 'And actually, we could consider looking at Little Waterlow's local rag. They still have the equivalent of a Lonely-Hearts column. Let me go online and check.'

'You must be kidding,' I said, spearing a piece of eggy bread with my fork. 'We won't find anybody suitable in the local paper.'

'Hold your horses.' Charlotte held up a finger. 'Listen to this.'

I put my knife and fork together. 'Go on. Surprise me.'

'Here we go.' She peered at the screen. 'I'm a forty-five-

115

year-old farmer looking for a good and steady wife. I have an acre of potatoes and another acre of mixed vegetables. I'm not looking to have a family, but it would be really nice to have a wife to look after the pigs while I'm milking the cows.'

'That'll be Farmer Gerry,' I snorted.

'Can you imagine his conversation?' Charlotte giggled.

'Udder nonsense,' I quipped.

'Oh my goodness, listen to this one: I'm already married but desperately trying to extricate myself. Meanwhile, if there's anyone out there up for some discreet get-togethers – at yours, not mine, for obvious reasons – let me know. I'm young and handsome.'

'I'll bet you're hoping that's Luke from the rehoming centre,' I said dryly.

'Oooh, I wonder.' Charlotte's eyes had gone a bit googly and I could tell she was tempted to reply.

'Don't even go there,' I warned. 'And never mind Little Waterlow's answer to Blind Date, where's this new app?'

'Ah, piqued your interest, have I?'

'Maybe,' I said carelessly.

'Good, but I'll show you later. Let's go and check out the waifs and strays of the moggy variety. You can drive. Then we'll sort out our love lives. Deal?'

'What have I got to lose?' I sighed.

Life couldn't deliver any more blows, could it?

Chapter Twenty-Three

When we arrived at the rehoming centre, we were greeted by Rachel, much to Charlotte's chagrin. As Charlotte's neck swivelled three hundred and sixty degrees in an attempt to catch any sighting at all of Luke, Rachel gave her a telling look.

'If you're looking for my husband, he's at puppy training classes this morning.'

'Is he?' said Charlotte carelessly. 'Oh yes, that's right. I remember him mentioning it now. Sadie was going to take her beagle along, but regrettably William was snatched back by his alleged original owner.' She gave Rachel a disdainful look. 'That should never have happened. This centre should make previous owners sign disclaimers to prevent them from unexpectedly turning up and demanding their pets back. Sadie has suffered major stress.'

'We do make patrons sign disclaimers,' said Rachel snippily. 'Unfortunately, the document is as much use as a chocolate teapot if the person bringing the animal in isn't the real owner. Now then' – she turned her attention to me – 'I understand you're thinking of rehoming one of our beautiful feline residents.'

'Yes,' I nodded. 'Maybe two, so they have each other for company.'

'That would be wonderful,' Rachel agreed. 'Follow me and I'll take you to the cattery.'

As we were led inside a bright airy building with caged units on either side, I peered within the first pen and immediately found my heart turning to goo.

'Oh look,' I gushed, grabbing Charlotte's elbow, and yanking her to a standstill. 'A mummy cat with all her kittens.'

'They have yet to be weaned,' said Rachel. 'But you can reserve a kitten, if you wish.'

'No,' I shook my head. 'Despite them being utterly gorgeous, I suspect you'll have no problem finding homes for such endearing fluffballs. I'd rather' – I paused to consider – 'yes, I'd prefer some kitties that aren't so popular. Maybe because they're older?'

'In which case, you might like Rosemary and Thyme,' she suggested, leading me further on and stopping in front of another pen. 'Here we are.' She stood aside to let me peer within. 'This is a sister and brother who have been here far too long, likely because they're middle-aged. Both are around seven, but there's plenty of years left in them.'

Silently, I studied the beautiful calico within. A pair of jade eyes regarded me curiously. Rosemary's brother, all black, nervously hugged his sister's side. From the safety of her flank, he glanced up with fearful yellow eyes.

'Hello,' I cooed, bending down. I pushed my hand

through the bars. Rosemary immediately came over and headbutted my fingers. Thyme was too scared and stayed welded to the spot under the heat lamp. I rubbed Rosemary's head and was delighted when she produced a deep purr. My decision was immediate. 'I'll take them,' I said, straightening up.

'Don't rush into anything,' Charlotte advised. 'Why don't you look at the others before making a hasty decision?'

'No, otherwise I'll be taking each and every one of them home. I'll be known as The Mad Cat Lady of Little Waterlow.'

Rachel smiled. 'Do you have a transporter?'

'I have William's old carrier in the car.'

'That will be fine. If you need anything else, remember we have an on-site shop. Litter trays. Tins of food. Grooming brushes. Collars. Toys. All the usual paraphernalia.'

'I'd love to have a browse and stock up,' I said gratefully.

'Sure. Let's do the paperwork first.'

We followed Rachel out of the cattery and into a designated office.

'Cats are a bit different to dogs,' she warned, indicating with one hand that we take a seat. She slid into a chair behind a desk covered in a row of colourful files. She reached for a purple folder and flipped it open. 'When you get Rosemary and Thyme home' – she removed a form and picked up a biro – 'I'd start off with them being in one room. It can be their safe place.'

'That's fine. They can have the spare room for

119

themselves. That said, I was kind of hoping they'd be in my bedroom with me. You know, the three of us snuggling down all together.'

'They can still do that. It's during the day that they need a safe place. Their own sanctuary.' As she spoke, she began filling in the form. 'For example, if the doorbell rings, most cats are startled. They can be quite nervous of visitors and usually make a run for cover. If they can scoot up the stairs to the spare room to hide under a bed, that's great. They will no doubt come out again when they feel confident. Cats are, after all, very curious. But make sure there's lots of hiding places for them while they're settling in. An old cardboard box will be instantly treasured. They love jumping in and out of them as a means of play, but boxes also provide a place to disappear. If you're going to visit our shop, I'd recommend picking up some plug-in diffusers. They're excellent at reducing stress.'

'Okay.' I wondered if the diffusers might work on humans. I could buy one for my bedroom and sniff it when insomnia paid a visit.

'Give them both time to adjust,' Rachel advised. 'Obviously they've had quite a bit of upheaval in the last couple of months. First, leaving their home. Second, getting used to this place. Now they're off again, so don't expect them to jump on your lap for a few days.'

'Right-oh,' I nodded. That was fine. I could be patient. 'Why were they put up for adoption?'

'Their owner died. It's often the case when older pets

come here.' Rachel slid the form across the desk. 'Have a read, then sign at the bottom.'

'Do you have cats?' asked Charlotte.

'No. Luke and I have enough feline company here.'

'And, er, how is Luke?' asked Charlotte, attempting nonchalance.

Rachel gave her a sharp look. 'You're the fourth female to ask after him this morning. The last one asked me if we were getting divorced following a certain advert that has appeared in Little Waterlow's Lonely Hearts column. Is that, by any chance, why you're asking after him?'

Charlotte immediately turned scarlet. 'Good heavens, no. Not at all,' she protested. 'I was just being polite.'

Rachel gave her a look that suggested she knew otherwise.

'Rest assured that Luke is fine. More importantly, *we're* fine. We're a happily married couple.'

'Excellent,' Charlotte warbled.

Chapter Twenty-Four

'I don't know why she got so snotty with me,' Charlotte complained, as we drove back to Clover Cottage. 'I'd bet my last fiver that was Luke advertising in the local for a new lady.'

Rosemary and Thyme were now stowed in William's old carrier wedged on the back seat. Every now and again they let out plaintive meows.

'Whoever placed the ad likely doesn't want a new wife,' I suggested. 'Rather, they just want a leg over.'

'That would be fine by me,' Charlotte nodded. 'I'd take a leg over with Luke.'

'No you wouldn't,' I tutted. 'Sooner or later, you'd be after some commitment. The last thing you want is some flake using you for sexual gratification.'

'I think you'll find that's a two-way thing,' said Charlotte wryly. 'I'm perfectly up for some sexual gratification without any strings. Which reminds me, when we get back to your place, we'll have a quick look at the dating app I was telling you about.'

'*You* can look at the dating app,' I corrected. 'I'll watch you set up your profile.'

'Sadie, have I ever told you that sometimes you can be

remarkably boring?'

'Yes, and I don't care.'

'You're twenty-nine years old. Don't you want a companion in your life?'

'I thought I had William for that, but now I have Rosemary and Thyme.'

'And what sort of exciting conversations will the three of you have?' Charlotte puffed out her cheeks. 'Oooh, coochy-coo,' she said, in a falsetto voice. 'How's Mummy's baby-waby today? What shall we have for din-dins? A little fishy-wishy?' She made a harrumphing noise. 'Such stimulating chit-chat.'

'I have you for that. And my parents.'

'Hmm. No mention of Flora.'

'Leave Flora out of it,' I muttered.

For a moment, neither of us spoke.

'Have you completely forgiven her?' said Charlotte eventually.

I sighed. 'She's my sister at the end of the day. Blood is thicker than water. And all those other clichéd sayings. Anyway, it happened ages. Water under the bridge, as they say.'

'Sod that. I'd have probably scratched her eyes out.'

I sighed. 'Can we just drop the subject? My life is fine the way it is, thanks. It's straightforward and without complications.'

'But are you *happy*, Sadie?' Charlotte persisted.

'I'm happy – whatever happiness is.'

'God,' she snorted. 'You sound like Prince Charles – but substituting the *love* word with *happy*.'

'Are *you* happy?' I said, volleying the question back at her.

'No!' she roared. 'I'm sexually frustrated. I should have been born a rabbit. They supposedly have a marvellous time.'

'Not really,' I disagreed. 'Leonardo Fibonacci posed a brain-teasing question. If a male and female rabbit are placed in an enclosed area together, and produce a litter after one month, then they have another litter, and so on, how many rabbits would you have after one year?'

'What?' said Charlotte. 'Are you trying to make my brain boggle?'

'The answer – theorised by Fibonacci – is one hundred and forty-four.'

'And your point is?'

'That if you were a rabbit with so many kids to look after, you wouldn't be sexually frustrated, you'd be bloody knackered.' I pulled up outside Clover Cottage and tossed my keys to Charlotte. 'Go and open up while I get my new additions unloaded.'

'*Meow*,' wailed one of the cats. My head swivelled round to look at them both on the back seat. '*Meowww*,' came the same plaintive cry. Thyme. He blinked at me, his sweet furry face both handsome and fearful.

'It's okay, little boy,' I soothed. 'I'm your new mummy, and I'm going to love you and your sister forever and ever.' I clambered out of the car and opened the rear door.

'Are you already talking gibberish to them?' said Charlotte, reappearing at my side.

'Yes,' I said happily.

'The front door is wedged open. What else do you want me to do?'

'Would you mind grabbing all the kitty shopping, please?'

'Gordon Bennett,' Charlotte puffed, a second later. She wrestled with one particularly huge carrier bag that was stuffed with three bags of litter. Others contained food, bowls, baskets, and an awful lot of toys, including a realistic looking mouse that, earlier, had made her shudder. 'If you ever become a mother to a tiny human being, I dread to think how overboard you'll go on baby gear.'

'Bonkers, probably,' I agreed, as we lumbered up the garden path.

'Not sure I'm cut out to ever be a parent,' said Charlotte, bringing up the rear. 'My sister told me that having a newborn was like a hangover that even hot water and lemon couldn't fix. On the upside she's mastered the one-minute poop and the half-minute shower.'

'Delightful,' I replied, as Charlotte kicked the front door shut behind us. 'Let me get these two upstairs and settled in the spare room, then we'll have a sandwich and a cuppa.'

As I reached the landing, the doorbell rang. Strange. I wasn't expecting any visitors. Perhaps it was the bible bashers recruiting.

'I'll get it,' Charlotte called after me.

I put the carrier down in the spare room, pausing to catch my breath, just as I overheard Charlotte expressing surprise at the unexpected visitor.

'Goodness. Whatever are *you* doing here?'

Chapter Twenty-Five

'Hi,' said a familiar voice. 'Is Sadie in?'

I froze. I knew who the surprise visitor was. Jack Farrell. And I was inclined to echo Charlotte's question. What, indeed, had brought him to Clover Cottage? Unless it was something to do with a certain beagle. My stomach flipped with anxiety.

'She's upstairs,' I heard Charlotte say. 'Hang on a mo.'

I quickly put the cats' carrier into the spare room, then leant over the landing's banister rail.

'Is William all right?' I called down, trying not to let panic get the better of me. Oh God, had this blasted man left his back gate open? Had William made a run for it? Got lost? I gulped as an even more terrifying thought crossed my mind. Had he been run over?

'He's fine,' Jack assured, peering up. 'Er, sorry to interrupt your Sunday, but can I come in for a minute?'

'She's been settling her new babies into their nursery,' said Charlotte cosily.

'Babies?' said Jack, sounding flabbergasted.

'It's okay, I haven't given birth,' I assured, moving along the landing. I positioned myself at the top of the stairs. 'Do you want to come up and see them?'

I had no idea why I was being friendly to a man I disliked.

'Um…'

'They're cats,' I assured.

'Ah. Okay.' Cautiously, Jack came up the stairs. 'Cats, as in moggies?'

'Well they're definitely not lions and tigers,' I retorted.

'It's just… I thought you were a dog person.'

'So did I,' I said, trying not to sound bitter. 'But for reasons beyond my control, it didn't work out.'

'That's why I'm paying a visit.'

'Oh?' I said, curiosity getting the better of me.

'Look, I'll talk to you about that in a minute. For now, I'd love to see your' – his lips twitched – '*babies*.'

Was he sending me up?

'They *are* my babies,' I declared. 'Aren't William and Sylvie *your* babies?'

'No. They're my dogs.'

'That's the difference between you and me,' I said, pushing down the handle to the spare room. 'My pets are my family.'

'Excellent,' he nodded. 'And my dogs are my pack.'

I had a sudden vision of Jack Farrell in a dog food ad, running across the hills, wind in his hair, coat tails flapping, with hundreds of dogs at his heels as he zoomed towards a bowl of meaty chunks.

'This is Rosemary and Thyme,' I said stiffly.

He hunkered down in front of the carrier. 'Hello, beauties,' he said softly. 'Has your mummy not let you out of your carrier yet?'

'I was just about to before you turned up,' I said irritably, closing the bedroom door. I then quietly crouched down alongside Jack. As I reached for the cage's latch, my hand inadvertently brushed against his. *Zinggg.* I let out a small cry.

'Are you all right?' he asked.

I shrank away from him in horror. Why had my body reacted like that?

'Fine,' I squeaked. 'Er, could you move over, please? Make a bit of room.'

'Sure.' He shuffled a few inches sideways but remained too close for my liking.

Trying to ignore his presence, I fumbled with the catch. The carrier's door swung open. Tentatively, heads bobbing, the cats slowly emerged. Rosemary led the way, pausing every now and again to stare at Jack, then me. Thyme brought up the rear, almost glued to his sister's bottom.

'Hello,' said Jack softly. His hand slowly reached towards Rosemary's head. She allowed his fingers to tickle her ears and then head-butted his hand for him to do it again. 'You're very beautiful,' he told her.

Like all new mothers, I felt my heart swell with pride. Rosemary was indeed extremely pretty with her marmalade, black and white markings. Seeing his sister enjoying some fuss and attention, Thyme crept towards me. Carefully, I

129

extended one hand. A wet nose momentarily bobbed against my skin as he investigated. Deciding that I was friend, not foe, he allowed me to stroke him… just as Jack made to fuss him too. Once again, our hands brushed together, and a sizzle scorched up my spine. I stifled a gasp and, like a jack-in-a-box, sprang upright, startling the cats and making them both run back into the carrier.

'Try not to do any sudden movements around them,' Jack advised, straightening up.

'Yes,' I wheezed. 'I mean, no. I mean…'

'Shall we leave them to explore this room in their own time while we talk downstairs?' he suggested.

I nodded, temporarily unable to speak. What the heck was going on with my body?

As we stepped out onto the landing, Charlotte was standing on the third stair tread.

'I was just about to come and get you,' she said, going into reverse. 'The kettle has boiled, and I've made some sandwiches.' She gave Jack an enquiring look. 'Do you want to join us? There's plenty for you too.'

'Why not,' he replied. 'It will be nice to sit down and eat without a beagle staring at me, drooling all over the floor and guilt-tripping me into sharing my lunch.'

'I always shared food with William,' I said.

'Funnily enough, I'd worked that out,' he replied. 'Yet another bad habit he's picked up.'

I opened my mouth to protest, but then shut it again. Oh, let the man moan. Heavens, according to him, William was a complete delinquent, and it was all my fault.

'As leader of your *pack*' – I gave Jack a tight smile – 'I'm sure you will soon have William sleeping in his basket downstairs, eating his meals in the back yard, and walking obediently to heel when out. And no doubt you'll go that extra mile and train William to pick up his poops and pop them in the bin before mowing the lawn and pegging out the laundry.'

'Unfortunately' – Jack's expression was grave – 'he's not that intelligent.'

'Sit down,' said Charlotte, sensing tension and wanting to diffuse it. 'So what brings you here, Jack?' she asked, handing out plates and then setting a platter of ham sandwiches on the table.

'Will.'

'You mean William,' I corrected, picking up a sandwich.

'Before you two get into a slanging match about a beagle whose name you can't agree upon' – Charlotte plonked herself down, her chair almost centre position between the two of us – 'how about we have our food, and then discuss Will' – she caught my arched eyebrow – 'or even William, afterwards?' She didn't wait for an answer and instead rattled on, determined to deflect any bad feeling. 'Now then, Jack. Sadie and I thought you and your band were absolute heaven. Didn't we, Sadie?' I didn't answer on account of having a mouthful of food but managed to curl my lip. Charlotte flashed me an exasperated look before prattling on. 'Cathy said she was so impressed she will be booking you again.'

'That's nice to hear.'

'Do you do a lot of gigs?' she asked.

'Not especially. It's just a hobby.'

'You should be professional.'

He smiled, and I noticed how it transformed him. From grumpy to, goodness, almost approachable.

'You're not about to tell me you and Simon Cowell are like that, are you?' he held up one hand and crossed two fingers.

'No,' Charlotte grinned. 'That's Flora's speciality.'

'Ah yes, Flora,' said Jack in a tone I couldn't quite fathom.

'What's that supposed to mean... "ah yes, Flora"?' I mimicked.

'I think I'm in enough trouble with you without dissing your sister.'

I straightened my spine. Diss my sister?

'Why, what did she do?' I said, curiosity getting the better of me.

Jack suddenly looked a bit bashful. 'Look, I'm sure she's a lovely girl–'

'But?'

'She doesn't know how to take no for an answer, does she?'

'In what way?' I frowned.

'Last night, all I wanted to do was pack up the gear and get home to Sylvie and Will, then relax with a cuppa. One way or another, yesterday had been quite fraught, what with the shock of unexpectedly finding my dog and then seeing you stressed and upset. I had a commitment to play the gig but didn't really want to be there. I spent the entire time fretting about Will getting out of his crate – he's a total Houdini – and then wrecking the house. The last thing I needed was Flora insisting on coming back to mine and being my hot water bottle for the night.'

I flinched. 'And was she?'

'What?' Jack frowned.

'Your hot water bottle,' I growled. Jack caught my tone and gave me a strange look. Oh dear. I seemed to be impersonating how William had always greeted Ted the postman. 'Sorry,' I cleared my throat. 'Frog.'

'Frog?' Jack's brow furrowed.

'Yes. In the throat. Ahem.' I made a show of clearing it. 'A-*hemmm*. That's better,' I chirped. 'So, you were saying?'

'What was I saying?' Jack was looking even more confused.

'You were telling us whether or not you slept with Flora,' said Charlotte helpfully.

'Really?' Jack looked staggered at being quizzed about his love life. 'Er, no. I didn't.'

'Why not?' I demanded, ridiculously pleased to hear this, but not sure why.

'Because I didn't want to,' he protested. 'Goodness me, what is this? The Little Waterlow Inquisition? Sorry, Sadie. I know she's your sister, and I'm sure you feel very protective

133

of her as a result, but she's really not my type.'

'Not your type?' I repeated, blinking rapidly. Since when had my sister *not* been a man's type, with her long flicky-blonde hair, tiny waist, enhanced bust and eyes the colour of delphiniums.

'A pretty girl' – he said hastily, as if trying to back-peddle and ingratiate himself with me – 'but she's way too pushy and, apart from anything else, she reminded me of my ex which put me right off. I'm not looking for a carbon copy replacement. And, just like Gaynor, Flora didn't take too kindly to rejection.'

'That's because she's not used to it,' Charlotte pointed out.

'What did she say?' I said, aware that I was holding my breath.

'She charmingly conveyed that I was probably the reason the middle finger was invented.'

'Oh dear,' said Charlotte. 'So you won't be seeing each other again any time soon.'

'Er, no. I'd like a girlfriend at some point, but not Flora.'

There was a silence as Charlotte and I both digested this.

'So' – the sandwich Charlotte had been about to bite into hovered mid-air – 'you're not dating?'

'Not yet. I'm still recovering from Gaynor.'

Charlotte raised her eyebrows. 'You're nursing a broken heart?'

'Hardly,' Jack snorted. 'By "recovering", I mean recuperating. Taking a breather. Like paying off the debts she ran up on my credit card and repainting my house where she graffitied the walls.'

'She's the woman who put William into the rehoming centre by way of revenge for being dumped,' I reminded Charlotte.

'Seems a bit over the top,' said Charlotte. 'Did you cheat on her?'

'No! Absolutely not. If you must know—'

'Yes?' Charlotte and I trilled in unison.

'We'd been dating for a few months and Gaynor wrongly assumed we were on track to getting married. She'd already semi-moved into my place without me inviting her. The stealth factor. A few clothes here. Some books there. Framed photographs. Then a lamp. Followed by a coffee table. The next thing was half my furniture disappearing and a John Lewis van turning up with a new three-piece suite, and a bed I knew nothing about until getting home from work. And while I was opening my credit card statement and trying to make sense of the spending on it, she prattled on about an autumn wedding and that she'd seen the dearest little flower girl dresses in House of Fraser. It was the last straw. I told her it was never going to happen and that I wanted her out. The rest of the story you already know. I left her to pack and got home to find chaos and damage but, even worse, William gone.'

'I see,' said Charlotte, suddenly looking shifty. She put down her sandwich and brushed some imaginary crumbs from her lap. 'Sadie and I were talking earlier about a new dating app.' She looked innocently at Jack. 'We're both going to try it out.' She picked up her phone. 'You should too.'

'Thanks, but no.'

'It's called *The Butter Half*,' she continued.

'Sounds like a café.'

'It is, sort of. The idea is that if you match with someone, you first meet in a café for a cuppa and, say, a cheese toastie, and then see how you go from there.'

'Actually, you've jogged my memory. I heard one of the band members talking about it.'

'Which one?' asked Charlotte, ears pricking up.

'The other guitarist. I'm a hundred per cent sure he's on it.'

'Is he now?' she said quietly, a smile playing about her mouth. 'How about you tell me your mate's name while I set up my profile?'

Chapter Twenty-Six

In the end, it wasn't just Charlotte who set up a dating profile. Despite Jack and me being reluctant, she bullied and cajoled and finally persuaded Jack and me to do the same. It was only when we were interrupted by the plaintive cries of Rosemary and Thyme from upstairs, that I pushed back my chair and leapt to my feet in horror.

'My babies,' I gasped. 'What sort of new mother am I?'

'Don't worry,' said Jack, looking amused. 'I won't report you to Social Services.'

'They're probably cross-legged and needing their litter tray,' I said, appalled.

'More like wanting some kitty food,' put in Charlotte. 'Go and sort them out while I clear up these cups and plates.'

'I must be going,' said Jack, getting to his feet.

'Yes, you need to get back to William,' I said firmly. 'You're clearly as negligent a parent as me.'

'I left him sleeping,' Jack protested. 'He was in the garden this morning having a marvellous time digging holes so deep I'm surprised he didn't end up in Australia. He came in filthy and exhausted and was out cold when I left home. Anyway, before I leave, he's the reason why I paid you a visit.'

'Look, let me see to the cats' – I scampered out of the

kitchen – 'and then we'll resume this conversation,' I called over my shoulder.

'No need to shout, I'm right behind you,' said Jack, following me up the stairs. 'Let me help you. I'll sort out their litter tray while you feed them, and then I can chat to you at the same time. We seem to have allowed your friend Charlotte to thoroughly distract us.'

'Okay,' I said, pushing open the spare room door.

There was no sign of the cats.

'They're hiding,' said Jack.

'Ten out of ten for observation, Sherlock.'

'Are you always sarcastic?'

'No,' I said honestly.

'Look, Sadie,' Jack sighed. 'I feel like we've got off on the wrong foot together.' He split open a bag of cat litter and began filling the two trays. The rehoming centre had advised that both cats should have their own tray from a *territory* perspective. 'I'm really sorry about the experience you had with Will... William... whatever you want to call him–'

'William,' I confirmed, levering open a tin of cat food and forking the contents into two new bowls.

'And if you must know, when I got home after the gig, he spent the rest of the night howling well into the early hours. I had to resort to ear plugs.'

'My poor boy,' I said, misery washing over me.

'That's why I found your business card. I remembered it had your address on it. I thought I'd pay you a visit and ask if you'd like to take Will...William... for a walk with me. He's obviously been spoilt rotten during his time at Clover Cottage. Also, seeing you might reassure him, so that he resettles at my place.'

At that moment, a head popped out from under the spare bed. Rosemary.

'Come on, little girl,' cooed Jack. 'Your mummy has some lovely din-dins for you.'

I regarded Jack in bemusement. 'I can't believe you just talked to my cat like that.'

'Neither can I. Guess I'm more sensitive than I realised.'

'A man in touch with his feminine side, eh?'

Jack laughed. 'I don't know about that.'

A moment later and Thyme's head poked out too.

'Come on, fella,' Jack adopted a wheedling tone. 'Smell this. It's yummy!'

The cats' noses quivered and, after a brief hesitation, they both minced over, the tips of their tails curling over like shepherds' crooks.

'Good boy,' said Jack, stroking Thyme's head as he tucked in, purr engine springing into life. Jack glanced at me. 'So what do you say?'

His hazel eyes met mine. There was a warm light in them now, and his expression was hopeful. Friendly. A truce of some sort being offered. I met his gaze and inexplicably found my heart skipping a couple of beats. Weird.

'Okay,' I nodded. 'You're on.'

Chapter Twenty-Seven

'Shall I pop back in about an hour?' asked Jack. We were downstairs again, standing in the hallway. 'Or do you want to drive over to mine, and we take the dogs for a walk from there?'

'The latter would probably be better,' I replied.

Realistically, I didn't want William seeing Clover Cottage and thinking, "Oh goodie. Home. Lead me to your bed so I can jump on it and roll about on the duvet." I was aware he'd picked up atrocious habits while with me, but I was never going to admit that to Jack. Also, I didn't want to risk William bounding into the house, catching a whiff of feline, scrabbling to get into the spare room and then traumatising Rosemary and Thyme on their first day at Clover Cottage.

'Okay, I'm only over at West Malling. Not far away. Shall I text you the post code?'

'Sure,' I said, aware that we were, in effect, officially swapping numbers, which went beyond the exchange of business cards. My stomach went a bit fluttery at the thought, although my brain quickly intervened.

This is about seeing William, Sadie. Not Jack. Do you

fancy this guy, or something?

I recoiled in horror at the very idea. *Most certainly not. He took William from me. Therefore, I could never fancy this man. No matter how attractive I think he is.*

The little voice didn't miss a beat. *What's that? You're attracted to Jack?*

I suddenly felt flustered. *Look, I didn't mean it that way. Yes, Jack is good looking. But I meant it in the context of… I dunno… like admiring a sofa. Or a bookcase. "My goodness, that's a mighty fine bookcase over there. Very handsome." See? Sure, Jack is handsome, but I don't fancy him.* Sorted.

Seconds later my phone dinged with a text containing Jack's full address.

'Fab,' I said, giving him a proper smile instead of a peel-back-the-lips-and-bare-the-teeth grimace like William did when he was grumpy. 'See you in an hour.'

'You will,' he said, returning the smile. Suddenly I found my heart lifting. 'Bye, Charlotte,' Jack called over his shoulder.

'Laters,' she yodelled, from the kitchen.

Shutting the door after him, I turned round to find my bestie standing in the kitchen doorway, hands on hips.

'What's with the silly smile?' she asked.

I'm seeing William in an hour,' I grinned. 'We're going for a walk.'

'Just you and William?'

'No. Jack and Sylvie too. The four of us.'

'How cosy,' she remarked. 'The pair of you *are* getting along. Quite a turnaround.'

'Hardly,' I protested. 'Want to come?'

'No. I really do need to do some work. I wasn't bluffing when I declined your mum's invitation for Sunday lunch.'

'Fair enough.'

'I'll leave you to do some quiet bonding with your new family members, and catch up with you later to see if you've had any matches on *The Butter Half.*'

'Oh, that,' I said, having completely forgotten about the dating app.

'Don't dismiss it,' she chided, wagging a finger. 'Right, see you later. I'll let myself out.'

I gave her a brief hug, then bounded up the stairs again, leaving Charlotte to lace up her trainers and shut the door behind her.

Letting myself into the spare room, I was surprised to see that both cats had snuggled up together on the spare bed. Neither of them made any attempt to make a run for it and hide, although they did regard me with saucer-like eyes as I slowly approached the bed.

'Hello again,' I said softly. I sat down carefully, perching on the edge of the old candlewick bedspread that I'd taken from my childhood home.

I then quietly told them my life story and included my deepest, darkest secret. Either the sound of my voice was comforting, or else they were bored to tears because, forty-five minutes later, the pair of them were fast asleep.

Chapter Twenty-Eight

When I arrived at Jack's place, I tried and failed not to be impressed.

The mews house was set back from the road within a swish gated development where the developer had blended old with new. Old, because the properties had once formed part of a rundown, red-bricked brewery, high ceilings and huge paned windows lending light and a sense of space. New, because a developer had bought the site, worked some magic, and – from what I could glimpse – made it thoroughly contemporary with open-plan rooms and floating staircases. My beagle was living in the lap of luxury. No wonder Jack's ex-girlfriend had made such a song and dance when he'd asked her to leave.

The heavy wrought-iron gates rolled back as I was buzzed in.

'Visitor parking to the right,' said Jack, his voice crackling through the squawk box.

I eased Grace, my ancient Citroen, into a space between a Mercedes and a Range Rover, then shimmied out, taking care not to scratch anyone's paintwork.

As I walked towards the house, I had a sense of déjà vu. Why was that? After all, I'd never been here before. I walked up three stone steps, then paused in front of a solid, black-painted door with a shiny knocker. Suddenly I was transported back in time. To another house with the same number of steps and a not dissimilar front door. The home of Tara Barrington-Jones, Felix's mother.

Ridiculously, I felt a netful of butterflies take off in my stomach, and marvelled at how the body could react, all this time later, to old programs of anxiety and discomfit. But instead of the door being opened by an ice-maiden in formal evening dress, I was greeted by Jack wearing the same old jeans and sweater from an hour ago. He was smiling broadly.

'Hey,' he said. But before he could say anything further, a bleary-eyed Sylvie bustled into the hallway, indignant that she'd been caught napping while on guard duty.

'Woof!' she said, giving an obligatory bark before wagging her tail.

'Hello,' I replied, patting her head, and suddenly feeling peculiarly tongue-tied and a little bit shy with Jack.

A high-pitched yelp came from deep within the house accompanied by the thumpity-thump of paws pounding along the upper landing. I watched, in delight, as a tri-coloured blur flew down the staircase, then used a rug as a launch pad to spring into my arms.

'Oomph,' I grunted as the impact of William's weight nearly sent me flying.

'Steady,' said Jack, grabbing my elbow. A whoosh of electricity shot up my spine. It was a wonder William and I didn't instantly self-combust.

144

'My goodness,' I gasped, still fizzing and popping as I hugged a wriggling William. He was doing his best to lick my entire face. 'What a lovely greeting.'

Which one, Sadie? goaded the little voice in my head. *The reception from the beagle with the terrible halitosis, or the greeting from the guy whose touch just pinged your bra strap and twanged your loins?*

Sylvie promptly goosed me, wagging her plumy tail, politely letting me know that she didn't want to be ignored. I made a long arm and rubbed a silky ear.

'Did you bring your wellies?' asked Jack.

'Walking boots.' I stuck out a foot by way of demonstration. 'Will they do?'

'Definitely. Right, let me take Will… William… from you.' Jack's expression said, "You win on the name". I flashed him a grateful look. He then slightly spoilt it by adding, 'His recall seems to be better if I use the formal version of Will.'

'Ah, so he did learn one good thing from his time with me,' I quipped.

'Just the one,' Jack winked. 'Here's his halti.' He passed me a small black headcollar with an attached lead. 'I'll let you pop this on him. Right, Sylvie.' He turned to the patiently waiting dog at his heel. 'Where's your lead?' She gave a joyful yip, then padded off to a concealed cupboard under the stairs. Patting a large paw against it, the door sprang open. Sylvie's front half disappeared for a moment, then she reversed out with a rope-lead in her mouth.

'Did you teach her how to do that?' I asked, astonished.

'Not really. She just caught on quick that the cupboard under the stairs is the place where shoes and doggy paraphernalia are kept. I've hardly had to train her. She's so clever. To be honest, she doesn't even need the lead, but I don't like to take any chances if we're walking alongside a road.'

'Well, quite.' If I'd ever attempted the same with William, there would have been traffic mayhem, not to mention a flattened dog.' I put the still wriggling beagle down and slipped the halti over his nose. 'Where are we going?'

'Manor Park. It's only around the corner.'

'Do you know, I was born and bred in nearby Little Waterlow, so how crazy is it that I've never checked out West Malling's country park?'

'Now you can,' he said happily, shutting the front door behind him and leading the way down the stone steps. 'I've worked at the park from time to time.'

'How come? I thought you were a landscape gardener,' I said, as we set off at a cracking pace. Goodness, my previous walks with William had been at half this speed.

'I'm a tree surgeon too.'

'Ah.'

'Manor Park is a large area. Fifty-two acres in all but divided into four sections. There's a lake which is very popular with moorhens, dabchicks, and swans. Then there's Chestnut Paddock and Abbey Field used for grazing but

146

providing an array of wildflowers in the summer. On the far side of the lake is the Ice House field.'

'That's a strange name.'

'Yeah. It came about from the building there that used to store ice. In the winter months, the lake froze over. The ice was taken for the manor house's kitchen. They took plenty of fish from the waters too, for their table, obviously.'

'You seem to know an awful lot about the place.'

'I ended up working there for several weeks and discovered its history along the way. The estate goes back to the eighteenth century and was created by a man called Thomas Douce. Douce's Meadow is an open grassland area where a lot of today's families like to congregate. There are several picnic tables and plenty of space for ball games.'

'Sounds wonderful.'

'It is. The woodland areas – particularly the veteran trees – are also home to bats.'

'Oh.' I tried not to shudder. 'I'm not so keen on them. They look sweet enough, but they always remind me of flying mice.'

Jack laughed as he led the way off St Leonards Street, taking us across a car park and along a leafy footpath. 'Don't worry,' he assured. 'I'm sure the bats won't flap around our heads. What we need to be more aware of – you in particular – are the squirrels. William is obsessed with them.'

'Yes, he was always chasing the bushy-tailed visitors in my garden,' I laughed. 'On one occasion he nearly got lucky and caught one.'

As we bowled along, I felt myself relaxing in Jack's company. We visited the lake and stood on its muddy banks edged with rushes. Jack kept up a running commentary about the birds that visited, including kingfishers and herons. Mr and Mrs Swan glided by, their paddling webbed feet leaving a trail of ripples fanning out behind them. The March sunshine beamed down as a cool breeze ruffled the surrounding trees' branches. Whilst all this was lovely, the best thing was having William by my side again.

Something deep within me began to unknot and relax. It seemed like a lifetime ago that I'd felt this carefree. To be more specific, since last seeing Felix. My mind instantly conjured up an image of my sister, way back, in that ballroom with Felix, but I swatted the thought away. My brain instantly substituted another picture. This time, Flora scampering after Jack at The Angel. *Go on,* my inner voice urged. *Ask him.*

I took a deep breath. 'So!'

Jack gave me an assessing look. 'Hmm. For a small word, that sounded pretty loaded.' He gave me a knowing look. 'Are you, by any chance, revving up to ask me a pertinent question?'

'Okay,' I tutted. 'Sussed.'

'Let me guess.' He pretended to think for a moment. 'Is it to do with Flora?'

How could I deny it? Despite being overjoyed to be with William on this heavenly walk, there was another part of me that wanted to probe a little bit more about last night.

Get down to the nitty gritty. In other words, hear exactly what moves Flora had made on Jack.

'Yes, it's to do with my sister,' I admitted.

'What do you want to know?'

'About what happened. You know, when she followed you out of the pub.'

'But I told you earlier, at your cottage. She wanted to come back to mine and–'

'Yes, yes. I know that bit. But… did she? Go back to yours?'

'She got in my car without being invited and said her place was on the way and I could drop her off.'

'Her place?' I snorted. 'She lives with my parents.'

He shrugged. 'Details. I told her I wasn't going home straightaway and was hanging out with the rest of the band for a while. That we were taking some downtime at Aran's place. Except that wasn't true. I was trying to fob her off. The reality was that I simply wanted to go home, let the dogs out for a wee, then chill for a while before going to bed. Obviously, I didn't tell Flora that. But she remained welded to the front seat of my car and said that she loved an "after party" and would come along too.'

'Wow,' I said, marvelling at my sister's thick skin.

'It was at this point that I said it wasn't that sort of gathering and vaguely suggested another time. I was still trying to politely give her the brush off, but she continued to sit there. Then she produced her mobile and asked for my number. She said she'd ring the following day and get a proper date in the diary for us to see each other again. I gave her a steady look, debating whether to be honest and say, "Look, sorry, but I'm not interested." However, she misread my silence as a cue to launch herself at me.'

'Goodness,' I gasped.

'That wasn't quite how I put it,' Jack murmured. 'I let slip a certain four-letter word which your sister then misconstrued as the green light. She squealed, "Oh yes, let's do that!" Suddenly, her tongue was halfway down my throat, and her hands had become octopus tentacles and were going everywhere.'

'I'm so sorry,' I breathed.

'I don't expect you to apologise on your sister's behalf, Sadie.'

'So what happened after that?' I couldn't, somehow, imagine Flora being totally peachy with rejection.

'She was very angry. I gave her that old line. "It's not you, it's me". She said, "Damn right." I explained that I'd recently ended a relationship and wasn't looking for another, and she snapped that she wasn't looking for a relationship. Just a f—'. He stopped abruptly. 'Sorry. Too much information.'

'It's fine,' I said faintly, visualising Flora's outrage and indignation. She wasn't so pretty when angry.

'Has Flora put you up to questioning me about what happened?' Jack looked at me, eyebrows raised.

I blanched. 'No! Absolutely not.'

'Why are you so interested then?'

I found myself flushing. *Yes, indeed, Sadie. It's none of your business.* Except...

I took a deep breath. 'Oh, I don't know.' I did. 'I guess it was old-fashioned curiosity. Wanting to hear what my sister is like in action. I've spent goodness knows how long not knowing. Not properly.'

Jack looked confused. 'You've lost me.'

'Sorry, I'm probably not making much sense. You see, at one point I suspected Flora was having an affair with my fiancé.'

Jack looked startled. 'I thought you were single.'

'I am. Now. The wedding was cancelled. Both Felix and Flora denied there was ever any shenanigans, but I was never quite sure. Not that it matters anymore. But I just wanted to know' – I stared blindly ahead – 'what my sister was like when she's determined to get what she wants.'

For a moment, Jack didn't say anything. 'Sneaky,' he eventually said. 'Would that be the right word to sum up?'

I nodded. 'Yes, I guess.'

We didn't say anything for a while and the only sounds were that of the dogs panting in time to our footsteps.

'So!' said Jack, breaking the silence and making me jump.

'Hm. Now it's your turn to say that same small word with a loaded tone.' I gave him a mischievous grin.

He smiled sheepishly. 'Maybe. Can I ask *you* something?'

'Fire away.'

'If Felix and Flora vehemently denied there was anything

going on between them, why did you call off your wedding?'

I opened my mouth to tell him, but the words died on my lips. I wasn't quite sure how to reply. Because although family and friends had known the outcome, none of them had been privy to the finer details of the tipping point from which there had been no return.

'Because' – my voice was low, but steady – 'something else happened. And it changed everything.'

Chapter Twenty-Nine

Jack didn't say anything further, perhaps hoping that the silence would provoke me into telling him exactly what had changed everything. But I didn't reply. Instead, my thoughts were elsewhere. Back at Tara Barrington-Jones' charity ball. Watching Felix disappear with Flora.

I'd hastened across the ballroom, threading my way through half-cut braying guests, out through the function suite's double doors, into a corridor, eyes flicking left and right, wondering where they'd gone.

A sudden draft had ruffled my hair and, instinctively, I'd turned left, heading in the direction of cool night air. I'd stopped short of a door that was ajar. It had led out on to a balcony. Silently, I'd paused for a moment. Taken a deep breath. And then I'd stealthily approached the door and peered through its opening. There had only been a gap of two or three inches, but it was enough to discreetly view the couple on the balcony. Felix and Flora.

I couldn't believe what had happened. Indeed, was still happening. Felix had always made me feel like the most adored woman in the world. And even though I knew I was only a notch above ordinary, he'd made me feel beautiful. I could remember telling him how I'd always wanted to be blonde, like my sister, but Felix had insisted he'd loved the dollop of strawberry God had added to my hair colour, and that my cool grey eyes were far more interesting than a pair of baby blues. Which was why I couldn't believe what I'd just witnessed. Felix going off with a blue-eyed blonde. My sister no less.

As I'd peered through that gap, I'd seen Flora with her hands on my boyfriend's shoulders. Felix's palms were cupping her bottom, thumbs inside the backless dress. From the movement under the fabric, it was plain he was massaging the cleft that divided her butt cheeks.

I'd wanted to throw up and had let out an involuntary whimper. Their heads had whipped round, and their bodies had sprung apart like deflecting magnets.

'Who's there?' Felix had demanded.

Shaking, I'd placed my palm on the door and gently pushed. It had swung outward revealing my ashen face.

Felix had blanched, but Flora hadn't so much as flinched.

'What are you doing here?' she'd asked, curiously.

'I could say the same of you?' I'd croaked. 'You haven't yet met my boyfriend, have you? Well, now is the perfect moment. Flora, meet Felix.' Then I'd rallied. 'Except he's now an ex-boyfriend.'

And then I'd turned and fled along the corridor, hurled myself through the main doors that led outside and then belted along the London pavement. I'd stuck up one hand as I'd run and instantly secured a black cab. Disappearing into its depths, it had trundled off just as Felix had burst out of the venue, his breath leaving clouds in the cold night air as he'd stared after my taxi.

As soon as I was back at the loft apartment, I'd been a whirlwind of activity. My suitcase had been pulled under the bed and I'd frantically grabbed clothes from hangers, tossing garments in any which way. Felix had returned just as I was zipping up the case. There had been no sign of Flora.

He'd been in a terrible state. Beside himself. Gibbering. Almost crying. A constant stream of apologies had fallen from his lips.

'Darling, please. I'm so sorry. I don't know what got into me. You must believe me. I'd never met her before in my life. I had no idea who she was. Not that that's any excuse. Please, Sadie, don't leave me. It's you I love. *Please.* Can we put it down to too much drink and a huge dose of stupidity?'

My face had crumpled. By that point I'd felt physically drained. So full of emotion I couldn't think straight and so full of tears, I couldn't see properly. My legs had buckled, and I'd sunk down on the bed, head in hands, and sobbed profusely.

Felix had got down on his knees in front of me. Taken my hands in his. Kissed them frantically, all the while apologising over and over. Telling me it was nothing. Meant nothing. That he'd had his head momentarily turned. So stupid. So utterly and completely stupid.

'It's you I love, sweetheart. *You.* Always has been.

Always will be. I know – let me prove it to you. Marry me.'

Whether it was the relief of knowing he still wanted to be with me, or the fact that his face was ingrained with regret, or his voice so desperate, I'd slowly found myself nodding. Despite Flora and I being two such very different people, and rarely seeing eye to eye, I loved her. She was my sister. However, by the time I'd allowed Felix to undress me, kiss his way down my neck, my torso and then between my thighs, I'd convinced myself that somehow, in some way, the whole thing had been Flora's fault... conveniently forgetting Henrietta Cavendish's words of warning.

Chapter Thirty

It was a while before I saw Flora again.

A social butterfly, she didn't let her brief clinch with Felix be anything more than a blip on her ambitious horizon. I was reliably informed that after confronting her, she'd returned to the ballroom and, before the night was over, mesmerised someone else. This time a businessman. Older. Richer. But not wiser.

My sister had subsequently attached herself like a beautiful barnacle, dumped her employer, and jetted off around various capitals of Europe followed by a stint in the States. She'd ended up in Miami and from there it had been a hop, skip and a jump to a private chartered yacht sailing around Exuma, Bimini, Eleuthera and, finally, Long Island. It was there that she'd blotted her copybook fraudulently appropriating the businessman's bank cards. She was lucky not to have ended up cooling her tanned heels in a foreign jail. By the time Flora was back in England, I was wearing an engagement ring.

My parents had now met my fiancé. Mum was predictably embarrassing. When she'd opened the door to us, for one horrible moment I'd thought she'd been about to curtsy. At the last moment she'd recovered herself and instead done a weird sort of half bob. Dad had simply been Dad. He'd taken Felix by the hand and given it a firm shake, but he'd had no airs and graces. Unlike Mum or, for that matter, Tara Barrington-Jones.

The wedding machine had swung into action. Mum had been beside herself with excitement when Felix had laughingly mentioned that he had a family connection that meant we could marry at St Paul's Cathedral if so desired. At the time I couldn't think of anything more intimidating. I was perfectly happy with Little Waterlow's tiny church. But then Tara had intervened and insisted the marriage take place at Kensington and Chelsea Register Office. Felix had been keen for me to agree. "Let's not ruffle her feathers, darling," he'd said. "Mother wants to be involved, and she knows what she's doing." The implication possibly being that Mum and I didn't. But frankly, I was so terrified by both Tara and Arabella, that I lacked the confidence to assert myself. And anyway, my own mother – who would never be a bosom buddy of Tara's – was firmly in agreement that I should let Felix's side of the family take control. "You only have to see how Tara dresses to know she's a real lady," my mother had declared, her hands clasping and unclasping in delight. "And anyway, why on earth would you want to get wed in the village church? The roof leaks and the whole place reeks of damp. No, Sadie. Tara is right. Kensington is far more appropriate." Mum's eyes had shone with a messianic light. "And just think, it's almost within spitting distance of

Kensington Palace!" I'd looked at her in disbelief. Dad had caught my eye and given a discreet shake of the head. *Let her be*, his expression had said. *Give her this moment.* And so, with both mothers – in their own way – at the helm, I'd conceded. "But you'll let Flora be bridesmaid, won't you," Mum had beamed. And my heart had lurched.

I'd met Flora in due course for a coffee. I'd left Felix in London and spent an entire week at Clover Cottage working in my studio in preparation for an exhibition. Flora had agreed to meet me at Chloe's Café along Little's Waterlow's tiny high street.

'So you're marrying him,' had been Flora's opening gambit. 'Well done on hooking such a prize. Mum is no doubt wetting her knickers as we speak.'

'Do you have to be so coarse?' I'd chided.

'Why not?' she'd shrugged. 'I don't have pretensions.'

'That's pretty rich coming from someone who actively pursues sugar daddies.'

'Wow, I didn't have you down for being a bitch, Sadie.'

'And I didn't have my own sister down for trying to nick my boyfriend.'

We'd glared at each other.

'Listen, when we were at that ball, I didn't *know* Felix belonged to you. Hell, I didn't even know you were there. I couldn't believe it when you appeared on that balcony. I didn't think London parties were your thing.'

'They're not. It was a charity ball organised by my future mother-in-law.'

159

Flora had wrinkled her nose. 'Tara B-J. That old bat.'

'You know her?'

'Know *of* her. Stuck up cow. Are you sure you're doing the right thing marrying into that family?'

'I love Felix,' I'd said simply.

'Love,' she'd tutted. 'That doesn't mean you have to marry the guy.'

I'd shrugged. 'Call me old fashioned.'

She'd snorted. 'I think I'd rather call you stupid. You certainly wouldn't catch me shackling myself to a man whose surname initials were BJ.'

'Do you have to bring everything down to base level?' I'd cried.

Flora had put her hands in the air. A gesture of exasperation. 'Sorr-*eee*,' she'd sighed. 'I'm thrilled for you. No, really.' She'd nodded her head. 'He's definitely a catch.'

'God, now *you* sound like Mum.'

'Except I don't mean that word in quite the same way as our mother.' She'd given a hard little laugh. 'Mum's definition would be with reference to the way Felix speaks. A bit of posh. And no doubt she's enamoured with his connections. That he will provide for his wife and future children who, when they come along will – in her head – be replicas of Kate and Will's kids. No, my definition is somewhat different, Sadie. More jaundiced, you could say. Felix is loaded enough to enable a wife to give up the day job, buy fabulous clothes, have numerous holidays, and regularly meet her girlfriends in Fortnum & Mason for afternoon tea rather than Costa for coffee and a sandwich. On the upside, if things don't work out, you can divorce him and take half his bank balance without too much sweat.'

'That really is the most mercenary statement I've—'

She'd instantly cut off my riposte. 'I'm a realist, Sadie. Something you're not. You're way too romantic and stupidly soft. Listen, you're my sister. Despite us not always seeing eye to eye, I love you.' That had brought me up short. Flora had never expressed sentiment before. 'But I'm on the same circuit as Felix's mates.' Her tone had hardened. 'He has a reputation, Sadie. I've heard he's a player.'

'Heard,' I'd scoffed. 'That's hearsay.'

'Call it what you like,' she'd said, getting to her feet. 'Just don't say I didn't warn you.'

Chapter Thirty-One

Over the ensuing days Flora's words had reverberated in my head, mixing uncomfortably with the echo of Henrietta's missive that had been delivered some months previously at Tara's charity ball.

But despite such cautions, Felix continued to behave like the perfect partner. He was attentive. Caring. Every day, sometimes several times, my phone would ping with romantic messages, whether at Clover Cottage's garden studio or at "home" in Felix's loft apartment. I also made sure our sex life was extremely active and imaginative. Sometimes the little voice in my headed goaded me.

Another basque, Sadie?

And why not?

But you already have six in your underwear drawer.

Felix likes them.

You must be Ann Summers' best customer.

And what's wrong with a little imagination?

Nothing! My concern is that you're simply exhausting the man in the hope that he doesn't have the energy to pop his willy into any other female's barely-there knickers.

Oh pur-leeze. I just have a high sex drive, that's all.

Hmm. Are you sure about that? You're looking a little peaky to me.

Bog off.

I was reluctant to admit that the nasty little voice had mentioned something that resonated. I was knackered. Indeed, I'd never had so much sex in my life. There was also a part of me that figured if Felix was well and truly put through his paces in the bedroom, then he wouldn't have his head turned elsewhere. Not when he had such an energetic and imaginative fiancée always ready, willing, and able.

And on the table, sneered the little voice. *Wherever next? The elevator?*

Don't be ridiculous. That would be wrong on so many levels.

Not funny.

Eventually the warnings of Henrietta and Flora had faded to nothing more than a soft whisper. Anyway, by this point I had something else to preoccupy me. Tara. For the first time since meeting her, she'd telephoned asking that I join her at lunchtime the following day. I'd been due to stock up on studio materials but told myself I could defer it to another time.

'How very kind of you to invite us,' I'd replied.

'Not Felix,' had come the brisk reply. 'Just you.'

'O-Oh,' I'd stammered, instantly feeling a sense of unease.

'And no need to mention this to him either,' she'd added.

I'd been so anxious about the impending meeting – for I couldn't imagine it to be anything else – I'd made an excuse to Felix that evening about needing to pop out for some milk. Once alone, I'd telephoned Charlotte.

'Why do you think Tara wants to see me?' I'd hissed.

'Gawd, I dunno.' I'd sensed Charlotte puffing out her cheeks at the other end of the line. 'Perhaps she finally wants to befriend you.'

'Yeah right. Do you think it's a ruse of some sort? Maybe I'll ring her doorbell and find myself greeting a hitman.'

'I think you'd have been a goner by now if that had ever been her intention,' Charlotte had chuckled. 'No, it's probably something perfectly trivial.'

'Tara doesn't do trivial,' I'd pointed out.

'You're right. It's likely wedding related. From what you've told me, the woman is an utter perfectionist. She probably wants to run through the guest list – final numbers. And then chat about the flowers, catering, and the seating plan. Perhaps she needs to be cautious about people who can't stand the sight of each other and need to be kept on opposite sides of the room.'

'Possibly,' I'd nodded. My brain had told me that this was a perfectly reasonable explanation, but my heart had sensed a different vibe. That night I'd found it hard to sleep and tossed and turned for a good couple of hours, fretting away, before finally nodding off.

The following day, I'd turned up at Felix's family home

with an armful of flowers and dressed, I'm embarrassed to say, in the sort of garb that Henrietta favoured – a silk dress with the hemline well past the knee. I'd almost put an Alice band in my hair but ripped it off at the last minute.

'Hey,' I'd smiled, as Tara opened the door.

'Sadie,' she'd acknowledged, relieving me of the blooms. 'I'll ask Consuela to put these in water later.' Tara had dumped them on the hall's console table.

There was a distinct lack of cooking smells coming from the kitchen, so I deduced that Tara's housekeeper had made some dainty sandwiches for us instead. The type with the crusts cut off and cut into triangles.

'Come on through,' Tara had instructed.

I'd followed her into the formal dining room, but no china plates had adorned the polished table. Instead, there were some papers neatly placed upon its surface. As I'd sat down, I'd realised it was a legal document.

'Take a seat,' she'd indicated.

I'd duly perched, trying not to reveal how nervous I'd suddenly felt. 'Is Freddie joining us for lunch?' I'd asked.

'Lunch?' she'd frowned. 'This isn't a social occasion.'

'O-Oh. I'd assumed that–'

'Then you assumed wrong.' She'd given me a chilly look. 'I asked you here to sign this.' She'd indicated the papers on the table.

'Okay,' I'd said, still unsure what this was all about. 'Do you want me to witness something?' I'd done that a couple of times, the most recent being Charlotte's *Last Will &*

Testament. We'd both shuddered theatrically as we'd scribbled our respective signatures.

'This is a prenuptial agreement,' Tara had explained. Her expression had dared me to challenge her. 'It's to protect Felix's financial interests.'

'W-What?' I'd stuttered.

'Do you know what a prenup is?'

'Yes,' I'd gasped. 'But surely there's no need for–'

'On the contrary.' Tara had smiled thinly. 'Freddie and I paid for Felix's apartment and we're not about to stand back and let you get your hands on our investment in the event of a divorce.'

'Does Felix know about this?' I'd demanded, suddenly finding my voice.

'Not yet, but he will. After all, he knows which side his bread is buttered when it comes to the family's finances.'

'You do realise that I'm a homeowner,' I'd asserted, managing to sound both furious and indignant. 'Why would I want any part of Felix's flat when I'm already on the property ladder?'

'Ah yes. Clover Cottage.' Tara had given me a withering look. 'With all due respect, Sadie, there is zero comparison between a tumbledown ex-farmworker's lodge and a state-of-the-art bachelor pad in a prime city location. Sign here, please.'

I'd duly scrawled my name, by which point Consuela had appeared to witness the signature. Then, wrapping my dignity around me like a cloak, I'd taken my leave. What sort of person did Tara Barrington-Jones think I was? Clearly a grasping gold digger.

As I'd drooped down the steps to the tube, a small part of me had acknowledged that my future mother-in-law was simply protecting her family's interests. Looking out for her son. After all, if I'd been someone like, say, Flora, Tara would have been deemed extremely sensible to ensure a signature was delivered on the dotted line. But despite telling myself this, it had left a bad taste in my mouth, and as the train doors had slapped shut, I'd found myself silently seething.

I'd kept my word to Tara and not mentioned anything about our meeting to Felix. He'd left for work earlier that morning believing that I was heading off to Little Waterlow for my stocktake and would be back in London much later. So it was with a sense of surprise on both sides when I'd walked back into the flat mid-afternoon and found him fresh out of the shower and wearing a dressing gown.

'Whatever are you doing here?' He'd looked flabbergasted as I'd swung into the hallway.

'Good to see you too,' I'd retorted, dredging up a smile while slipping off my jacket.

He'd instantly looked bashful. 'Sorry, darling.' A peck had landed on my cheek. 'You just surprised me, that's all.'

'How come you're home so early?'

He'd pulled a face. 'I'd had enough at work. Dad was in, anyway. Some client or other that he wanted to butter up. So I left him to it and pushed off early.' He'd looked me up and down. 'What's with the silk dress?'

'Oh,' I'd shrugged. 'The stocktake got delayed by something else. Short notice. I was trying to impress someone.'

'And did it work?'

'No,' I'd said economically, dumping my handbag on the floor and kicking off my high heels. 'Let me get changed and we'll have a glass of wine together. I feel like I need one.'

'Great idea,' said Felix. He'd headed off to the kitchen while I'd peeled off to the bedroom. And then I'd paused. Sniffed. The faint smell of perfume had hung in the air. I'd sniffed again, but the scent had then eluded me so that I'd no longer been sure if it had been real or imagined.

Chapter Thirty-Two

'Do you want to talk about it?' said Jack, bringing me back to the present. He was looking at me curiously.

'No. Not really. It's over and done with.'

He nodded. 'Best not to linger in the past otherwise you can never walk into the future.'

'Yeah.' God knows how many times I'd heard lines like that one. Too many. 'Anyway, you've had your own heartache to get over.'

He snorted. 'At the risk of sounding like an insensitive plank, I didn't sob into my pillow night after night over Gaynor. I did, however, lose sleep wondering where William was. I didn't know if he was dead or alive.'

'Instead, my boy was at Clover Cottage. Oh, sorry,' I reddened. 'I need to remember that he's no longer my boy. He's your boy.'

'Tell you what' – Jack looked at me kindly – 'how about we refer to him as *our* boy?'

My cheeks went from pink to puce. Partly from pleasure. Partly, embarrassment. Jack's words made it sound as though William was a link between us. Which, I suppose, he was. But I couldn't deny that it was also a link I rather liked.

Because, ever since turning up at Jack's house, there had been a thaw going on in my feelings about this man. When I'd met Jack – was it only yesterday? It seemed like a lifetime ago – I'd been angry at him reclaiming William, but now… well, now I understood what he'd been going through.

We spent the next hour or so walking around the country park until, reluctantly, I had to make my excuses. I had two new family members to go home and check upon, which was comforting, although it didn't make it any easier saying good-bye to William.

'We'll have to do this again,' said Jack, as we returned through a side gate into his development.

'I'd like that. Seeing William today has made things…' I paused, trying to put into words how my heart felt. 'Just better,' I said softly. I bent down to fuss "our boy". He responded by putting his front paws on my thighs, instantly imprinting my trackie bottoms with muddy marks.

'Oh, look what he's done,' Jack tutted.

'It's fine,' I said, stroking William's silky ears.

'I can be flexible with work if you want to walk again tomorrow.'

'That would be great,' I beamed. 'What sort of time?'

'Either early – around seven in the morning – or between four and five in the afternoon. What suits you?'

'Four o'clock would be perfect.'

'Great. That's a date then.'

I felt myself going a bit pink again. *A dog walking date, Sadie. Not a DATE date.*

'Um, do you mind me asking' – I trailed off, aware that I needed to word my question carefully – 'but when you're at work all day, don't you worry about William being bored at home. Beagles aren't great left to their own devices for hours on end. And' – I gabbled – 'this isn't a criticism. It's simply an observation which I learnt from experience.' Memories came flooding back of an upended kitchen bin, chewed sofa cushions and a snoring beagle sprawled across my newly laundered duvet. At least Rosemary and Thyme wouldn't behave like that.

'No offence taken,' Jack assured. 'Now that I have Sylvie, I'm hoping she'll prove to be not just company for William, but also a good example of how to behave when I'm not around.'

'Hm. I wouldn't count upon it.'

'Well, I know you don't approve of me crating William, but while he's settling back in, it might be a necessity. But only for a while,' Jack added, catching the look on my face. 'If he proves to be an utter nightmare, like howling and upsetting the neighbours, then he'll have to come to work with me. Before Gaynor dognapped him, he occasionally came along with me. No, I'm not kidding,' he said, catching the look of disbelief on my face. 'I'd pop William in a hi-vis jacket and let him trundle around a customer's garden while I got on with, say, a patio job. There's ways and means of getting around it.'

'That's good to know.' I trailed off awkwardly, and gave William a final pat. 'Well, um, see you tomorrow then.'

'You will,' Jack smiled.

'Same time, same place.'

'Yep.' He was still smiling. 'I'm glad we're now friends, Sadie.'

I felt my neck reddening and prayed that the stain didn't travel up to my face. *Blush, flush, blush, flush.* What was wrong with me?

'Yes, me too,' I said shyly.

Then I turned and fairly skipped towards Grace, my trusty Citroen. And when the automated gates swung open and Jack put up a hand in farewell, I had to resist the urge not to frantically wave back, like an overexcited kid on a school excursion. But it was fair to say I drove home with a silly smile on my face.

Chapter Thirty-Three

'Hello, you pair of pickles,' I cooed, peering around the door to the spare bedroom.

Two small faces with huge wide eyes stared back at me, but other than the owl-like surprised expressions, it was evident Rosemary and Thyme hadn't moved. The pair of them were still snuggled together on the candlewick bedspread.

Slowly, taking care not to make any sudden movements, I tiptoed in and shut the door quietly behind me.

'What have you both been doing?' I murmured, perching on the bed beside them. Neither made any attempt to make a run for it and hide. 'Have you both had lovely snoozes? Did you enjoy happy dreams? Did dancing butterflies or dicky-birds feature?'

Carefully, I reached out and began to stroke them. Rosemary first, under the chin. She immediately began purring. Thyme shifted his weight, then headbutted my hand to do the same to him. Soon he was purring too.

'Isn't this nice,' I beamed. 'And do you know what? Despite losing my lovely William, I've gained two beautiful fur-babies. Because that's what you are. My babies.'

Encouraged by their relaxed demeanour, I let my fingers stroke their backs. Neither tried to claw or bite, so I repeated the action. 'Do you like me talking lots of silly nonsense?'

Purrrrrrrrrrrrrrr, said Thyme, getting up and languidly stretching.

'I'm not sure you'd like William Beagle, although he's sweet-natured and does funny things that make me laugh. Like barking at the television or running round and round the house with a pair of old socks dangling from his mouth. You'd probably find him too boisterous. That said, his heart is in the right place. A bit like his owner,' I nodded, thinking of Jack. 'I was a bit mean to him in the beginning, but he's been very accommodating. We went for a lovely walk together, with William and Sylvie. Sylvie is William's sister,' I prattled. 'And we're going to do it all over again tomorrow. He's really rather handsome, you know. Jack, not William. I mean, William is handsome too. Obviously. But I'm talking about Jack. In fact, I don't mind confessing that I like him. You know, as in' – I lowered my voice furtively – 'fancy him.' My heart sped up upon saying that out loud. Goodness. What was happening to me? 'I haven't felt this way about anyone since Felix. I've simply not been interested. At the time, it was like a light going out. But now it's as if someone has switched it back on. And you know what?' Rosemary yawned and rolled onto her back, waving all four paws in the air, while Thyme crept onto my lap. I smiled as he walked in two tight circles then collapsed down in a heap. 'Okay, I'll tell you anyway. Liking Jack feels good, but scary too. I

174

mean, nothing is going to happen, is it? So it's silly being scared about having a crush on him. After all, the guy is out of my league. If Jack rejected a beauty like Flora, then he's hardly going to be interested in me. Not that I'm going to be making any advances,' I added hastily. 'Anyway, I'm glad the two of you have been settling in nicely while I was out. I'm going to have a bath now and get changed. My mother is cooking Sunday dinner as we speak, and I'd better not turn up in my grubby old jogging bottoms or this t-shirt with holes in it thanks to William chewing the sleeve, otherwise I'll get told off for not making an effort. My mother likes to keep up appearances,' I told Thyme conspiratorially. He promptly stuck one leg in the air and began washing his bottom. 'Try not to do that when she next visits.'

I arrived at my parents' place with five minutes to spare.

'Be a love and lay the table,' said Mum, her face pink from standing over the gas hob which was full of steaming saucepans. 'Your father is holed up in the bathroom with the Sunday papers and your sister' – Mum rolled her eyes – 'is watching some must-see vlogger putting on eye make-up in a way that's never been done before and it's vital Flora doesn't miss a second.'

'Sure,' I said, giving Mum a sympathetic grin. I opened the cutlery drawer and began selecting utensils.

'Don't forget napkins. No, not those paper ones. The linen ones in the next drawer down.'

'Won't it make extra laundry?'

'Yes, but they look far more elegant than tissue serviettes

covered in primary colours. I don't know what your father was thinking of when he put them in the shopping trolley.'

Flora and Dad appeared just as Mum was getting ready to dish up.

'Hello, love,' said Dad, giving me a kiss on the cheek.

'I hope you've washed your hands, Bill,' said Mum, draining broccoli through a colander.

'Yes, Cynthia,' said Dad mildly. 'Have you washed yours?'

'Very droll,' Mum tutted. 'Do something useful and see to the wine.'

'You're looking very glowy,' said Flora, scrutinising me as she sat down at the table. 'And furtive,' she added. 'What have you been up to?'

I pulled a face. 'Nothing much.' Suddenly I didn't want to tell her all about my magical afternoon with Jack and the dogs. 'What about you?' I asked, deflecting attention away from me. 'Been anywhere?'

'Nope,' she said, taking a sip of the wine Dad had placed in front of her. 'I'd had plans to spend the day with that Jack guy. You know, the singer who stole your dog.'

'Oh?' I said, ignoring the dig about Jack stealing William. I sat down too and took a sip of my own wine. 'So why didn't you?'

'Because it turned out he's gay.'

'What?' I spluttered, nearly spraying wine everywhere.

'I reckon he's having a fling with that other guitarist.'

'How on earth did you reach that conclusion?'

'Well it's obvious, isn't it?' She made sure Dad had moved away and was helping Mum. 'He turned me down flat,' she hissed. 'I mean, *hellooooo*! What man in their right mind would do that to ME?' She mistook my stunned silence as agreement. 'Exactly. He couldn't wait to hot-foot over to Aran's house and spend the night with him.'

'Jack recently ended a relationship. With a *woman*,' I emphasised, as Flora rolled her eyes.

'Then he must have ended it because he knew he swung the other way.'

'Who swings what way?' said Mum, setting loaded plates in front of Flora and me.

'Er, nothing,' said Flora, picking up her knife and fork and hastily popping a potato in her mouth.

I didn't think it wise to comment further. I still had memories of how Flora had allegedly reacted after Felix had left her at the ball. Despite Flora ending up with a businessman later that night, prior to that she'd apparently pursued Felix out into the cold night air claiming SHE was the right woman for him, not me. I only had Felix's word for it, and it wasn't a conversation I wished to ask Flora about. The whole Felix-and-Flora thing had been a taboo subject ever since.

'Are you all right, Sadie?' enquired Mum, pulling out a chair to sit down.

'Yeah, I'm good, thanks.'

'That's the ticket, love,' she beamed. 'I'm so glad Charlotte insisted you go back to the rehoming centre. Tell us all about the new additions.'

So I brought them all up to date about Rosemary and Thyme and then casually dropped into the conversation that I'd seen William earlier, and Jack saying I could see William whenever I wanted.

'That's very decent of him,' said Mum.

'Huh,' said Flora, pulling a face. 'That's probably so he can dump William on you when he wants to spend the night with his lover.'

'Who's this we're talking about?' said Dad, bringing his own plate over and sitting down.

'Jack,' I said, blushing slightly as I said his name again. 'William's owner.'

'He's gay,' put in Flora.

'Who? William or Jack?'

'Both probably,' said Flora grouchily. 'By the way, have you seen that new dating app?'

'Which one?' I said cautiously.

'It's called *The Butter Half.* I thought I'd check it out later. Everyone I know is raving about it. You should look into it too.'

'Oh that,' I said vaguely. 'Yeah, I already did. Charlotte talked me into setting up a profile.'

'Darling, that's wonderful,' said Mum. 'Dad and I were only recently saying how nice it would be to see you dating again. After all, it's been such a long time since–' She trailed off awkwardly. My parents never said the F word.

'Steady,' muttered Flora. 'After all, Sadie hasn't actually

swiped right yet.' She looked up at me under her eyelashes. 'Or have you?'

I shook my head. 'No, and I probably won't either.'

'I don't think it works like some of the other apps,' said Flora thoughtfully. 'Carmella told me that someone can "like" your profile and then you can decide if you want to reply, and there's also an option to have a live conversation.'

'Oh, right,' I said, feigning disinterest.

'I know *just* the photo I'm going to use for my profile. It will guarantee me over a hundred likes within an hour,' she smirked.

'I didn't think dating apps were your sort of thing,' I said mildly.

'They're not normally,' she snapped.

Her abrupt tone let everyone know that the dating subject was now closed. At the time of Flora's debacle with the businessman, ripples had flowed out into her social circle sullying her reputation. And whilst she'd eventually clawed her way back, I'd since heard – more recently – that my sister had been involved with a wealthy married man. I had a sneaky suspicion that Flora's reputation now preceded her. Maybe it wasn't such a coincidence that Minty and Jonty had gone off abroad without her. Perhaps they'd dropped her. After all, nobody liked being associated with a tea leaf – whether it was stealing credit cards or nicking another woman's husband.

By the time I was back at Clover Cottage, it was dark. Going into the hallway, the house felt chilly. Pulling off one shoe, I hopped over to the thermostat whilst simultaneously pulling off the other shoe, then turned up the temperature dial.

Meowww, came a plaintive cry, immediately followed by a second one, then two at the same time.

'Coming,' I called, picking up my shoes and tossing them into the cupboard under the stairs. One of these days I would invest in a proper shoe rack. I hastened up the staircase and opened the spare room door. 'Hello, my kitties,' I said, surprised to see both apparently waiting for me. Rosemary weaved around my ankles while Thyme stretched his front legs up my jeans using the fabric as a ladder to reach my arms. 'Ow, ow, *owwww*,' I protested, as sharp claws pierced denim and skin. 'Well, hello, boy,' I said, delighted that he'd been brave enough to do such a thing. 'Are you feeling more settled? And where are you off to?' I said to Rosemary, as she disappeared between my feet and minced along the landing. 'Exploring? Come on then,' I said, following her. 'Let me give you both a guided tour.' Thyme remained in my arms as I followed Rosemary into my bedroom. She did a swift scan of bed, drawers, wardrobe and dressing gown flung across the duvet, following by a perfunctory look inside the bathroom. She peered over the rim of the tub, dismissed it as nothing special, and then pattered down the stairs to the lounge. Her eyes swept over the room's contents in a nano-second. Finally, she made her way into the kitchen, sitting her bottom down near the larder. A marmalade tail curled over dainty paws as she looked up at me expectantly.

'What?' I said.

'*Meow.*'

Thyme leapt out of my arms and joined his sister, mimicking her position.

'Oh, I get it,' I said. 'The pair of you couldn't be clearer. *Feed me.* Okay, I understand. It's time for more kitty food. You're both very shrewd sussing where the tins are kept.'

I dished up some rather whiffy sardine and tuna mixture which, judging from the loud purrs, was going down a treat. I'd been at Mum and Dad's for hours and it was almost bedtime. Leaving the cats to their late-night dinner, I went upstairs and changed into my pyjamas.

It was only as I was snuggling under the bedcovers that I reached, on a whim, for my mobile. Maybe, before reading my kindle, I'd have a little mosey through *The Butter Half.* Not that I was looking for anybody to date. But my curiosity was piqued after also hearing Flora talking about the dating app.

I clicked on the icon and was surprised to see half a dozen notifications. Oh! I had some "likes". Astonished, I clicked to see who was waiting for me to potentially reply. And then my heart skipped a beat. I didn't know who Tom Biggins was. Nor Christopher Holmes, Sam Wilkins, Harry Thomas, or Ryan Beasley. But I recognised the next name. Indeed, I'd only seen him a few hours ago. Jack Farrell. And he was waiting to start a conversation with me.

Oh don't be ridiculous, Sadie. He's just being polite after Charlotte made the pair of you set up profiles. He's probably liked Charlotte's profile too.

Yes. Probably. After all, Jack seemed very decent like that. In which case, it would be rude not to reply. Right. Absolutely. With slightly shaking fingers, I double-clicked.

Chapter Thirty-Four

Having clicked "reply", I hadn't a clue what to write. What about:

Hi! Thanks for liking my profile pic. Does this mean you want a date? If so, I'm up for it. I'd love to have a coffee and croissant with you. And then watch you get crumbs all around your mouth. And let me lick them off.

Geez, Sadie, you really do need to get out more. How peculiar is it that you're lying in bed on a Sunday night thinking about a man who, twenty-four hours earlier, you couldn't stand?

Yes, well, things have changed.

Evidently. But your imagination is behaving a bit like William when he sees a squirrel. Over-excited. Settle down. Write something boring. After all, that's what you are.

Thanks for that. You really know how to make me feel good.

I gazed ahead at a framed picture on the wall. It was a print of a field full of flowers. Pretty but predictable. I'd once overheard Felix saying the same thing about me. My brain instantly shied away from that scenario. It was time to be bold. Less "pastel" like those flowers and more "colourful".

Outgoing. Gregarious.

Fired up, I began to type.

Hello, Jack. Thanks for liking my profile. That's really kind of you.

My inner voice immediately chimed in. *Wow, what a scintillating reply. He'll be mesmerised by your prose. Not.* Before I could tell my inner voice to get stuffed, I was shocked to note that the "live" icon had activated. Oh my goodness. Jack was online. Was he going to reply?

Hey, Sadie! Really enjoyed our walk this afternoon, and I know William was thrilled to see you too.

William was thrilled to see me too? *Too?* Did that mean that Jack had been thrilled to see me *as well as* William? I chewed the edge of my thumb as I thought about it. Why was the English language sometimes so complicated?

It was a lovely afternoon made even more special for seeing William.

Oh hell. Would he now think that it had been a special afternoon even if William hadn't been in the equation?

My mate has liked your friend's profile. Aran and Charlotte have been chatting this evening.

I raised my eyebrows and typed back. *That's great. She's a lovely girl. A lot of fun.* Best keep quiet about Charlotte also being a sex-mad lunatic, especially if she'd shipped a bottle of Prosecco.

They are meeting tomorrow evening for The Butter Half's stipulated coffee, but I have a feeling they'll be going out for a proper drink afterwards. Charlotte apparently dropped a lot of hints about having a glass or two of Prosecco.

I'll bet she did. *Ha ha, Charlotte is a bibbly girl who likes her bibbles.*

There was a pause while Jack typed. *Do you mean *bubbly* and *bubbles*?*

I rolled my eyes. Damned predictive text. *Yes! My phone does that sometimes. Comes out with completely different words. It's so annoying. Anyway, I'm really looking forward to tomorrow and seeing William again.* There. I'd stipulated I was looking forward to seeing William. Not Jack. Although, secretly, I was totally looking forward to seeing Jack. *And Sylvie too,* I added. *She's gorgeous.*

Jack was now typing. *Sylvie is my girl.*

I sighed, momentarily wondering what it was like to be Sylvie. I certainly wouldn't mind rolling over and having Jack rub my tummy. *Have you had any other likes?* Oooh nooo. Why had I asked him that question? That was plain nosey and surely taking a small step away from keeping things neutral.

Yes, a couple. What about you?

A couple? What, just two? Bet he was being modest. *There are currently five other men waiting to see if I start a conversation with them.* I chewed my lip. Perhaps I should have lied and said ten. Bigged myself up a bit. Too late. I'd said it now.

I expect you'll be inundated in due course, ha ha.

You're too kind.

Are you going to reply to any of them?

Unlikely. Although I'd have a proper date with you, Jack. *What about you?*

I'm not planning on starting a conversation with anyone else.

Oh goody! But maybe it would be better to steer *this* conversation to more neutral subjects. *How's William been this evening?*

Naughty. He beheaded Scruffy.

Omigod. A neighbour's cat? The local fox? A visiting hedgehog? *Who is Scruffy?*

William's toy.

Ah! *Yes, he likes soft things. All my socks are holey thanks to William.*

You should treat yourself to new pairs.

It's fine. I like them. Makes me feel that William is close.

I really am sorry about how things worked out for you.

It's okay. Especially as I'm seeing him again. And you.

How are the cats?

In bed with me. I wish you were too.

Confession time. I'm in bed and William is beside me.

What? Lucky, lucky William. *You said you'd stop his bad habits.*

He kept howling. Arooooo! I couldn't take it.

What part of arooooo do you not understand? It means "feed me"!

Ha! Did you hear the beagle pizza joke?

No.

Never mind. It's too cheesy…

Oh that's bad!

Sorry, sorry. So you're still up for tomorrow?

Yes, definitely.

Give Rosemary and Thyme a hug from me.

And give William and Sylvie one from me. And I'd like to hug you too, Jack.

Night x

Omigod, he'd signed off with a kiss. Not that it was anything other than friendliness, obviously. And to be honest, it wasn't even real. Just a little cross. Hardly a cheek smacker. More's the pity. But at least it gave me an excuse to sign off with one too.

Goodnight x

I sighed and sank back against the pillows, my head full of a man called Jack Farrell and, for once, not a guy by the name of Felix Barrington-Jones.

Chapter Thirty-Five

'When can I see you again?' Felix cooed.

I stood stock still in the loft apartment's entrance while, internally, my heart began to pound as if running a marathon. Felix hadn't heard me come in. To my right, the bedroom door was ajar. From the lounge, the sound of an unwatched television burbled in the background.

Quietly shutting the entrance door behind me, I tiptoed a few steps forward and paused outside our bedroom.

'That's too long,' I heard him say.

My heart rate steadied, but only a smidgen. Thankfully there wasn't a woman in there. Instead, Felix was on his mobile.

'Yes, I know I have a fiancée.'

Who the hell was he speaking to?

'Yes I know she's very attractive. You don't need to remind me.'

Whoever it was, the person on the other end of the line obviously knew me.

'She's pretty, but predictable. Whereas you, my darling, are anything but.'

I felt my legs become rubberlike. Without a doubt, I was

eavesdropping on a lover's conversation. Oh. My. God. There was only one female I knew who was never predictable. We shared the same surname. The same DNA. But in this case blood was not thicker than water. Presumably Flora had, somehow, somewhere, had another crack at Felix. Except this time, she'd succeeded in getting beyond first base.

To say I was stunned was an understatement. How the hell was Felix finding the time to have an affair? He had a busy life. He worked hard and was out of the apartment, as far as I could tell, for hours and hours at a time. He could hardly rock up at my parents' house and announce himself. "Hello there, Mrs H. That floral crimplene dress goes so well with those washing-up gloves and today's hair-do matches HRH's to perfection – but without the pearl rinse. Meanwhile, I've popped round to give Flora a seeing to. Okay if I go upstairs? No need to mention this to Sadie, eh? I'm sure you're the soul of discretion. Just like Her Majesty. So let's keep mum. Oh, I say, you *are* Mum. Ah ha ha ha!"

No. Flora's love nest was most definitely not her bedroom at our parents' house. Nor could it be here, at Felix's apartment. At least, not on a regular basis. It was too risky. Maybe the pair of them were running up hefty bills booking hotels for their sexy sessions? But then again, I couldn't imagine Felix forking out indefinitely. Whilst my fiancé wasn't tight with money, he didn't splash it needlessly.

My brain raced ahead checking out possible places for an uninterrupted rendezvous. The art gallery? It had a miniscule staff room and a cramped stock room. Somehow, I couldn't

189

imagine Flora spreadeagled over a stack of canvasses while Felix pumped away. That left the antiques shop in Dering Street. There was a small flat over the shop which Tara and Freddie rented out. But perhaps the tenant had left, and it was currently empty? But, then again, the shop had a decent staff room. It was like a studio flat with its micro-kitchen, tiny shower room and a sofa that converted into a double bed. Felix had mentioned that his father had, in the past, sometimes stayed overnight at the shop if he was expecting a crack-of-dawn delivery and didn't want to disturb Tara with a five-a.m. alarm call. And although Felix had an assistant at the shop, it would be the work of a moment to say, "Hey, John. We're hardly rushed off our feet this afternoon. Tell you what. I'm feeling generous. Take the rest of the day off. So off you go. See you tomorrow." And then, the moment John had disappeared around the corner, Felix flipping the *Open* sign to *Closed*. Yes. That's where my sneaky sister and treacherous fiancé must be meeting up for their shenanigans.

However, before confronting either of them, I needed to be one hundred per cent certain my sister was the other woman.

Silently, taking care not to make any giveaway noises, I foraged in my handbag. Seconds later I was holding my mobile. Switching it to silent – the last thing I wanted was the damn thing erupting with an inopportune caller – I scrolled through the contact names and found Flora's details. My trembling finger pressed the handset icon. It took less than a second for the screen to flash "User Busy". Right.

190

Either it was a coincidence that Flora was using her phone at the same time as Felix, or else the pair of them were chatting to each other. I felt it was the latter.

'So what do you say then?' prompted Felix.

Yes, what was Flora going to say? Right now, I'd give anything to be able to listen to what my sister was coming out with. Murmured sweet nothings? Oh hardly, Sadie. Probably filthy phone talk.

'Do you know you've got the sexiest voice. I just love it when you talk dirty. In fact, you're giving me quite a reaction.'

I knew it. I bloody *knew* it. What should I do? Burst into the bedroom, arms in the air, handbag aloft, then bring it crashing down on Felix's steepled trousers and shriek, "So I'm predictable, eh? Well, I'll bet you've never had me *and* Michael Kors going down on you at the same time! *Wallop, wallop, wallop.*

But I couldn't move. There was something both shocking and paralysing by overhearing this sexy bit of chit-chat which, this time, left me in no doubt that action had been taking place. It was one thing to have caught them in a clinch at Tara's charity ball where not so much as even a kiss had been exchanged thanks to Yours Truly interrupting them. But it was quite another to hear that the two of them had since met up behind my back and were carrying on together. I couldn't understand it. Why didn't Felix just dump me and take up with Flora instead? I wouldn't be the first woman in history to have a two-faced deceitful sister.

191

There were many people out there who'd been treated duplicitously by those they loved. And not just sisters. Mothers had been known to do the unspeakable too. Best friends. The secretary at the office. They were everywhere. Smiling to your face before stabbing you in the back.

'You bad girl,' said Felix, giving a throaty chuckle. 'Yes... yes... that's what I want you to do... oh yes, please...' – his voice became slightly hoarse – 'darling, I can't stand it. I need you. Can I see you this evening? I can make up an excuse to get away. Are you sure your parents will be out all night?'

I frowned. Mum and Dad never stayed out overnight. As far as I was aware, they weren't planning on going off anywhere for a little jaunt either. How strange. Something wasn't quite stacking up here. Maybe I'd ring my folks. Just to check.

'Okay, you're on,' Felix was saying. 'The usual place in about an hour. Give me a ring and I'll make out it's Dad calling me with a problem that he needs my help with.'

Wow. Such glib lies being smoothly trotted out.

'Great. And make sure you greet me with nothing on under your coat,' chuckled Felix. 'Laters.'

He was ending the call. Stealthily, I crept back to the entrance, quietly opened the door, then banged it shut noisily.

'Yoo-hoo,' I yodelled. 'I'm home.' I made quite a racket dumping house keys and handbag on the console table.

'Sweetheart,' said Felix, coming out of the bedroom. My

eyes flicked briefly over his trousers. No sign of a flagpole. The slam of the front door must have helped with a rapid recovery. 'You're home early.'

'Tough day at the kiln,' I said, flashing him a dazzling smile. 'But I thought to myself, "Sadie, you have more than enough pots for your next exhibition. Go home to Felix and enjoy a glass of wine together."'

'Great idea,' he said, coming towards me and dropping a kiss on my cheek. 'I'll go and crack open a bottle of something nice while you start on the dinner.'

I tried not to lose the dazzling smile. If he thought I was rustling up something fabulous to satisfy his belly before he went off to satisfy his willy, he had another thing coming.

'Oh I don't know,' I trilled, following him into the kitchen. 'What about we go out for dinner? I'm starving.'

A shadow passed across Felix's face as he paused by the well-stocked cooler. 'That might be tricky.'

I raised my eyebrows and expressed surprise. *Careful, Sadie. Don't overdo the acting otherwise he might smell a rat.*

'Problem?' I queried.

'Yeah,' Felix sighed, removing a bottle. 'Dad was having some issues earlier at the gallery. The burglar alarm is playing up. An engineer is on his way, but Dad's a little edgy about the ETA. Apparently, he and Mother are attending some must-go-to dinner party this evening. So I said I'd be available to take over if the guy doesn't turn up within the hour. Hopefully it won't happen, and we can have a nice evening snuggling in front of the telly.'

'Oh, okay. What about a takeaway? I fancy a Chinese. Let's get something super garlicky,' I beamed. Yes, Felix. See how far you get snogging Flora while you're wafting whiffy spices.

Felix looked mildly horrified. Clearly the same thought had occurred to him. He popped the cork and set about filling two flutes.

'I'd much prefer something quick and easy.' He passed a glass to me. 'Fishfingers and baked beans would be just as nice.'

'Really?'

'Really,' he smiled. 'Anyway, cheers.' He clinked his glass against mine. 'Shall I do something useful, like laying the table.'

As opposed to laying my sister?

'Sure,' I nodded, sipping the wine. Outwardly, I was the epitome of calm. Inside I was raging. Best not to drink too much alcohol on an empty stomach. I needed to keep a clear head and decide on a plan of action.

For a moment, I surreptitiously watched Felix pottering about. Opening a drawer. Picking out cutlery. Absentmindedly humming to himself.

Placing my glass upon the worktop, I went to the freezer and peered within. There were the fishfingers. Captain Birdseye winked back at me, without a care in the world. What would he know of treachery? "I've just grilled four fish fingers, but I couldn't get any information out of them."

Never mind, Captain. There were other ways of getting a confession.

Ripping open the packet, I shook the entire contents onto a baking tray. Even though I had no appetite, I would be sure to eat my share. After all, a betrayed woman had to keep up her strength when her head was full of dark thoughts.

Chapter Thirty-Six

We'd barely put our knives and forks together when Felix's mobile rang. The phone was in the back pocket of his trousers. After the fifth ring, I looked at him curiously.

'Aren't you going to answer that?'

'Yeah,' he said vaguely. 'I'll just...' He got up and moved towards the television. Picking up the remote control, he lowered the volume, at the same time extracting the mobile, making sure his palm covered the screen, hiding the identity of the caller.

'Dad!' he said jovially. 'How's it going? Oh. I'm sorry to hear that. Okay, no problem. I explained the situation earlier to Sadie and said I might have to pop out. That's fine, we've just eaten. You're starving? Well perhaps you can grab something en-route to the theatre, so you don't upset Mother.'

The theatre? Earlier, Felix had mentioned a dinner party. My fiancé was having trouble keeping track of his lies.

'I'll leave now. Hopefully the traffic won't be too bad. See you soon.' He disconnected the call and looked at me with regret. 'Sorry, sweetheart. Looks like I have to go out after all.'

'That's all right,' I smiled. 'I'll come with you.'

Felix looked aghast. 'Whatever for?'

'To keep you company, of course.'

'There's no need for that, darling. I'll be in and out in a jiffy.'

Yes, one could describe your recent lovemaking as thus.

'But I want to,' I insisted. 'Honestly, it's no bother. I haven't seen you all day. We'll have a nice chat while waiting for the engineer.'

'No, darling. If you don't mind, it gives me a chance to catch up on some paperwork. I won't be able to concentrate on the figurework if you're chattering away.'

I'll bet. You'll be preoccupied with another number. Sixty-nine briefly flashed into my mind. *Stop, Sadie. This whole situation is bad enough, don't torment yourself further.*

'Felix.' My voice caught in the back of my throat. He looked at me, startled, and, for a moment, a look of wariness crossed his face. 'Don't go,' I whispered. 'Please.'

His face relaxed and he walked over to me. 'Stop being a silly goose,' he said, sweeping me into his arms and giving me a big squashy bear hug.

'Do you love me?' I quavered.

'More than words can say,' he said, hugging me harder. 'Come on, Sadie. This isn't like you. Make the most of me being out. You can pore over the wedding planner without me making comments that drive you potty. Give it a tweak. Add another adorable bridesmaid. Email the florist and triple the size of your bouquet. Be a bit of a bridezilla.'

'No chance of that,' I replied. Not with Tara Barrington-Jones at the helm.

Felix planted a kiss on the top of my head. 'I must go. Dad's waiting. See you later.'

I watched silently as Felix grabbed his car keys. Following him out to the hall, I said nothing as he laced up his shoes and then plucked his jacket from the coat stand. He gave me one final hug before opening the door and stepping out onto the landing.

'Drive carefully,' I called out, as he disappeared down the stairwell.

Chapter Thirty-Seven

I didn't waste a second. Reaching into the console table's drawer, I removed the spare keys to both the art gallery and the antiques shop. I didn't know which location Felix was heading for. Maybe neither. For all I knew, my parents might really be away on some unexpected jaunt leaving Flora with the house to herself. I would ring my parents to verify shortly, but right now I didn't have a moment to lose.

Jamming my feet into shoes, I didn't even bother wasting precious seconds putting on a jacket. Instead, I grabbed my mobile and slipped out of the flat on to the landing. Pausing, I tried to ignore my hammering heart. It seemed to have noisily relocated to my eardrums, so that I struggled to hear if Felix had yet reached the bottom of the stairwell. A moment later and the main door to the street creaked back on its hinges, then slammed shut.

I belted down the steps two at a time, then pushed my weight against the entrance door. It swung open, and I remembered in the nick of time to ensure it clicked shut quietly behind me. Alerting Felix to my presence would wreck everything.

Outside, it was already dark. The building's courtesy

lights were dotted about, lending a warmth that was at odds to the chill in my heart. There was no sign of Felix, but I knew he'd be heading towards the small private car park at the rear.

Feeling like a spy, I bobbed my head around the corner of the building. Felix was getting into his sportscar. For a moment, he looked up causing me to panic. Had he spotted me? Pressing myself into the shadows, I ducked down behind a row of wheelie bins. Moments later came the unmistakable roar of a turbo engine. Seconds later, the vehicle shot past. Heavens, Felix was in a hurry. I remained hidden, waiting to see whether he turned left or right. A moment later, the brake lights went out as the car whooshed away. Felix had turned left.

Suddenly I was up and running, head down, arm out, key fob extended as I belted towards Grace.

'Please don't let me down,' I muttered, yanking open the door.

My Citroen wasn't always the most reliable for starting first time, especially in rain and cold. Fortunately, it wasn't raining, but it was flipping freezing right now. Certainly my teeth were chattering away, although that could have been from nerves and lack of a warm jacket.

The ignition momentarily whined but the engine coughed into life. Sending up a silent prayer of thanks, I lurched forward, mentally keeping my fingers and toes crossed that that I'd catch up with Felix and not get caught out by the traffic lights a mile further down the road. Those lights were at a crossroads. If Felix was off to Little Waterlow, he'd need to turn right to head out of London. However, if the destination were the art gallery, then he'd need to take a left. But if his assignation was at the antiques shop, then Felix would be heading straight across the junction.

I hit the accelerator and pulled out of the car park just as an old boy in an ancient Lada was approaching. He put up a gnarled fist and shook it at me. Sorry, Mister. But I can't afford to get stuck behind you or I'll never catch up with my fiancé.

Grace's engine protested noisily as I zoomed off. I wasn't a fast driver, but Felix was. Feeling horribly out of my comfort zone, I watched the speedometer climb to fifty. I gulped. This was a thirty zone. Please don't let a policeman catch me speeding.

And then, miraculously, I spotted Felix ahead. Dramatically slowing down, a Mini took advantage and pulled out from a side-on residential road. Okay. That was fine. As long as its driver didn't hold me up at those lights – which were now coming into view. Green… amber… red. Thank you, God. Thankyouthankyouthankyou.

Felix's car purred to a standstill. The Mini came to a halt behind the convertible, and I carefully tucked Grace squarely behind the Mini so that Felix wouldn't see me if he happened to look in his rear-view mirror. Taking advantage of the temporary pause, I punched out Mum and Dad's number on my mobile's keypad. No Bluetooth in Grace. I rested the phone on my lap, out of sight, aware that I was breaking the law for a second time in as many minutes.

'The Harding residence,' said my mother, in an elocuted voice.

'Mum,' I panted.

'Darling, how are you? You sound *fritefly* out of breath.' I did wish my mother wouldn't speak like that when on the phone. It sounded so artificial.

'That's because I *am* out of breath,' I gasped, staring up at the lights. Still red. 'Where's Flora?'

'Out.'

'She told me *you* were going out,' I lied.

'Whatever did she tell you that for?' Mum sounded puzzled.

'Perhaps I misunderstood,' I lied again. So Flora had misinformed Felix. Perhaps she was messaging him right now, as he sat in his car. *Felix, hunny-bunny. Bad news. The blasted rents have let me down. Thought they were pushing off to the local for the night. We urgently need to change the venue. Love from Flora Flopsy-Ears. PS I can't wait to show you my cottontail xxx*

'Where is she?'

'Gosh, I don't know,' said Mum, sounding mildly defensive. 'I can't keep up with your sister's social life. It's a whirl of activity. Now, let me think.' I sensed my mother pondering. 'She mentioned a drinks party. Or was that last night? Yes, it was last night. Tonight, she's seeing Jemima.' I'll bet she isn't. 'That's her latest bestie. It looks like Flora and Minty have had a little tiff. Apparently Minty is going

202

away to the Caribbean and is a total you-know-what for not asking Flora to go along too, all expenses paid. Apparently Minty's brother–'

'Mum, fascinating as this tale might be, I just wanted to check that you were in, and Flora was out, and not the other way around.'

'Oh, right,' said Mum, sounding peeved that I wasn't up for a gossip. 'Can I ask why you wanted to know?'

I hesitated. The urge to splurge the details of Felix's telephone conversation was immense. But how would my mother feel hearing that her own flesh and blood was being so sly and duplicitous. Apart from anything else, if my mother thought that there was just the smallest chance of my wedding being cancelled, she'd probably have the screaming heebie-jeebies. No, best not to say anything. Not until I'd caught Felix and Flora together and screeched a few big fat fuck-offs at them.

'Sadie, are you still there?'

'Yes.' The lights were changing. 'I simply wanted to ask Flora's advice about my bridal bouquet.'

'Sooo exciting,' Mum gushed. 'But you can always ask me, darling. After all, I have walked down the aisle myself, even if it was a long time ago.' She gave a tinkle of laughter. 'And people do tell me I'm very stylish. Why, only the other day, Marjory Epson stopped me right outside the post office and said, "Cynthia, that navy suit is so chic. You're the best dressed woman in Little Waterlow. Unfortunately, I couldn't return the compliment. Marjory looks a total fright. Instead, I said that her allotment was amazing and that I expected her courgettes to win a prize at the village fete next week. You should see the size of them. Total whoppers. There's going to be quite a few noses put out of joint when she's awarded–'

'Mum! Sorry, I'm in a hurry. So, just to conclude, you're sure Flora is in London.'

'Yes, darling. Shall I tell her you–?'

'No, no. Leave it. Sorry, Mum. Must go.'

I disconnected the call and rammed the gear into first, my eyes straining to catch the taillights of Felix's sportscar. Okay, my mother had unwittingly confirmed that Felix's destination wasn't Little Waterlow. But might he indicate left and go to the art gallery?

Instead Felix accelerated across the junction. I followed, keeping a discreet distance, immediately knowing where we were heading.

Destination: one sofa bed at an antiques shop in Dering Road.

Chapter Thirty-Eight

'What's this?' I said to Jack, as he pressed a squidgy and badly wrapped package into my hands.

'A gift from William.'

We were sitting on a bench, once again at the park near Jack's house. But unlike yesterday's dog walk, instead of heading home immediately afterwards, Jack had suggested we sit down for a few minutes and simply enjoy the scenery.

I was more than happy to sit alongside him – although William had jumped up and stationed himself between us like an old-fashioned chaperone. Not that I was in any danger of being leapt upon by Jack. But I was secretly delighted to be in such close proximity to him. His twinkly eyes, tousled hair and slow sexy smile had been playing havoc with my heart for the last sixty minutes. I estimated we had another hour before the sun disappeared, and an early evening chill drove us out of the park to seek the warmth of a heated home. Or, in my case, the frigid interior of Grace thanks to her broken heater.

'Aren't you going to open it?' Jack prompted.

I ripped the wrapping paper apart and gave a squeak of delight. 'Socks!'

'And not any old socks,' said Jack, pointing at the knitted-in pattern.

'Beagles,' I grinned. 'Seven pairs, too.'

'One for every day of the week.'

'They're amazing. Thank you.'

'William had a word in my ear. He said he was very sorry for chewing all your socks and asked that I buy some more on his behalf.'

I played along. 'How very thoughtful of him.'

'And he wanted them to be covered in beagles to remind you of him.'

'They most certainly will,' I agreed. *And shall, in turn, also remind me of you. Pity there aren't any socks here with your face upon them.* 'You kept them well-hidden on our walk.'

'My pockets are deep,' said Jack, pointing to them on his wax jacket.

For a moment neither of us said anything, and I took the ensuing silence as a cue for heading back. Stuffing the sock bundle into my own pockets, I made to stand up.

'Er, Sadie?' said Jack tentatively. My bum momentarily hovered, mid-air. 'Sit back down again for a minute.'

'Okay,' I said, suddenly feeling fingers of dread. Oh no. Please don't let the sock gift be a pre-cursor for a gentle brush off. My spirits sank. Was Jack about to say, "Look, it's lovely that you're up for walking William with me and Sylvie, but I don't want to be tied to doing this every day. Shall we revise the arrangement? What about once a week?

Although once a month would be even better. After all, you can see William is happy. Let him continue to settle in with me while, from this point, you take a back seat." I looked at Jack, resigned to the conversation. 'Go on. You can say it.'

He gave me a curious look. 'Say what?'

'That you don't want this to become a habit. I'm a big girl, Jack. I can take it. Thanks for the socks, and everything, but you didn't need to soften me up before telling me.'

'How do you know what I want to say?'

My shoulders drooped. 'It's obvious isn't it. Anyway, now I've saved you the trouble.' I made to stand up again.

Jack's hand reached over William and pushed me down again. *Zingggggg.*

'I didn't have you down for being a psychic,' he said.

'Female intuition,' I muttered, fidgetting on the bench.

'Well, on this occasion, it's let you down.'

I looked up sharply. 'What do you mean?'

He gave me that heart–flipping lopsided smile again. 'I am more than happy for you to walk William with me and Sylvie, and whenever you want. I've already told you that and meant every word. I'm not about to change my mind.'

I stared at him. 'O-Oh.' I stammered. 'So, so' – my brow furrowed – 'why did you ask me to sit back down again?'

'If you stop trying to pre-empt me, I'll tell you.'

'Okay.' I looked at him expectantly. Was it my imagination or was Jack starting to look a little… awkward?'

He took a deep breath. 'I wanted to talk to you about

207

My frown deepened. The dating app. 'What about it?'

'I liked your profile pic. And… um… you went on to start a conversation.'

'Oh, that.' I felt myself blushing. 'It's okay. I'm aware of the rules. It means that we matched and are meant to have a date. But we both know that Charlotte railroaded the pair of us into joining, so it's okay. You don't have to do anything about it. I know you were simply being polite when you liked my profile and… well' – my blush deepened – 'obviously I totally get that. And… er… that's why I started the conversation. To also be polite.'

'Right,' he nodded, squirming slightly.

'It's okay,' I grinned. 'You're off the hook. There's no pressure to ask me to have a coffee and a toastie at the nearest café.'

'Right,' he said again.

Thank goodness we'd cleared that matter up. Once again, I made to stand up.

'Sadie, I haven't finished telling you what I wanted to say.' For the second time my bum hovered mid-air as I crouched, like a skier, neither standing nor sitting. My thigh muscles were certainly getting an excellent workout. 'Sit down,' he said softly. Intrigued, I slowly lowered my derrière. 'I double-clicked your profile for two reasons.'

'Oh?'

'First, because, yes, I was being polite.'

I looked at him kindly. 'As I said, I'd already worked that

out.'

'Second' – he ploughed on – 'because I like you.'

For a moment I didn't know what to say and gawped at him.

'You like me?'

'Yes.'

'As in… *like* me?'

'As in… wanting to go for that coffee and toastie with you.'

'Oh.'

'Is that an "oh" as in *omigod-how-do-I-get-out-of-this* or an "oh" as in *yes-please-I'd-really-like-to-do-that*?'

'The… um… latter,' I whispered, my blush deepening. Any minute now I'd be making a strawberry look anaemic.

'That's… great,' he said, starting to look a bit pink in the cheeks himself. My goodness, was the utterly gorgeous Jack Farrell a little shy when it came to asking a woman out? *It's only an invitation for coffee and a toastie* – sneered my inner voice – *not a marriage proposal.*

'When would you like to go?' he asked.

Now, please.

'Tomorrow?' I suggested.

Best to play it a tiny bit cool.

'After we've walked the dogs?' he said.

'That would be great.'

'It's a date,' he said, giving me a wink.

Chapter Thirty-Nine

I gave Charlotte a nonchalant look and tried to act cool. 'And then Jack said, "It's a date."'

'Oh wow, I'm really pleased for you,' she grinned.

The pair of us were in her workshop on this bright Tuesday morning full of March sunshine although there was a distinct nip in the air. I was leaning casually against the doorframe, arms folded, watching as she applied a final coat of black paint to a previously non-descript writing bureau. By the time Charlotte had finished transforming it, the bureau would look like it belonged on the pages of *House Beautiful* magazine.

'So what time are you meeting him?' she asked.

'It was meant to be immediately after walking Sylvie and William, later this afternoon, but I had to postpone when I realised that I'd overlooked a Zoom meeting in the diary. It's a new client. The gentleman in question has a restaurant on the other side of Little Waterlow and wants a dozen bespoke pots made, then painted to match the restaurant's interior. He's dotting olive trees around the place and has offered me such a generous commission I'd be mad to jeopardise it. So walkies with William will have to be either after the coffee date, or the following day. I'm meeting Jack at half past six.'

'I'm sure William won't mind forfeiting his walk. Anyway, if you go back to Jack's place afterwards, you'll see William.'

'Mm, maybe,' I said, attempting carelessness. The thought of going back to the house had already crossed my mind as a possibility. But then again, why should there be any need? Surely not for coffee? Not when we'd already had coffee. Well, maybe to see William. Or, depending on the time, maybe for a nightcap. Or something. I found myself getting a bit hot under the collar at the thought of *or something*.

'So where are you going?' asked Charlotte as she expertly stroked the paintbrush back and forth.

'Chloe's Café in the High Street.'

'Brave,' she murmured. 'Before you know it half the village will say you're stepping out with a brain surgeon.'

'Tree surgeon,' I corrected.

'Yeah, *I* know that. But you need to remember your immediate neighbours like to embellish everything. Watch yourself, Sadie. Before you know it, Mabel and Fred Plaistow will have their binoculars trained on your garden gate, making sure you don't bring the road into disrepute as you lead your latest man over the threshold for a nightcap. Fred will then inform Mabel to fetch him a glass. The next thing, it will be upside down and pressed against the party wall, as Fred tries to hear if your bed springs are creaking.'

'Give over.' I rolled my eyes. 'Jack and I haven't even

had the coffee and toastie yet.'

'Or the hot crumpet,' she joked. 'But it will happen.' She paused mid-stroke to look at me properly. 'I have a funny feeling about the two of you.' She sniffed theatrically. 'I can smell romance.'

'You think?' I said, perking up but trying not to get too excited. Yesterday evening, I'd failed to contain my joy. I'd kept making involuntary squeaking noises of delight. Rosemary and Thyme had regarded me curiously, perhaps wondering if their new human mummy had morphed into a vast mouse.

I'd floated up the stairs in a haze of happiness, beagle socks clasped to my chest. Pushing through to the bathroom, I'd filled the tub with foaming bubbles. Once in the bath, I'd lain back and shut my eyes to relax. However, my mind had instantly conjured up an image of Jack. There he'd been. Standing in the bathroom doorway. Eyes feasting on my naked body. Obviously, the soapy bubbles had done sterling work hiding the rampant cellulite, but the better bits had peeped enticingly through the Radox froth, getting Jack into a lather of his own. My heart had leapfrogged all over the place as I'd imagined him saying, "Make room for me because I'm coming in." Naturally he'd had to rip off his t-shirt and undo the zip on his fashionably distressed jeans before leaping on top of me and causing a tidal wave to slop over half the bathroom floor. In my head, I'd imagined much giggling and shrieking as he'd kissed my mouth then worked his way down my neck... my body... his head disappearing under the bubbles and–

'Sadie?'

'Sorry?'

'Blimey, where did you just float off to?' Charlotte gave me a sly look. 'I asked what you're going to wear for the date.'

'Ah.' Best not to mention my X-rated thoughts. 'I'll probably opt for my jeans and–'

'Jeans again?' Charlotte wagged a finger. 'No, I think you should pull out all the stops and get your knockers out.'

'I beg your pardon?' I gasped.

'Grab his attention.'

'Are you suggesting I do a Flora on him? I seem to recall that Jack went straight into reverse when she displayed her own billowing cleavage.'

'Well, okay, perhaps not be quite so obvious,' Charlotte agreed. 'But you do want things to develop, don't you?'

'Not in Chloe's Café,' I tutted. 'Anyway, enough about me and Jack. What's going on with you and Aran?'

'Hmm?' said Charlotte, suddenly terribly interested in her bureau again.

'You heard. How come you didn't get on the blower earlier to tell me all about it?'

'How do you know there *is* anything to tell?'

'Because Jack told me. He mentioned it yesterday.'

'Oooh, what a gossip Jack is!' Charlotte trilled.

'Why, is it a secret?' I said, feeling a tiny bit hurt at being excluded.

213

'No, of course not,' she sighed, brushing paint back and forth over a knot in the wood. 'Put simply, I'm a bit wary of chatting about it because I don't want to jinx things.'

'You won't,' I assured, mentally crossing my fingers. I knew what she meant. If you raved about a guy, everything turned to ashes. Whereas if you played things down, everything came up trumps. '*C'mon*,' I coaxed. 'Spill the beans.'

She adopted a careless expression, as if the date had been nothing special, but her body language told me otherwise. 'We went for our coffee over at Borough Green.'

'And?'

'And had the toastie,' she smiled.

'That's not what I mean, and you know it.'

'Okay, I had a blueberry muffin.'

'Charlotte,' I said warningly, transferring my hands to my hips. 'This isn't like you to be so secretive. Normally you're on the phone telling me whether you got to first base and giving me the guy's snog rating.'

'Ah,' she said, suddenly looking dreamy.

'So you kissed.'

She chuckled. 'And some.'

'This is like pulling teeth. Painful. I want more information and I want it now.'

'His kisses were a definite ten.'

'I'm presuming that bit of action didn't take place in the coffee shop. So where next?'

'Oooh, Little Miss Nosy!'

'Don't pretend you won't be giving *me* the third degree after my date with Jack.'

'Oh okay,' she said, chucking down the paintbrush. 'You win. From the café we moved on to a dear little pub. I'm not sure what the place was called, but it was in Otford. Really quaint. It overlooked a roundabout that was actually a duck pond and the whole thing was edged in a froth of daffodils.'

'Sounds pretty.'

'It was,' she agreed. 'But not as gorgeous as Aran.' She gave a satisfied smile, like a cat who'd discovered its regular saucer of water had magically transformed into a mini lake of double cream. 'He held my hand and led me inside the restaurant. The place was so cosy. All knotted beams and romantic candlelight. We sat in a window seat and then he gazed at me across the table and did the flattery thing. You know. "Your eyes are like the sea – I feel like I'm drowning in them."'

'In other words, he'd noticed the size of your boobs.'

'Of course,' she dimpled. 'And then I, too, gave him a couple of compliments.'

'Which translated as wanting to unbutton his shirt and run your hands over his chest.'

'Naturally. And then we just sat there staring at each other across the table, drinking each other in, and there was all this chemistry zipping back and forth. He was giving me such smouldering looks it's a wonder my eyelashes didn't get singed.'

'So did you actually get around to ordering any food, or

did your knickers self-combust in front of all the other diners?'

'The waiter came over and, yes, we did order, but don't ask me what because I honestly can't remember. You know me. I love my food. But I hardly ate a thing. Talk about a waste. But we managed to have a decent enough conversation, despite the major undercurrents. Aran told me that in his head he's a rock star and plays the guitar like Brian May, but the reality is he's a maths teacher at a secondary school in Dartford. He also added that he's more like a social worker than a teacher, so he destresses by doing gigs with Jack and the boys. He says it's only a hobby. There's no chance of them writing a song, getting a lucky break, and then going on a world tour. That's good news for you and me because I don't think I'd like to be a rock star's girlfriend and have to see off endless adoring groupies.'

'Quite,' I agreed.

'Anyway, needless to say, we both declined the waiter's offer to conclude the meal with coffee. Instead, Aran invited me back to his place to check out his various guitars.'

'Hmm. The melodic equivalent of looking at his etchings.'

'Indeed,' Charlotte smirked. That took... oooh, a good couple of minutes.'

'Whereupon Aran gave you a lift home and you gave him a chaste goodnight kiss on the cheek.'

She grinned good-naturedly. 'I think we both know that didn't happen. We're seeing each other again tonight.'

216

'Good for you,' I smiled.

'I really like him,' she said softly, picking up the paintbrush again. 'In fact—'

'Don't say it,' I warned. Every time Charlotte announced she'd met *The One*, it turned out that the man in question was instead *The Waste of Space*.

'That's right,' she nodded. 'I mustn't jinx it. Anyway, enjoy your date with Jack tonight and I shall keep my fingers and toes tightly crossed that it goes as brilliantly as it did for me and Aran.'

'Thanks. So, I take it you're over your crush on Luke from the rehoming centre.'

For a moment, Charlotte's brow wrinkled, as if she couldn't quite remember who Luke was. Then her vision cleared, and her eyes widened. 'Oh my goodness, I knew I had some juicy gossip to tell you.'

'About Luke?'

'Yes! I saw him in the restaurant last night. He didn't see me on account of us being in a tucked-away corner, but even if we'd been sitting next to him, I don't think he'd have noticed us. He was very' – she chose her next word carefully – 'preoccupied.'

'Are you going to tell me he wasn't dining out with his wife?'

'Got it in one.' Charlotte gave me a triumphant look. 'So much for him being a happily married man.'

'Maybe he was out with an acquaintance,' I pointed out. 'Some men do have platonic female friends.'

'Not in this case,' she harrumphed. 'Want to have a guess who the woman was?' She raised her eyebrows enquiringly.

'Don't tell me, Luke is into older women, and you caught him all gooey-eyed with Mabel Plaistow,' I teased.

'Not even close,' said Charlotte with satisfaction. 'He was gazing into the eyes of a certain pneumatic blonde. Ah, I can see from the look on your face that the penny is starting to drop.'

'You're kidding,' I said hoarsely. Not again. Why couldn't she find her own man – one that didn't belong to another woman?

'Yup,' Charlotte nodded. 'Luke was with Flora.'

Chapter Forty

I left Charlotte's workshop with a bee in my bonnet. How dare my sister pursue a married man. Didn't she have any morals? It was one thing to have a brush with the species. A close encounter. To throw your hands in the air and angrily say, "The bastard! I didn't even know he had a wife until Tina in Accounts put me straight. I hope his dick turns green and falls off."

However, Flora's track record was *waaaay* higher than the average unsuspecting female's, which told me that my sister simply didn't care. So what if there was a wife patiently waiting for her cheating husband to come home? As far as Flora was concerned, it was the wife's problem, not hers.

On the drive back to Clover Cottage, I resolved to contact Flora and give her a piece of my mind. I didn't understand what she was playing at. Okay, so she'd been spurned by the London circuit and was no longer pursuing filthy-rich businessmen. I'd also heard that her unpopularity had knocked other invitations on the head. Like weekends in Gloucestershire where previously she'd hoped to bag the attention of Lord Many-Acres. Evidently, she'd now turned her attention closer to home. I wasn't quite sure what she thought the co-owner of a pet sanctuary had to offer, other than an aggravated wife on the warpath, but she needed to have some sense shaken into her. When it came to men, Flora was like a missile that had been programmed to the wrong destination. The ensuing explosion would not only end in tears but also attract major retaliation.

The moment I arrived home, I flopped down in an armchair and rang her from my mobile. Rosemary and Thyme ventured into the lounge and suddenly my lap was full of purring fluffballs demanding cuddles.

'Okay, okay. Settle down,' I cooed, as I waited for the line to connect. 'There, my darling. Who's a lovely... oh, hello? Flora?' Damn. Voicemail. 'Hi, it's me. Listen, I have it on very good authority that you were out with a guy last night. Flora, I know him. His name is Luke, and he is married. Do you hear me? *Married.* I also know his wife. Rachel was key in assisting with my rescued cats. She's a pleasant lady and doesn't deserve to be betrayed. It's bad enough that her husband is cheating on her, but I was mortified to discover that you're the "other woman". Drop him, Flora. Please. He's not worth it.' I took a deep breath. 'In fact, I think he's a right git.' I wouldn't add what I thought of Flora. After all, there was just an outside chance that she didn't know the blasted man was married. I hoped that was the case anyway. 'Sorry if you didn't know any of this, by the way. I wasn't on a mission to be the bearer of bad news. Anyway, I'm here if you want to talk about it. You know, let off a few eff words. Either that or let his tyres down. Catch you later.'

I heaved a sigh. God help my parents finding out. Mum would be horrified. I could imagine her now, shrieking, "Oh the shame. I'll never again be able to look Mrs Quinten-Smith in the eye at the Bring and Buy Sale." Our village was small. Idle gossip was a pastime in a place like Little Waterlow. Despite not always liking Flora, she was still my sister and – perhaps because she was younger than me – I often felt ridiculously protective of her. It probably stemmed back to the school playground. Those innocent days where she used to zoom up to me, crying, on account of some kid snatching her skipping rope. Sadie to the rescue. Red hair flying as I marched over to some skinny child and then taking pity on the girl in question because she was fostered – father in jail and mum shacked up with a drug dealer. Telling Flora to gift her skipping rope and that I'd use my pocket money to buy her another. It wasn't quite the same with married men though. I could hardly turn to Rachel and gasp, "My sister has stolen your husband? Never mind, I'll buy you a new one."

I stroked Rosemary's head as she narrowed her eyes and gave me her best superior look. 'It's all right for you and your brother, pretty lady.' I rubbed her muzzle, flattening the silky whiskers. 'You'll never know the meaning of broken hearts and fresh starts. Sometimes it's tough for us humans. Falling in love is a minefield. Look how it was with Felix. Not that you knew my fiancé. But I've told you all about him and you know that it ended badly.'

I sighed as a blanket of gloom threatened to descend. Mentally I pushed it away. No, I would not let it envelop me and cause me to sink. It was time for the past to stop popping up with its surprise attacks. Not when the future was giving such promising glimpses of hope, and that things might be about to change for the better.

Chapter Forty-One

After my scheduled Zoom meeting with the new client, I felt flushed with success. My little business was doing brilliantly. If only my private life could be the same. *All in good time, Sadie. Be cool. Keep your head. Don't chase love. It will come when the time is right.* Even so. Charlotte was right. I needed to pull out a few stops to encourage any romance.

Upstairs in my bedroom, I emptied out my entire wardrobe. The weather, while getting milder every day, wasn't yet warm enough to expose white winter legs. Layers were the answer. I settled on a pair of black jeans – sorry Charlotte – and a floaty top. It didn't showcase my boobs in quite the way Charlotte had suggested, but hinted at a pair of fairly decent C cups.

Adding a three-quarter-sleeve cardigan, I then rammed my feet into my best high-heeled boots before standing back to regard myself in the long mirror for the *overall effect*.

A pale face with huge grey eyes stared back at me. I was wearing my hair down tonight. Instead of its habitual frizz from exposure to the elements, it had been coaxed to fall past my shoulders in a cascade of waves. I had the type of hair that rain or humidity could wreck in seconds.

Reaching for my cosmetics bag on the dressing table, I dabbed some extra blusher over my cheeks. They instantly turned into two pink apples. Oh to be blonde like Flora and turn the colour of toffee the moment the sun shone. Instead, I'd have to make do with being an English rose. I chucked the blusher brush back into the bag's depths.

Thyme minced into the bedroom to see what I was up to. He leapt on top of the dressing table and promptly patted the cosmetics bag over the edge. It landed with a thump on the carpet, startling him in the process. He instantly fluffed up like a porcupine and fled.

'Silly billy,' I murmured, stooping to pick it up. 'Right, kitties' – I called out, grabbing my handbag – 'I'm off. See you both later.'

I clattered down the stairs feeling a sudden frisson of excitement. 'And don't wait up,' I added skittishly, banging the front door behind me.

''Ello, luv,' said a voice. I turned to see Mabel Plaistow putting some empty milk bottles on her doorstep. Little Waterlow was a village where the milkman still paid a visit. 'You look nice.'

'Thanks, Mabel.'

'Makes a change not to see you in them overalls all covered in clay.'

'Yes,' I agreed, edging towards Grace.

'I expect you're goin' out then.'

'That's right,' I nodded, taking another step towards the car.

'Off anywhere nice?'

'Only to Chloe's Café,' I said.

Mabel's eyes gleamed. 'I've heard that place is even more popular than previously thanks to some dating thingybob.'

'Is that so?' I feigned surprise.

'Yeah. Our Sharon told me. It's called' – she screwed up her wrinkled brow trying to recall – '*The Buttery Somefink.* Sharon joined it. She wants to get 'itched again. Although I've told 'er it ain't goin' t'be easy. Not at 'er age. She's 'eadin' towards sixty. She said if she don't meet no one by the end of the year, she might invent 'er own dating club for people like 'er of a certain age. Said she'd call it *I've Fallen for You and Can't Get It Up.* No. Hang on. That's not right. *I've Fallen for You and Can't Get Up.*'

'Ah. Right. That's a great idea,' I said, managing to take three more steps towards Grace.

'Is that why yer dressed up? Because yer meetin' a young man?'

I tried not to groan aloud. Oh, so what? Was it such a big deal if I told her? It wasn't exactly as if Mabel had loads of excitement in her life. Maybe when I was a spritely octogenarian, then I'd want to fill my days with gossip and remember what it was like to be young and enjoy romance.

'That's right,' I smiled. 'I'm meeting someone. But it's only for coffee. Nothing wildly exciting and I'm certainly not expecting it to lead anywhere.'

'As long as it don't lead into 'is bedroom, lass. Make 'im wait. Make 'im take yer out for an expensive meal a few

225

times. An' not round 'ere neither. Somewhere posh. Like that restaurant in London owned by that telly cook. Mind you, in my day the only celebrity chef we 'ad was that Fanny Craddock. Back in the day my Fred loved a bit of Fanny.'

'Er, quite. I'd best be off Mabel.'

'Yes, you be on yer way. Toodle-oo, duck.'

I finally hopped into Grace and turned the key. She didn't let me down and started first time. Moments later, I was off. As I looked back in my rear-view mirror, I spotted Mabel's curtains twitching violently. Charlotte was right. I had a horrible feeling an ancient pair of binoculars would later be trained upon my return.

Chapter Forty-Two

Outside Chloe's Café, I squeezed Grace into a very tight parking space. I'd already spotted Jack's Ford Ranger so knew he was inside waiting. Without any warning, a netful of butterflies erupted in my stomach.

Come on, Sadie. Don't be silly. This is William Beagle's dad. No need to be nervous.

My brain instantly careered off in a panic and flashed up an urgent list of *What Ifs.*

What if the date is a disaster and Jack never wants to see me again?

What if – consequently – I never see darling William again?

What if

My mobile pinged with the arrival of a text. I grabbed the phone. Flora.

How DARE you assume I'm going out with a married man. Yes, I did have dinner with Luke and guess what? His wife was there too!

I sighed. Here we go. The lies. Always so glib. I tapped out a reply.

Not according to my informant. You were seen sitting opposite Luke and apparently gazing at him with dewy eyes. Just the two of you.

Seconds later an angry voice note came winging back.

'Hello, Sadie. You can tell your useless mole that if they'd bothered to stick around spying then they'd have seen Rachel coming out of the Ladies and then joining Luke and myself at the table. No gin bottles went flying and no accusations were made. Quite the opposite. You see, I responded to an ad in the local paper and, as a subsequence, Luke and Rachel have offered me a job at the pet rehoming centre. I've had enough of London and phony friends, especially after the mistakes I made. But now I'm a little older and wiser and want a fresh start. At least our mum's airs and graces are harmless, whereas I've been completely deluded thinking I could bag myself a lord or an earl. I went to a comprehensive, for God's sake, not Cheltenham Ladies College. So I'm starting the new job next week taking over the admin and secretarial duties, getting stuck into the digital marketing and dollying up the centre's website. Rachel and Luke are both worked off their feet and need more staff. So thanks for your "concern"' – Flora's voice dripped with sarcasm – 'but you'll now understand it isn't required.' Her voice hardened. 'And tell Charlotte to keep her nose out of my business. It's obvious that she's the one who fed you this info because I saw her with that drippy guitarist. Does she know he's gay?'

The voice note abruptly ended. Flora was evidently in high dudgeon. Oh dear. Well, at least she wasn't running true to form. In fact, if she was telling the truth, it would seem my sister was in the process of turning over a new leaf.

In which case…

Okay, sorry sorry sorry. Regarding the new job, I'm really pleased for you. Charlotte obviously got her wires crossed. By the way, Aran is not gay xx

And neither was Jack. Oh dear. In for a penny, in for a pound.

Might as well tell you, am on a coffee date with Jack tonight xx

I wasn't sure how Flora would react to that. She wasn't used to being spurned and certainly not with me succeeding where she'd failed.

It's okay, Sadie. It doesn't matter. Jack isn't really my type anyway. Have a lovely evening xx

I puffed out my cheeks. Well! Flora had taken that better than expected. Good heavens. Things really were changing around here. The phone pinged with another text, but this time it wasn't Flora. It was Jack.

Hey. I can see you through Chloe's window. You've been sitting in your car for the last five minutes. Have you had a change of heart? Xx

My head flew up and my eyes snagged on Jack's. He put up a hand and waved. I smiled and waved back, then quickly replied to his text.

I'm on my way xx

And then, chucking my phone in my bag and scrambling out of Grace, I set off towards the café with a spring in my step.

Chapter Forty-Three

'For a moment there, I thought you were going to stand me up,' Jack grinned, getting to his feet to greet me.

'No,' I laughed. 'I wasn't about to change my mind.'

It seemed the most natural thing in the world for him to kiss me on the cheek. I momentarily inhaled an unknown scent – citrus and sandalwood – which sent my senses reeling. As Jack's lips brushed against my skin, a distinct bit of knee-tremble came on and I had to refrain from touching my face and checking for scorch marks. My fingers coiled around the table's edge to steady myself.

Careful, Sadie. Don't make it obvious that you think he's hotter than Chloe's selection of toasties.

It was hard though. Especially as Jack was looking utterly divine. A black t-shirt seemed to be showcasing just about every muscle in his upper body, accentuating his athletic build. I tore my eyes away from well-defined pecs, broad shoulders, and some seriously impressive biceps. Mmm. Mmm.

'You look lovely,' he said.

'So do you,' I said without thinking. 'I mean' – my cheeks reddened – 'as in… smart. You look smart.'

'What, this old thing?' he mocked, raising his arms so that my eyes were automatically drawn again to the muscle t-shirt before feasting greedily on his torso and the way it tapered perfectly into the distressed denims that hugged strong thighs and–

'You okay, Sadie?' Jack asked, frowning slightly.

'Yes,' I trilled, giving a slightly manic smile. 'Just feeling a bit... hot.'

'You look it,' he agreed.

'Th-Thank you,' I stuttered, surprised but nonetheless delighted at the boldness of his compliment. Well, how about that! My gorgeous date thought I was *hot*. Go me!

'Um' – he looked momentarily awkward – 'as in, red. You're sort of... clashing with your hair.'

'Oh, I see,' I faltered.

Idiot. *Hot* as in *bothered*. Not *hot* as in *God-you're-so-sexy-I-want-to-rip-off-your-clothes-in-front-of-all-these-customers*.

I stood there gormlessly as Chloe squeezed past me with a tray of coffees and cakes for the table to my right.

'Not that you're not,' muttered Jack. 'Hot,' he added, colouring up a bit himself.

Oh Lord. This was so cringey. How on earth had we suddenly become so uncomfortable with each other? When the dogs were with us, barking at our heels, conversation always flowed effortlessly. But here, in this café, without grubby boots and muddy paws, we were suddenly behaving like a pair of tongue-tied teenagers. The situation needed rescuing. Urgently.

'I'm definitely hot,' I agreed, now puce in the face. To my right, Chloe had dropped her notepad on the floor. 'But all I need to do is strip off' – I mentally winced at the phraseology – 'and all will be well.' I ripped off my cardigan and tossed it to one side, just as Chloe stooped to pick up her notepad.

'What the–?' she squawked, as the cardi landed on her head.

'Sorry,' I said, as she staggered blindly upright. I quickly grabbed it. 'My aim was off.'

'Just a bit,' she said, smoothing her mussed-up hair.

'Sorry,' I repeated, sinking down on my chair. Except it wasn't there and I ended up descending – like an elevator with no brakes – to the floor. 'Oomph,' I exhaled, as my coccyx made painful contact with Chloe's quarry tiles.

Jack instantly leapt to his feet and peered at me over the table's edge.

'Are you okay?'

'The chair had moved,' I groaned, hauling myself upright. I dumped the wretched cardigan on the seat next to me and, ignoring amused looks from those around me, gingerly sat down.

How humiliating. I should have stayed at home with Rosemary and Thyme. Curled up on the sofa with them. Opted for a less stressful pastime, like enjoying a brew and mindlessly munching chocolate biscuits while my eyes glazed watching television.

'So what shall we have?' said Jack, settling down opposite me and attempting to steer the date into calmer waters. 'Coffee? Or would you prefer tea? Chloe has a wonderful variety on the menu. Ginger. Camomile. Earl Grey. There's also a couple I've never heard of. Peach Cobbler Guayusa and' – he frowned – 'not sure I pronounced that correctly or if I'll get this one right either, but there's another called Black Forest Cake Pu-erh Tea. Wow. Sounds like having your cake but without the guilt.'

He looked up at me and smiled, and I suddenly felt myself relaxing. This was more like it. Normal conversation. Even if the topic was tea. At least it was more interesting than discussing the weather.

'That Peach Cobbler one is pronounced *gwhy-you-sa*,' said Chloe, materialising at our side. 'So, if you've finished chucking your clothes about and wrecking my café' – she flashed a forgiving smile – 'are you ready to order something adventurous?'

'Er, maybe,' I said nervously.

'Well I usually recommend this one to my truckers' – she pointed at the menu with her pencil – 'because it perks them up after a long shift when there are still several miles to drive. I could wax lyrical about it being a rare tea native to the Amazon Rainforest but the only thing my lorry lads are interested in is knowing that it is heavily caffeinated and has a major awakening effect,' she laughed. 'Are you planning on staying up all night?' She looked at me speculatively.

I felt myself blushing again as a mental picture of me and

233

Jack – definitely in the early hours – began to play in my head. Naked. In his bed. A table lamp glowing ambiently. My fingers tracing Jack's snail trail. Down. Down a bit more…

I hastily pushed the images away. 'I think I'll stick to a pot of your usual.'

'PG Tips it is,' she said, licking the tip of her pencil and scribbling away on the pad.

'I'll have an Americano,' said Jack.

'And what are you both eating?' asked Chloe.

'I'll have a cheese and ham toastie, please,' said Jack.

'Make that two,' I said, too flustered to peruse the menu and make a speedy choice.

'Back in a bit,' Chloe smiled, tucking the pencil behind one ear.

'Where were we?' Jack asked.

'Harvesting tea in deepest Peru.'

Jack laughed. 'You know, my grandmother reads tealeaves.'

'No! Are you pulling my leg?'

'It's absolutely true.' Jack drew a cross over his heart with an index finger. 'A list of regular clients claim she's good at it too.'

'Has she ever given you a reading.'

'Several.'

'Have they come true?' I asked nosily.

'They've all been quite accurate so far.'

'I'm intrigued. Tell me more.'

'Well, if you went to see her for a reading, she'd make you a drink with loose leaves, using a special cup solely for this ritual.'

'Ritual?' I frowned. 'That makes it sound like witchcraft. You're giving me goosebumps.'

'It's not scary, honest. If you were looking for advice about something, my nan would ask you to formulate a clear and concise question in your mind, then ask you to sip the tea while contemplating your question. Then, when you're down to the last tablespoon of liquid in the cup, she'd ask you to swirl it three times from left to right. Next, she'd instruct you to invert the cup over its saucer, leave it upside down for about a minute, then rotate it three times.'

'Why is everything always in threes?'

Jack shrugged. 'No idea. Nan would then ask you to put the cup upright again and position the handle south. The tealeaves would be stuck in various shapes and clusters, and that's when she'd start interpreting the patterns and configurations.'

'But I don't understand how a bunch of leaves can translate as information.'

'It's quite straightforward. She'd look for five types of symbols – animals, mythical beings, objects, letters, and numbers. Sometimes a symbol is obvious, like the wings of a bird.'

'A journey?' I hazarded.

'Yes, but it could also mean a new-found freedom. On the other hand, something like a cross could signal unforeseen trouble ahead. The handle of the teacup plays an important part acting as an energy conduit. It's supposed to connect both the physical and abstract realms. Any leaves near the handle relate to the querent's immediate surroundings, like external issues and outside influences.'

'Which bits of the reading tell you about the future or the past?'

'The rim relates to the present. The sides refer to the near future, and the base of the cup signifies the far future.'

'You sound very knowledgeable. Are you sure it's not you who does the readings?' I teased.

'I'll let you into a secret,' he whispered, leaning in. 'When I was a kid, Nan used to childmind me after school before Mum got home from work. Many a time I was present on a client's reading – quietly sitting in a corner with my crayons and colouring book. Consequently, I saw first-hand how it all worked. I've also been known' – he gave a furtive look – 'to occasionally do my own readings.'

'Have you indeed?' My eyes widened. Would it be too presumptuous to ask Chloe to rip open a few teabags for Jack to give me an impromptu reading? Hm. Perhaps I'd just let the future look after itself for now. 'So does your nan have a special name? You know, like Mystic Meg or Psychic Sally.'

'Sort of. You see, she also writes a weekly column in a Sunday newspaper supplement. *Tessa's Tasseography*. She uses the same name for her private readings too.'

My jaw dropped. 'But I've heard of her! My mother is a big fan of your grandmother. Ever since *The Great Toilet*

Paper Fiasco of 2020, Mum swears by Tessa. She said we'd never have run out of loo rolls if we'd taken Tessa's advice to "think ahead and take stock."'

Jack laughed. 'It's all a bit vague in Nan's column, but then it has to be to have the masses identifying with what she predicts.'

'Toasties,' interrupted Chloe, clattering down a couple of china plates.

I leant back, making room for the drinks to be set down too. 'Thanks.'

'You're welcome, lovely. Enjoy.'

'I will,' I assured, trying not to dribble at the sight of golden bread oozing melted cheese. Picking it up, I resisted from greedily moaning aloud and instead took a huge bite. Delicious. I realised that Jack wasn't eating. Instead, he was watching me. 'What?' I mumbled, suddenly self-conscious.

'Nothing.' He shook his head. 'It's simply nice to see a girl eat.' He bit into his own toastie. 'My last girlfriend existed on lentils.'

His *last* girlfriend? I chewed thoughtfully. Did that make me his *current* girlfriend?

Don't be silly, Sadie. It's just a figure of speech. He could just as easily have said "ex-girlfriend".

'She must have been very slim.'

Jack nodded. 'Gaynor had the build of a waif.'

'Lucky Gaynor,' I said lightly, trying not to appear piggy by consuming the toastie in four mouthfuls. How had we suddenly got on to the subject of his ex?

237

'I prefer my women curvier,' said Jack, making his own considerable inroads with the toastie. I mulled over his words. *My* women? Heavens, now it sounded like he had a harem.

'Yes, me too,' I nodded. 'Not that I'm into women,' I added hastily. 'I simply meant…' – what had I meant? – 'you know, bums and boobs are best.'

Oh terrific, Sadie. Now you've thrown bottoms and breasts into the conversation.

Jack's mouth twitched. 'I totally agree. And how do you like your men, Sadie?'

'Um,' I reddened. 'Preferably without the boobs.'

He roared with laughter. 'I think you mean *moobs*.'

'Yes, those too.' My phone, sitting by my plate, let out a merry tinkle. A text message from Charlotte. 'Excuse me,' I mumbled. 'Work.'

'Carry on,' Jack gestured, his eyes still dancing with laughter.

Yes, carry on and keep making a berk of yourself. I wiped my greasy fingers on a paper napkin and picked up the mobile. A text from Charlotte.

How's the date going?

I quickly replied.

I keep making an idiot of myself.

Relax! Aran says that Jack really likes you.

I'd better go. I think Jack is trying to read my texts upside-down.

'Everything okay?' asked Jack, still looking amused.

'Yes, that was Charlotte wanting to know if I'm sharing a stall with her at her next exhibition.'

'And are you?'

'What?'

'Sharing the stall?'

'Oh, yes, probably.' I popped the last of the toastie into my mouth. 'I said I'd let her know.'

Jack nodded as he finished off his own sandwich, then wiped his hands on a serviette. 'Would you like another tea, Sadie, or perhaps you'd prefer to go on somewhere else?'

I brightened at the prospect of having more time with him.

'Somewhere else would be nice,' I enthused. After all, I was dressed up. Not that jeans were particularly smart, but I looked a damned sight better than my usual scruffy self. Shame not to make the most of it.

'Do you want to move on to a bar? Or go for a walk, work off the toastie, and then have a late dinner somewhere? Or come back to mine for' – he kept his voice deliberately casual – 'something alcoholic while seeing a certain wayward beagle?'

At the thought of cuddles with William, my eyes lit up and I didn't hesitate to reply. 'The last option, please.'

Which had nothing to do with also being at Jack's house with a comfy sofa to possibly recline upon, or a bed being conveniently placed upstairs. Good grief, the thought had never entered my head.

Chapter Forty-Four

I followed behind Jack on the drive back to West Malling. Once inside his house, we kicked off our shoes and said hello to Sylvie. She greeted me politely and very gently. William, however, launched himself at me in a frenzy of delight.

'He always goes berserk upon seeing you,' said Jack, as I patted my boy. Despite now having Rosemary and Thyme, my love for William hadn't diminished. 'I mean' – Jack continued – 'he's always thrilled to see the postman, or me, and even my parents, but when you come to the house, he goes completely nuts.'

'Well, I was his mummy for several weeks,' I pointed out.

'Yes, and he's not letting either of us forget it.' Jack held out a hand. 'Do you want me to take your cardigan? Unless you want to throw it over my head,' he chuckled.

'Funny,' I tutted. 'Yes, please. Take it. After all, it's not cold.' I slipped the garment off while Jack scooped up our footwear. 'I'd better chuck these in the cupboard too, otherwise a certain beagle will have the soles off in seconds.'

While Jack disappeared briefly inside the coat cupboard putting everything out of William's way, I quickly glanced around the hallway. It was bigger than that of the average home and easily contained William and Sylvie's baskets, also a large jungle-like potted plant and a huge wooden box that reminded me of a pirate's treasure chest. 'That's nice,' I said, pointing to it.

'Yes,' Jack agreed, reversing out. 'It was a birthday present from Gaynor.'

Oh God, her again. I tried not to grimace.

'She has good taste,' I said, dredging up a gracious smile.

Best not to be bitchy, even though I owed the woman nothing. She'd caused such a fiasco over the doggy ownership of William. Funny how you didn't necessarily have to meet someone to have them impact upon your life, but to also know instinctively – should you ever come face to face – that you wouldn't like them. Indeed, I was already feeling like I'd swallowed several sour grapes.

'Now then,' said Jack, shutting the cupboard door. 'I know it's not long since we had the toasties, but it was very light.' I followed him through to the kitchen where he picked up some leaflets. 'Shall I order a takeaway? There's a fab Chinese just around the corner. West Malling also has its own Indian restaurant that does a mean Vindaloo.' He passed me the menus. 'We could eat off our plates in the lounge and ignore the dogs salivating while watching a mindless Netflix movie.'

I suddenly had a rose-tinted vision of sitting alongside Jack. The dogs curled at our feet. Meal consumed. Feeling replete. Relaxed. Snuggling together. Me leaning into that wonderfully fit looking body. A muscular arm draped lightly around my shoulders.

'Shall we choose a movie first and then, maybe in an hour or so, order something?' I suggested.

'Sure.' Jack took the menus off me and put them on the worktop. 'Meanwhile, drink?'

'Erm...' Heavens, at this rate my body would be swimming in tea.

'I meant a proper drink,' Jack grinned. He opened a cupboard and peered within. 'Gin and tonic? Vodka and orange?' His hand delved inside. 'What's this? Heavens. Something left over from last Christmas. Baileys. Do you like the stuff?'

I wrinkled my nose. 'I'd rather have a glass of wine – if you have any.'

'I do.' He shut the cupboard and went to the fridge. 'Prosecco all right? I always keep a bottle for when my family come over. Mum's a bit partial.'

'Don't open it just for me,' I protested.

'It's okay. I'll join you. I know it's popular with you girlies, but now and again I like it too,' he laughed. 'Grab me a couple of glasses from that cupboard you're standing next to.' He busied himself popping the cork while I opened an overhead door. The shelves were impressively tidy, which surprised me. Somehow I'd presumed that Jack, being a bachelor, might be a bit chaotic. But all the glasses and mugs within were neatly lined up. And quite minimalistic too, I noted. Unlike my own cupboard where odd-sized tumblers

242

and mismatched cups jostled for space.

'Here you are,' I said, passing him two flutes.

'Cheers,' he said, a moment later. We clinked glasses. 'Shall we?' He gestured with a hand, indicating I lead the way out of the kitchen. 'Door on the left is the lounge.'

I went in and mentally raised my eyebrows. Blimey. This guy was *way* tidier than me. And look at the carpet. Vacuum lines. My beady eye travelled around the room taking in the tasteful décor. Attractive coffee table. Bespoke shelving system. Some abstract art on the wall. Not one mote of dust resided on anything. I couldn't even see any dog hairs. When William had been with me, his white tummy hair had left a fine layer over everything.

'How on earth do you keep this place so spotless with two dogs?' I blurted.

'That's a secret,' he said, suddenly looking furtive. He looked over his shoulder, left and right, as if someone might be listening, then dropped his voice to confide. 'I have a cleaning lady and she visited earlier.' He laughed. 'You're seeing the place at its best. Give it twenty-four hours and there will be biscuit crumbs on the sofa and muddy paw marks over the kitchen floor.'

'And there was me thinking you were one of those fastidious guys who liked everything spick and span.'

'Ha!' he chortled. 'Sadly not. Poor old Doreen despairs of me. I pay her twenty quid an hour and she earns every penny of it, from mopping the floors and bleaching the loos to stripping my bed and wielding the iron. I'm housetrained enough to work the washing machine and switch on the dishwasher, but that's about the extent of it. That said' – he gave me a dazzling smile – 'my garden is the best for miles. Not one weed dares to infest the lawn and there isn't a leaf out of place. Well' – he pulled a face – 'it *was* the best garden for miles until William dug several vast holes.'

I grinned and flopped down on the sofa. 'Yes, he made my postage stamp of a lawn occasionally look like it had been infested by a gang of giant moles.'

Jack sat down next to me, and his thigh momentarily brushed against mine. A zinger whizzed up my leg. I momentarily closed my eyes and clung on to my wine glass as if it were a lifebuoy.

'So, what shall we watch?' he asked, reaching for the remote and pressing a button. 'Action? Comedy? Or horror?'

'Um…' I peered myopically as the screen trying to read the blurry options. I screwed up my eyes, opened them a little wider, then narrowed them again. 'What does that say? *Money Hiss? Lost in Pace?* I concentrated harder. '*Am-er-ic-an Ginger?* I was suddenly aware of Jack shaking with laughter.

'Sorry, I shouldn't giggle. What's that ad? You should have gone to SpecSavers,' he chortled. 'Okay, how about I read it for you?'

'If you don't mind.'

We grinned at each other. And suddenly I couldn't tear my eyes away. It seemed that he couldn't either. We continued to sit there, saying nothing, our smiles slowly fading until we were simply staring at each other. I was aware of a highly charged silence. My eyes remained pinned to his. I felt helpless to do anything. I couldn't move. Blink. Speak. In fact, I could hardly breathe.

'You're very beautiful, Sadie,' he murmured.

I didn't know how to respond. I wanted to say, "Don't be absurd!" but my vocal cords seemed to be paralysed.

'Can I kiss you?' he whispered.

As my voice box had seized up and I couldn't reply, instead I nodded dumbly. As his lips met mine, the ensuing zinger was so forceful it jolted my arms. They ricocheted upwards, looped around his neck, then pulled him down on top of me. Good God. What must he think of such a brazen hussy? "Bloody hell! Is she desperate for me, or what?" But my body was doing its own thing now, reacting to all that chemistry and without consulting my brain either, so that I was totally lost in the rapture of it all. The thrill of his mouth on mine. The joy of my body responding – after so long in an emotionally arid desert. Fireworks were going off in every erogenous zone. My heart was hammering away, and every pore of my being was fizzing and popping with anticipation. As the kiss went on and on, it became apparent that sooner or later we were going to have to come up for air. Oxygen was required.

'Sadie,' he gasped.

'Jack,' I panted, putting my tongue away and hoping I didn't look like William when pursuing a squirrel.

'Shall we–?'

'Yes,' I agreed, springing to my feet. To the bedroom. Now.

He was on his feet in an instant, taking me by the hand, leading me up the stairs and – oops, tripping over William's squeaky toy – then we were pounding across the landing and into a bedroom with a vast bed slap-bang against the far wall. It seemed to be flashing, like a neon light, in and out of my vision, beckoning the pair of us over. Jack's mouth on mine again which rather hampered a smooth transition across the room. Instead the pair of us stumbled towards the bed, his hands on my jeans, my fingers lifting his t-shirt for a quick feel around – lovely – before moving down to his zipper. Oh God. Where was the zipper? Oh, I see. Buttons. Now his hands were pulling down my jeans and – oh! – taking my pants with them – while I carried on wrestling with that first button. His fingers were exploring now. Moving upward. Disappearing under my floaty top. Stroking my skin. Making me shiver as, all the while, I tugged at that button. Now he was loosening my bra strap. Releasing my breasts. They fell like two ripe peaches into his cupped palms while I tugged and tugged on that flipping button. His thumbs brushed across my nipples. They sprang to attention like two sentries, while I privately wondered why the hell he'd opted to wear jeans with button flies rather than a good old-fashioned zipper. His hands swept down. As they cupped my bare buttocks, I mentally bashed out a quick letter of complaint to the manufacturer of Jack's jeans:

Dear Sir

Please be aware that, at the time of my new boyfriend initiating a sexy grapple, I was completely unable to get to first base on account of your product having ridiculous stud buttons that were comparable to a male chastity belt. In future would you please refrain from making garments in this manner to prevent an army of women experiencing similar frustrations.

Yours sincerely

A thoroughly irritated female deprived of a–

'Fuckity-fuck!' I cursed as the button pinged off the denim and ricocheted across the floor. Only three more to go!

Jack unglued his mouth from mine. 'You do it like this,' he gasped, effortlessly sliding the buttonhole over the stud. Moments later he'd stepped out of them leaving me standing there, mouth hanging open gormlessly as my eyes feasted. His legs had biscuity-brown skin with strong thighs sculpted like a footballer's. *Beautiful*, I mentally sighed, suddenly aware that he might not be thinking the same about me with my own jeans hanging unattractively at half-mast.

Get them off, Sadie, screeched my inner voice.

I yanked at them, but they were skinnies, and became wedged around my ankles. There was a choice. Either pogo about, attempting to free one leg at a time, or perch on the bed and whip off the trousers in one swift move. I opted for the latter and began to totter towards the bed which – hell, how big was this bedroom? – was still twenty pigeon steps

247

away. Right. Keep tottering, Sadie. That's it. Left, right, left right. Getting there. Only fifteen more pigeon steps. Twelve… ten… eight. My bare bum jiggled away as I shuffled seductively onwards. Why hadn't I taken lessons in undressing like a temptress? There were probably loads of videos on YouTube. I'd bet my sister had never seduced half the men in London like this. Flora would have no doubt performed an eye-popping striptease, elegantly and effortlessly shedding clothes as she shimmied across the bedroom. I gritted my teeth and kept shuffling. Six more pigeon steps. Five. Four–

'Look out!' cried Jack, as I tripped over yards of denim and nose-dived down to the carpet. I was aware of my bottom wobbling long after the rest of me had stopped moving.

'I'm okay,' I trilled, rolling over. Like an awkward yogi, I raised my ankles to my ears and pulled off the hateful trousers. Why had I worn them? Charlotte had been right. A dress would have been so much easier for sexy action. A simple zip followed by the rustle of silk slithering to the floor, and everything instantly revealed.

I hauled myself to my feet, a vision in a dishevelled top and woolly socks, just as the intercom buzzed. 'Leave it,' I said, anxious to get back to where we'd left off.

'Yes,' Jack agreed, peeling his top off in one effortless move and, once again, rendering me speechless at his physique. Oh. My. God. Look at that torso. That chest. Those pecs. That snail trail. Those–

248

But I didn't have time to gawp further. His mouth was once again on mine. Mmm. Oh yes. Mmm. Perfect. Mmm. What a great kisser. I could do this all day. I inwardly sighed with joy as the zings once again started up but, unfortunately, the buzzer was keeping time with them. Whoever it was, they weren't going away. The visitor was now giving short, sharp presses on the button. Downstairs, Sylvie and William were starting to vocalise their displeasure, letting out a series of growls and woofs. Then suddenly everything went silent. Deep joy. But... wait. Oh no. Whoever this person was, someone must have let them in through the side gate because they were now attacking the doorbell. The dogs went potty.

Ring. Bark. Ring. Woof. Ringgggg. Bark-bark-bark-bark-growlllllllll.

'I can't stand it,' said Jack, pulling away. 'Let me see who it is and get rid of them. I'll be two minutes,' he promised, picking up his jeans and quickly slipping them back on. 'Don't worry,' he said, grinning wickedly. 'Two more minutes and these will be off again.'

'Good,' I answered, trying not to leer, and thinking that at least I'd now be able to quickly strip and arrange myself artfully across the bed. Yes, good idea, Sadie. Oh God, this was so thrilling. So exciting. Sex for the first time in, well, ages and ages and ages! And, happily, all the important bits and pieces seemed to be working properly. Everything was harmoniously sizzling and spitting.

I peeled off my top and bra, the latter of which was like a ship that had lost its mooring. A moment later and the socks had gone too. I heaped everything on a handy chair, then dived under the duvet.

The sheets were cold against my skin, and I shivered. At the thought of Jack soon being beside me, I shivered again. I mentally hugged myself and only just stopped myself from shouting aloud, "Yippee!"

Now then. Time to arrange myself. I lifted my head so that my hair fanned across the pillowcases, prettily framing my face. Okay, cleavage next. I fluffed up the quilt, then wedged it under my bust. Oh dear. That didn't look right. The trouble with laying on one's back was that one's bosoms parted company. Currently my nipples were snuggling up to my armpits. Maybe prop up the pillows and *then* lean back. I wriggled upright and then… yes… that's it. Let the hair fall seductively over the shoulders instead, then use upper arms to squish the boobs together. Finally, showcase one's formidable looking cleavage, wait for the man in question to return, then watch as his eyes pop out of his head.

And wait.

And wait a bit longer.

I frowned.

Blimey, how long did it take to see off an unwanted doorbell ringer?

My ears strained to hear. Downstairs, an agitated conversation seemed to be taking place.

'… really not convenient right now… have company…'

Jack's fragmented words floated up the staircase, but his voice was low, and I couldn't catch everything he was saying.

I wondered who he was talking to.

'… tried calling… never pick up… ignore texts…'

The voice was female.

'… told you it was over…'

'… don't want that… sorry for *mumble mumble*… so stupid to have *mumble mumble* … all I want is to try again and…'

I froze. Oh dear God. I had a horrible feeling who this visitor was. A moment later I heard Jack's footsteps coming up the stairs. I experienced a sinking feeling in the pit of my stomach. I didn't need his nan to read the tealeaves and predict that he wouldn't be getting into bed with me. I knew it in my heart. A second later he appeared in the doorway. His face told me everything.

'Sadie,' he said softly, picking up his t-shirt and popping it over his head. An entirely retrograde action in my opinion. 'Sorry, but we're going to have to reschedule. My visitor is refusing to go away.'

I stared at him. 'Gaynor?' I whispered.

Jack nodded miserably. 'She's in a state. Threatening to jump off Dartford Bridge if I don't talk to her.'

'Right,' I nodded. Well, wasn't this just peachy. And what about if *I* threatened to do such a thing too? My shoulders drooped. That wasn't my style. Apart anything else, I remembered how awful it was when you were in love with a man who didn't hold you in his heart. 'Well, I'll just…' I nodded at my clothes on the chair. Suddenly it didn't seem right that I should slip out of bed completely starkers when Jack hadn't yet fully revealed himself to me.

'I'll go and...' he jerked his head at the bedroom door, awkward now.

'Yes,' I agreed. Slip away and let me get dressed in peace.

'I'll be downstairs.'

'Right,' I nodded.

A moment later and I was alone. Feeling slightly sick, I flung back the cover and hastily stuck my legs into my jeans. Too late I realised they were inside out, but I didn't care. A moment later and the floaty top was back on, minus the bra. My feet were devoid of socks too. I didn't want to waste a second getting out of here. Scooping everything up, I hastened across the bedroom and down the stairs. Jack was waiting for me in the hallway. The door to the lounge was shut. Beyond, I could hear a woman softly weeping.

'My bag,' I gasped. It was in the living room, but Jack produced it along with my cardigan and boots. He was two steps ahead of me. 'Thanks,' I muttered, stuffing my undies and socks inside. Romantic. Not.

'I'll be in touch,' he whispered, brushing his lips against mine and instantly leaving a trail of fire.

I looked at him sadly. 'Do me a favour?'

'What?' His eyes searched my face.

'Only contact me when this situation has completely resolved.'

'It already *has*,' he insisted. 'She's just beside herself at the moment, and I don't want her doing anything stupid or–'

At that moment the door to the lounge flew open. A woman stood there. Despite having tear-stained cheeks, she was incredibly pretty with piled-up fair hair, huge eyes, and the sort of figure I could never achieve in a million years unless I existed on plain yoghurt and edamame beans.

'Thank you so much for looking after my boyfriend,' she said, in a voice that could have cut glass. 'But now I'd like him back.'

Chapter Forty-Five

I didn't hang around to hear Jack protest about Gaynor's claim on him, instead pushing past the pair of them and running full pelt towards Grace.

Anger and upset seemed to be whooshing up from the very soles of my feet, through my abdomen and into my oesophagus, clogging up my throat and choking me. I let out a strangled sob as the tears started to fall. Oh God, get me out of here. I hadn't even had time to say good-bye to my boy.

'Oh, William,' I moaned.

If I couldn't see Jack again, what were the chances of seeing William? If ever? Especially if that manipulating cow got her own way.

My thoughts returned to the bits of conversation I'd overheard. "Sorry for *mumble mumble*... so stupid to have *mumble mumble*." Gaynor must have been apologising for taking William to the rehoming centre and trashing Jack's house. I had no doubt that Jack would forgive her because he wasn't the sort to hold grudges. After all, William had found his way back to him, and a decorator had put things right on the home front. No harm had been done in the grand scheme of things – no one had died.

Driving home, I illegally reached for my phone. *Breaking the law again, Sadie?* Last time, I promised my inner voice. My bestie answered immediately.

'Sadie! How did the date g–?'

'It didn't,' I said, cutting her off.

Charlotte caught the tears in my voice. 'What's happened?'

As I drove back to Clover Cottage, I shrieked and stuttered my way through the story of Gaynor and Jack's grand reunion.

'Doesn't sound like they're getting back together to me.'

'But what choice does he have?' I wept. 'She told him she'd commit harikari if he doesn't take her back.'

'That's just to get his attention,' Charlotte assured.

'Well she's got that all right,' I spat. 'But that's not all. Not only did Gaynor thank me for looking after her boyfriend, but she also said she'd now like him back.'

'That doesn't mean to say Jack will oblige. And anyway' – I sensed Charlotte choosing her words carefully – 'I seem to remember Jack saying *he* was the one who ended it with *her*. In fact, I'm sure of it. The whole ensuing saga over William was due to Gaynor taking revenge for being dumped.'

'Yes,' I sniffed. 'That's true.'

'Well there you go then,' said Charlotte calmly. 'Your imagination is running away with you. What man in his right mind would reignite things with a woman he didn't want to be with, especially after her pulling such a mean stunt?'

'Jack's a very forgiving type,' I sobbed, eyes brimming again.

'Forgiving is one thing. Being a pushover is something else. Apart from anything else, he doesn't want to be with her.'

'But Charlotte, you haven't seen her,' I bleated. 'She's stunning. All swingy hair and goo-goo eyes and–'

'And a cruel streak in her heart. Why else would she have dognapped William? That's just downright nasty. For goodness' sake, Sadie, get a grip on your emotions.'

'You don't understand.'

'Yes I do, sweetheart,' Charlotte soothed. 'You've been triggered.'

Charlotte's words crashed into my brain. For a moment I couldn't speak. Instead, I stared, wide-eyed, through Grace's windscreen. It had started to rain. On autopilot I toggled the stick for the wipers. The rubber blades made me jump as they scraped across the glass. Triggered. Now *there* was a word.

'Do you think?' I croaked.

'Without a doubt,' Charlotte assured. 'Listen, I know you've only known Jack for five minutes and this was a first date that – due to unforeseen circumstances – got rudely interrupted, but–'

'You can say that again,' I muttered.

'*But* we both know that Jack is a nice guy. He isn't your ex,' she said gently.

'My ex was nice in the beginning,' I said, on the defensive.

'He had way too much charm, darling.'

'What's wrong with that?' I protested.

'It becomes smarm,' Charlotte countered. 'And that isn't so attractive.'

'I don't know what to do,' I wailed, wiping the back of my hand across my nose.

'Do nothing,' Charlotte advised. 'Sit tight. Let Jack deal with the obnoxious Gaynor. He'll be in touch soon. You'll see.'

'I told him to call me only when she was well and truly off the scene.'

'Fair enough, and I'm sure that won't take long. Now then, are you feeling a bit better?'

'I don't know,' I whispered, as Grace shot through a traffic light on the change. An amber light. Another trigger.

'Do you want me to come over? Sadie? Are you there?'

I didn't reply. My mind was flipping back in time. Back. Back a bit more. Driving. At speed. Well, not to begin with. At the start of the journey, as I'd followed Felix on the drive to Dering Road, everything had been fairly calm. Moderate traffic flow. Reading the road. No erratic driving. I peered through the screen and into the dark night, trying to shut out the memories.

Chapter Forty-Six

When Felix arrived at the antiques shop in Dering Road, he drove into the small customer car park at the rear of the shop.

Following Felix into the car park was a big fat no, unless I wanted to blow my cover. As parking anywhere in the area was at a premium, I hesitated, not knowing what to do. Dering Road was full of double yellows.

Instead, I sailed past the shop, cruised on for another couple of hundred yards, then came to a standstill at the side of the main drag. A strategically placed sign warned that this action was prohibited and carried a fine. Switching on Grace's hazard lights, my eyes did a sweep of the surroundings. No ticket-wielding traffic warden was currently in the vicinity. Good.

Instead, via the rear-view mirror, I watched for signs of activity. Would Felix enter the building via the staffroom just off the car park? Or would he walk around the shop's perimeter and go to the front entrance? Logic screamed the former. Nonetheless, I made myself sit, wait, and observe for a full ten minutes.

When there was still no sign of Felix, I started up the engine, made a U-turn, and doubled back. Seconds later,

Grace's right indicator light was blinking away. There was a pause as I waited for a gap in the traffic. An oncoming car flashed me to go, and I pressed the accelerator. As Grace bounced over the ramp and into the car park, I cut the engine. She rolled silently across the tarmac and came to a muted standstill next to Felix's sportscar.

I glanced over at the building. My fiancé's face didn't appear at a window. Phew. I'd succeeded in the first part of my mission. Arriving without alerting the occupants within.

I paused for a moment, taking in the initial surroundings, looking for clues that might help process immediate information. There was a distinct absence of an engineer's van – no surprises there – but, more importantly, there was no sign of Flora's car. She must have used London's Underground. I peered upwards. The overhead flat was in darkness. I had no idea if that meant it was empty, or whether a tenant was in situ and simply not yet home from work. However, the shop's lights were on, which indicated that this was the setting for the romantic rendezvous.

I slipped quietly out of the car. Instead of slamming the driver's door, I leant on it, using my bottom to push it into the locking mechanism. Taking a deep breath, I crept over to the shop's rear door. For a moment I just stood there, straining to hear anything, but the passing traffic drowned out what might otherwise be heard. I fingered the spare key in my pocket. Pulling it out, I looked at it in dismay. It was a Yale. I could now see that the rear door was secured by a mortice lock. Damn. The key in my hand was for the front door. The last thing I wanted was to enter street-side and risk being seen. The shop's frontage had large picture-windows, although there was a possibility that Felix might have since drawn the blinds within.

I puffed out my cheeks and dithered. What to do? The rear door had a handle, like that of an internal door. I stared at it and then, on impulse, quietly levered it down. To my surprise, there was no resistance. Good God, Felix *had* been in a hurry when he'd hot-footed into the place. Fancy not securing the back door! But then, almost immediately, another thought occurred to me. What if he'd deliberately left it unlocked for Flora's arrival?

I gulped and peered anxiously over my shoulder, half expecting to see my sister standing behind me. There was no one. However, best not to linger. My aim was to catch them at it, not have the situation reversed so that I was the one caught out.

Taking a cautious step forward, I peered around the door. There was no inner hallway. Instead, a functional staff room met my gaze. It was practical, but cosy enough. My eye was drawn to the sofa against one wall. It hadn't yet been pulled out to become a makeshift bed. Still, there was plenty of time for that, especially if Flora had yet to arrive.

Get a move on, Sadie, urged my inner voice.

Galvanised into action, I stepped over the threshold, quietly shutting the door behind me. I needed a place to hide. Somewhere to lurk until hemlines were raised, trousers were dropped, and I could calmly step out of the shadows and say, "Well hell-*ooo*! Did you know that a cheating bastard instructs karma to deliver the bitch he deserves?"

The staffroom was devoid of any convenient nooks and crannies to melt into. There was a small shower room which, at this moment, offered the only plausible sneaky space in which to disappear. Earmarking it as a possibility, I crept across the room and paused by an internal door. From past visits I knew that, on the other side, was the shop's counter complete with old-fashioned working cash till. If Felix were truly busy with paperwork, he'd now be stationed inches from me. I strained to hear a chair creaking, or a calculator being tapped. Nothing. But wait. What was that?

I pressed my ear harder against the wooden panels. A cry for help. And from a woman. My heart began to gallop. What was going on here? Was Flora being held against her will? Surely not! Carefully, I cracked open the door and put one eye up against the gap. There was nothing to see other than a glimpse of the shop's windows. Felix had indeed drawn the blinds so that eyes couldn't see within.

'Help!' came the voice again, but something told me this wasn't a genuine call of distress. The plea wasn't frantic. In fact, it lacked any authentic urgency. This wasn't a female needing to be rescued. 'Oh God help me,' came the voice again. More of a moan this time.

'Why do you always make a racket?' gasped a male voice. Felix. My eyebrows shot up into my hairline. From the sound of it, he was panting. I slipped silently around the door and dropped down on all fours behind the counter.

Where were they?

'*He-l-ppp*,' bleated the woman.

Something else was off. The wailer didn't sound like my sister. Crawling forward, I bobbed my head around the counter. And that was when all was revealed.

Felix was facing me. I sent up a silent prayer of thanks that he'd not noticed the staff room door inching open – but, then again, right now he was busy. From my ankle-viewing perspective, I could see he was naked to the waist. Any further view of my fiancé was blocked by a woman lying on her back. She was sprawled across a solid-looking oak table with barley-twist legs. Her own legs were coltishly long and draped gracefully over Felix's shoulders. Despite being devoid of clothing, she'd opted to keep on her Alice band. The pink velvet strip held back mousy-coloured hair and revealed a long, thin face devoid of any make-up. The horse-like features were screwed up in what some might have thought to be pain, but which I knew to be pleasure.

Shock reverberated through me. This woman clearly had her own key to the premises and was the last female I'd ever have suspected of duplicity. It was Henrietta Cavendish.

Chapter Forty-Seven

I gaped at the scenario going on in front of me, unable to tear my eyes away.

One part of me was hugely relieved that it wasn't Flora being serviced by Felix, the other part was devastated. And of all the women to have a dalliance with. Henny!

So many times, Felix had ridiculed her. Behind her back he'd called her Horsy Henny. He'd often joked about her unfortunate Ken Dodd dental arrangement. At parties, he'd been known to make whinnying noises behind his hand whenever she'd entered the room. At Tara's charity ball, Felix had even cantered on the spot, drunkenly saying, "Giddy up!" to an audience of bemused onlookers.

And then another memory surfaced from that night. Henny had buttonholed me. Asked me if I'd ever caught Felix out. She'd said, "Looks like you're about to." At the time I'd assumed she was commenting upon Flora leaving the ballroom with Felix. But in fact, I realised she'd been giving me a subliminal message. After all, she'd pointed out that Plain Janes like her took infidelity on the chin before going on to tell me I was in another league, and that consequently she hadn't thought Felix would muck me about. *That* was what she'd meant about not yet catching Felix out. Not with Flora, but with *her*.

'Oh, help-me-help-me-help-*meee*,' Henny moaned.

'No one's gonna help you, babe' – Felix gasped, speeding up his thrusts – 'so you might as well shut up.'

Another part of me wondered what Tara would make of this coupling. And I just knew that Felix's mother would be thrilled. She'd be cancelling our wedding invites in a jiffy before rushing off to buttonhole The Archbishop of Canterbury for the marriage of Miss Henrietta Cavendish to Mr Felix Barrington-Jones.

But I was puzzled. If Felix had a thing about Henny, what the heck was he doing with me? Why not simply marry Henrietta, and thrill both her and his mother at the same time with a splashy society wedding?

'Ooooooooh,' Henny gasped. She let out a final shriek as her body convulsed. 'I'm com-*inggg*.'

Felix's hip thrusting went into overdrive. 'I'm right behind you,' he panted.

'And I'm in front of you,' I announced, standing up and revealing myself.

Henny let out a screech that was nothing to do with climaxing but everything to do with shock. Felix's head jerked up and, upon seeing me, he turned grey.

'Sadie!' He instantly decoupled and deflated. 'Oh my God.' Suddenly he was reaching for his shirt. 'Darling, I'm so sorry. It meant nothing–'

'How DARE you,' screeched Henny, wiggling off the

table and looking outraged.

'But it's true,' Felix protested, hastily stepping into his pants, and grabbing his trousers. 'You knew it was nothing other than sex.'

'For God's sake,' I croaked, tears now pricking my eyes. '*Why?* Why did you ask me to marry you? Why have you been shagging around while your mother plans our wedding? Surely it should be Henrietta walking up the aisle, not me.'

'I can't marry Henny,' said Felix incredulously, stuffing shirttails into his waistband. 'I'd be a bloody laughingstock.'

Henrietta's mouth dropped open. 'Well thank you so much for that, Felix.'

'Sorry, but it's true. I mean, have you looked in the mirror?'

'YOU BASTARD!' she cried, her eyes brimming.

'Sweetheart, you have the body of an angel, but I never once looked at your face while fucking you. And that's all it ever was. A fuck.'

Henrietta had made no attempt to cover herself and I wasn't really surprised. If I'd had a figure like hers, I'd have paraded it at every given opportunity. She stood there, openly weeping, and I almost felt sorry for her as she put her head in her hands. Meanwhile Felix was still hopping about, now attempting to put on his socks.

'You disgust me,' I said quietly, as my fingers worked to release the ring on my left hand. 'Obviously we're over.'

Seconds later, the diamond flew through the air and smacked Felix on the bridge of his nose.

'Ouch,' he yelped. 'For fuck's sake, Sadie,' he said crossly, scrabbling for the ring. 'Listen to me.' His head reappeared over the other side of the table as he pocketed it. 'Let's not be hasty.' But I was no longer listening. 'Sadie, come back! I love y–'

I was off. Belting through the staffroom. Out the back door. Scampering over to Grace. Throwing myself behind the wheel. The engine coughed into life. Tyres momentarily spun before the vehicle shot backwards. Horns blared as I reversed, kamikaze-style, into oncoming traffic. And suddenly I was screeching off, swiping the back of my hand over wet cheeks as the tears began to flow. I was crying so hard it was a struggle to see the road.

My phone, on the passenger seat, began to ring. A sideways glance revealed Felix as the caller. I dithered on whether to answer. What if a passing police car caught me? But then the furious part of me decided I didn't care. They could put me in jail and throw away the key because, as far as I was concerned, my life was already over. I snatched up the mobile.

'What?' I snarled, steering Grace with one hand. I shot past a cyclist who was wobbling all over the road.

'Henny means nothing to me.'

My eyes flicked to the rear-view mirror. I could see Felix a few cars behind me, his sportscar weaving through the traffic. Now the cyclist was in *his* way.

'It obviously meant something to Henny,' I said scathingly. 'She looked shattered.'

'Listen, she's a nice enough girl. Hands up, I admit it. I took advantage of her having a crush on me.'

'The woman is clearly in love with you, Felix.'

'Well it's not mutual. *You're* the woman I love.'

My chest was starting to squeeze so hard I wondered if this was how it felt to have a heart attack. Such deep pain. There was so much of it, swilling around under my ribs. I didn't know how to respond to Felix's declarations of love when I'd just witnessed the ultimate betrayal.

'I can't believe this has happened,' I cried, as a fresh round of sobs ambushed me.

'Don't cry, darling. Please. I'm sorry I've been such a shit. I don't know why I keep doing this but–'

'*Keep* doing this?' I whispered, as a fresh wave of shock slugged me in the solar plexus. 'You mean it's not just Henny? There have been others?'

The question was met with a resounding silence.

'Stupid,' Felix muttered. 'So stupid.'

'Oh my God,' I wailed. 'Am I really hearing this?'

'Sadie, please. Darling, slow down. I'm worried you're going to have an accident. You're driving way too fast.'

'Then stop chasing me. Just turn around and go home. Or back to Henny – or whoever else you've been seeing.'

'But I don't want to. I want you. Listen to me, Sadie. I'm aware that I don't look like God's gift to women. Oh sure, I have money in the bank and come from an affluent family. But strip all that away, and I have zero confidence.'

'Oh pur-leeze.' I gave a bark of mirthless laughter. 'You

have more bluster than anyone I know.'

'But it's true, Sadie. I lack self-esteem. That's why I do it. I mean' – he hastily amended '*did* it. But no more. I give you my solemn promise. I'll even go and have counselling. Would you like that, hmm?'

'Sorry, Felix. I'm sure therapists are excellent for helping people with many things. Bereavement. Loneliness. Depression. But I'm not convinced they have a magic wand to help serial adulterers keep their dick in their pants.'

'Of course they do,' Felix assured, finally swerving past the cyclist and hitting the accelerator to catch me up. 'Look at all the famous men who have had therapy and sorted themselves out. Kanye West. Russell Brand. David Duchovny.'

'Oh so you're saying you're a sex addict now?' I cried. 'Is that it? Because a few moments ago, you were telling me you waved your willy at women due to lack of self-esteem. So make up your mind. What's it to be?'

'A combination,' said Felix quickly. 'It's because I have no self-esteem that I need to see if I can attract other women to bolster my confidence.'

'Well you can carry on,' I shouted. 'But from now on it will be without me.'

'But I love you,' he bleated.

'You don't know the meaning of the word.'

A bus loomed ahead, and I pressed down hard on the accelerator to get past it.

'Sadie, you're driving like a lunatic. Please, sweetheart.

I'm worried for you.'

'Oh cut the crap, and stick your fake concern where the sun doesn't shine,' I hissed, grateful that Felix was now stuck behind the bus and unable to overtake. 'You're a total SHIT.'

'Yes, yes,' he acquiesced. 'But that's all in the past. Please, Sadie. In a quarter of a mile or so, there's a three-lane junction. If you take a left, there's a pub on the corner. Pull into its car park. You're in shock, which is perfectly understandable, but it's imperative you calm down. All I want to do is put my arms around you and hold you tight.'

'Hold me tight?' I sneered.

A pedestrian crossing was looming, and I knew I was driving too fast. Thankfully nobody was waiting to use it. I shot over its black and white lines and zoomed on. The junction was in the distance. I could now see its traffic lights. I had no idea where I was going. The journey so far had been a blur.

A quick look in the rear-view mirror revealed that Felix had finally got past the bus, negotiated the pedestrian crossing and was roaring up behind me. Oh God. The last thing I wanted was getting stuck at the lights. They were currently green, but still some way ahead. I needed to go faster to avoid the unwanted change to red, otherwise Felix would take advantage of Grace being stationary. I had visions of him jumping out of his car, dashing over to mine, jiggling the door handle, or banging on the driver's window, demanding I pull over and allow him to make everything right between us. That couldn't happen.

My foot once again hit the accelerator, urging Grace to go even faster and cover the ground to that traffic light. Shit... it was on the change. I gasped as my Citroen rattled and shook, and the circle of bright green switched to amber. It was time to brake... slow down... stop. Taking a deep breath and half-closing my eyes, Grace shot across the junction just as the amber light switched to red.

'Sadie!' Felix roared. 'Come back.'

'GO TO HELL!' I screamed.

My entire body was now shaking with adrenalin. I really did need to slow down. My foot eased off the accelerator. Oh thank God, I'd escaped him. I exhaled shakily. By the time those lights were green again, I'd be long gone, being sure to take several quick lefts and rights, not knowing where I was going, but putting an ever-increasing distance between my car and his.

I jumped with fright as an angry horn blared. Where had it come from? My eyes automatically flicked to the rear-view mirror. It was at that moment that I lost track of what was going on in front of me, and instead became transfixed by the scene unfolding behind.

Oh no. Please God, *noooo*. Felix had taken a chance at the crossroads and jumped the red light. My eyes widened with horror as an articulated lorry headed towards the sportscar. Moments later it ploughed into the driver's side, almost tossing the vehicle across the painted yellow lines of the junction box. I caught a flash of Felix's face. White.

Wide-eyed. Appalled. And then everything slipped into slow motion. My car. Felix's car. The lorry. Frame. By. Shocking. Frame. The roar of sound. Then the absence of it. Vision turning to snow. Like an old-fashioned television with a bad signal.

My brain instantly scrambled the image that continued to play out behind me. I knew, later – much later – that it was a coping mechanism. The mind's way of ensuring that the image of a man's broken body in the twisted wreckage of a vehicle could never, ever be revisited.

Chapter Forty-Eight

I have a hazy recollection of what followed.

Traffic coming to a standstill in all directions. My vehicle screeching to a halt. Of abandoning Grace and running back towards that jack-knifed lorry. Of traffic lights repeatedly changing from red to amber to green with nothing moving. Of the lorry driver climbing out of his cab and promptly throwing up. Of me hysterically screaming Felix's name. Of arms holding me back.

Eventually a fire engine barged its way onto the scene as did two police cars and two ambulances. A screen was put up as firemen cut Felix from the wreckage. Not that I saw this. Incredibly – and thankfully – nobody else was injured. I was ushered into the rear of an ambulance along with the lorry driver, who was in deep shock. The other ambulance was for Felix's body.

A kind policewoman retrieved my car. A policeman explained that they had a primary duty to investigate and establish the circumstances that led to the accident. I was asked if there was a family member I could ring. Absurdly I didn't give them my parents' details. All I could think of was my mother's potential reaction. "You were speeding? You went through an amber light? You mean you INCITED Felix to jump a red in order to keep up with you? In other words, YOU CAUSED HIS DEATH?" Okay, maybe she wouldn't have reacted quite like that, but then again, maybe she would have. Shock does strange things to the mind.

Instead, darling Charlotte met me at the hospital. She was white-faced but calm. She was the one who listened to everything the police had to say while I was checked over by a tired overworked doctor. Charlotte was the one who tracked down Henny. She was also the one who gave the police details of Felix's next of kin. The police said they would pay Tara and Freddie Barrington-Jones a visit to inform them that their son had deceased. And all the while I stared into space, my brain replaying images of Felix shagging Henny on that table and then – less than fifteen minutes later – meeting his demise. On a loop. Over and over.

How could someone be here one minute and gone the next? Road deaths and the wellbeing of the individuals connected aren't just devastating and tragic – they're situations from which all involved are deeply affected and may never fully recover.

Charlotte nodded as a policeman talked in hushed tones. He advised that an investigation would take place and that it was important to understand anyone involved in road casualties may also be party to a criminal act. I remember shaking violently upon hearing that. The weight of those words. Knowing that if we hadn't been rowing… if I hadn't raced across the crossroads… if I'd done as Felix had requested... slowed down... promised him I'd turn left as he'd suggested... gone to the pub he'd mentioned... parked in the car park... let him talk to me... if I'd done all those things, then he'd still be alive. He might even have persuaded me after a hefty gin and tonic – yes, Sadie, why not add drink-driving to the list of your crimes? – that we were a match made in heaven. Especially once he'd had his counselling for sex addiction. Or was it lack of confidence? He'd probably have suggested I go along too. After all, perhaps I'd played a part in his poor self-esteem issues. Not been a good enough girlfriend. Not praised him adequately about being a whizz in bed. Not flattered him on his looks. Not complimented him for dressing like a film star. Not verbalised my admiration about him having a brain like Einstein. Yes, it was probably all my fault. Everything. My fault. But was I going to tell anyone all this?

From somewhere in the recesses of my shocked mind, something else kicked in. The survival instinct. Or, in this case, the need to keep myself out of jail. I fretted that this scenario might indeed be a possibility if the police got wind of what had really happened – Felix and I rowing on the phone and driving dangerously.

Instead, numerous witnesses told how a flash sportscar driven by a boy racer had taken a chance and paid the consequences. Months later, the investigation was formally closed. Accidental death.

Except I knew otherwise.

Chapter Forty-Nine

For a long time afterwards I seemed to exist in a twilight world. I simply retreated from reality. Who wants to experience life when you feel that yours is over?

Every morning I opened my eyes to the light of another day and knew my heart wasn't in it. Don't get me wrong. I wasn't suicidal. Just... terribly disinterested. And so utterly tired. The world seemed so drab, like putting a bundle of whites in the washing machine and having everything turn grey thanks to a rogue black sock. In one split second, everything had irrevocably changed.

Of course, it didn't take long for the truth to come out about Felix's infidelities. I was aware of a certain phone call. Of my mother speaking into the handset and sounding shellshocked. Then squawking rather loudly. In the same conversation, I heard her seesaw from anger to crying. Eventually Dad intercepted and I heard him address the caller calmly but firmly. It left me in no doubt that he meant business.

'I don't give two hoots about your wishes, Tara. We will be there. As will our daughter.'

My head had briefly reared up from the pillowcases. Oh

God. Tara. How must she be coping? And then I'd flopped listlessly back down again. I didn't have the energy to think about anyone else's grief. I was too consumed with my own. Selfish? Of course. But that's how it was.

Dad didn't tell me that Tara had told him about Felix's affair with Henny. But I later found out that Tara had opined a lot of presumptions. She'd been emphatic that Felix would never have gone ahead with the wedding. That it would only have been a matter of time before he'd dredged up the wherewithal to end it and marry Henrietta, his true love. That, consequently, it was pointless I attend the funeral. As I said, everyone handles grief differently. There's no rule book. If Tara's dogged beliefs were her way of coping, then I forgave her.

After being discharged from hospital, I'd stayed at my parents' house in my old childhood bedroom. I'd had every intention of returning to Clover Cottage just as soon as I'd found the strength to get out of bed. But the energy to do that had eluded me.

Instead, I'd stayed under the duvet, peering over the covers to occasionally spoon up soup or scrambled eggs, looking at the room's four walls with disinterested eyes. The posters of popstars had long gone, but my old corkboard had remained hanging over the built-in desk. I'd spent most of the time pondering how many hours I'd sat at that desk as a teenager. Poring over textbooks. Diligently doing homework. Back then, the corkboard had been full. The school's term timetable had been neatly pinned upon it.

Coloured highlighter pens had marked occasions that were important. Neon green had drawn the eye to the last announcement on the sheet: *End of Term*. Every student had salivated over those three words. Hurrah, the start of the holidays! Back then, little did we know that *real life* awaited us. Not failure to deliver a tricky maths piece or fretting about the possibility of a detention, but instead the warts-and-all experience of being an adult. Surrounding the timetable had been invitations to classmates' parties, bits of artwork, and an armful of rosettes from my pony-riding days. But as I'd lain there in my old childhood bed, I'd observed that the corkboard was now devoid of anything. Just like my new life.

About a week after the fatal accident, I'd had an unexpected visitor.

'Sadie?' Mum had called up the stairs. 'There's someone here to see you.'

Blearily, I'd peeled back my eyelids. It was two o'clock in the afternoon, but I'd been out cold. Who was this person who'd dared to haul my mind out of the peaceful blackness and into the bright light of day? I hadn't had long to find out. There'd been a tappity-tap on the bedroom door.

'Who is it?' I'd croaked.

'Can I come in?' a refined voice had answered.

I hadn't replied on account of my entire body, including my voice box, freezing. Seconds later, Henny had stepped into the room.

Chapter Fifty

'What do you want?' I said listlessly.

'To see you, of course,' said Henny timidly. 'Is it all right if I sit down?'

I shrugged. 'Whatever.'

She looked awful. Her beautiful curvy figure had all but disappeared. The weight loss wasn't flattering, and her eyes sat in sunken sockets. She looked like a malnourished horse bound for the knacker's yard.

Henny perched on the edge of the bed and, as the mattress shifted, I felt a flash of irritation. At this proximity I wouldn't be able to zone out, especially with the mattress shifting about from her fidgeting. When she spoke, her voice was little more than a whisper.

'I'm here to say sorry.'

I pulled a face and closed my eyes.

'I mean it,' she asserted, her voice cracking as she ploughed on. 'I am so ashamed of myself. Ever since the accident, I've been eaten up by guilt.'

I opened my eyes a fraction. 'Why?'

She gave a mirthless bark of laughter. 'Why? Why do you think?' she cried, emotion staining her cheeks. The pinkness looked at odds with her otherwise grey pallor. 'It's all my fault that Felix is dead. I as good as killed him.'

I closed my eyes again and sighed. It came out as a hiss. 'No, it's my fault.'

'Don't be ridiculous,' she sobbed, tears flowing down her cheeks. 'If I hadn't been having a fling with him, everything that followed wouldn't have happened. You wouldn't have caught us out. Nor would you have fled, wide-eyed and in a terrible state. Felix wouldn't have given chase. He'd never have jumped that red light and consequently he'd still be alive. I've shattered so many people's lives. Yours. Arabella's. Freddie and Tara's–'

'How are they?' I interrupted.

'Devastated.'

I nodded. 'Understandable.'

'I've wrecked everything,' she shrieked. 'Your wedding–' She broke off, overcome with sobs.

I shook my head slowly. It felt so heavy. 'You didn't wreck it.'

'Of course I did,' she wept, foraging up her sleeve for a tissue. 'The invitations have long been sent out and wedding gifts have been steadily rolling in. Even now Tara's drawing room is full of presents that need returning. Instead of ticking off another name on the RSVP list, she's now organising a funeral.' She trumpeted into the tissue. 'That's the other reason why I'm here.' Henny opened her handbag and dug inside. 'Here.' She removed a sheet of paper. 'The details of the memorial service.' When I didn't take the sheet, she set it down next to me on the duvet. 'It's next Tuesday.' She took a great shuddering breath. 'I'm going to be honest and relay some information. Frankly it's downright hurtful. Prepare yourself, Sadie.'

'I can guess. Tara doesn't want me there.'

Henny blinked in surprise. 'How did you know?'

I tutted. 'My face never fit, Henny. Oh, Freddie was sweet enough. Always kind and courteous. But Felix's sister and mother never liked me. Tara has already been on the phone to my parents. I semi-overheard the conversation. One doesn't need to be psychic to put together the gist of what was said. She regards you as the woman who should have been her daughter-in-law. Who *would* have been her daughter-in-law.'

'That was never going to happen,' said Henny, shaking her head. 'Despite Felix playing around, it was you he loved.'

'I don't agree. In my book, if you truly love someone, you don't cheat.'

She gave the ghost of a smile. 'No disrespect, Sadie, but you've not mixed in the same circles as me. My upbringing' – she was choosing her words carefully – 'was... colourful.' She nodded to herself, satisfied with that description. 'Mummy and Daddy were married at a very young age – and they're still together. However, they've produced their children. Done their family duty. And whilst they're terribly fond of each other and will never divorce, they've found other partners who resonate with them.'

'Lovers?' I gasped.

'Yes. Well, not so much Mummy these days.' She gave the smallest of laughs. 'A little while ago she confided that she was done with "all that nonsense". Nowadays she much prefers lunching with her friends and tending to her roses. But Daddy has always had a mistress. He's been with Carmen for the last ten years.'

I regarded her in amazement. 'So why doesn't your father leave your mother and set up home with his mistress?'

'That's not the way it works.' She smiled sadly. 'Family fortunes. Established businesses started by our forefathers – to be passed on to the next generation. Trust funds...' she trailed off. 'Carmen understands all that. After all, she has her own husband. And no doubt Carmen's husband has a mistress. Even Tara and Freddie aren't exempt,' she added quietly. 'My goodness. That was remarkably indiscreet of me. It's one thing for me to talk about my family, but quite another to talk about Felix's.'

'Don't worry, I won't be ringing up the glossy magazines to share the gossip.'

'Quite,' she said, suddenly looking jittery. 'Anyway, these things, it's just the way it is.'

'Messed up,' I muttered.

'Call it what you will.'

I blew out my cheeks. 'So why didn't Felix simply marry you and then take a mistress afterwards?' I pointed out.

She looked wistful for a moment. 'Good question. And one which Tara vocalised several times.'

My mouth fell open. 'You mean–?'

'Yes,' she nodded. 'I was up for it. I knew I'd never completely have Felix's heart, but I'd have been perfectly happy playing second fiddle.'

'Well I bloody well wouldn't have,' I gasped.

'The answer to your question is that Felix liked to be contrary. He had a peculiar relationship with his mother. Loved to do the opposite of what she wanted. I think he enjoyed winding Tara up. Anyway, he wanted a pretty wife, and you were very much that, Sadie. Actually, no. Not pretty,' she amended. 'Stunning. And your own person too. A successful artist with her own business.'

'A potter,' I scoffed. 'My business is hardly a dynasty.'

'Don't knock what you have. Remember Arabella is an artist too, except she lacks any real talent and uses the family's name – and fortune – to big herself up. Her work is pretentious crap, and everyone knows it.'

I gaped at Henny's frankness. Well, it was all coming out today, wasn't it.

She stood up. 'I must go. But before I do, can you...' – her voice quavered and she blinked rapidly several times – 'can you find it in your heart to forgive me?'

I looked at her long, narrow face. The mournful expression. The desperately sad eyes. 'There's nothing to forgive,' I assured.

She brushed her cheek with one hand as another rogue tear leaked out. 'Thanks,' she sniffed. 'That's very decent of you. So, shall I see you at the funeral?'

'You will.'

'And never mind Tara. I'll save you a seat at the front.'

'No.' My voice came out like a pistol shot and Henny flinched like a whipped dog. 'I want to slip in and out of the church unnoticed.'

'What about after the funeral? Tara is organising a huge wake and–'

'Felix will be at the church, so that's where I'll be. I have no desire to attend anything else.'

'Fair enough.' She smoothed down her skirt. 'Well, good-bye for now then, Sadie.'

'Bye, Henny.'

Chapter Fifty-One

When the day of the funeral rolled around, I felt dizzy. After spending so much time in bed, my legs didn't want to work properly. The effort of standing up, instead of lying horizontal, kept giving me moments of vertigo.

Slowly, I dressed in a simple black dress and jacket. Both hung off me. As I stared at my reflection in the mirror, I didn't recognise the person gazing back. The usually vibrant red hair, despite being freshly washed, hung limp and lacklustre. My grey eyes looked so dull it was as if an internal light had been flicked off.

'Ready?' said Mum, popping her head round the bedroom door. She looked immaculate apart from lipstick on her teeth. I followed her meekly down the stairs and out of the house.

'Come on, love,' said Dad, helping me into the rear of the car.

My sister wasn't sitting beside me. Flora had opted out.

'I might be tempted to do a reading' – she'd ranted earlier – 'and tell the congregation the truth. That Felix Barrington-Jones was a tosser.'

'Now then, Flora,' Dad had cautioned. 'Let's not speak

ill of the dead.'

'After the way he treated my sister, why ever not?' she'd demanded, nostrils flaring with indignation. 'Sadie hasn't been right in the head since. These days she's like a zombie.'

I'd been touched at Flora's show of sisterly concern. A first on her part. She'd then slightly spoilt it.

'Anyway, I've been invited to go skiing with Pierre in the French Alps, and I'm not turning him down. He may be prematurely bald and four inches shorter than me, but he's stinking rich. You should see the size of his–'

'Flora,' Mum had warned.

'What?' She'd adopted an innocent expression. 'I was going to say *chalet.*'

As Dad's car weaved along the lanes of Little Waterlow and then headed towards the M20 and London, it was inevitable that my eyes eventually shuttered down. The fatigue was endless.

When we arrived at the church, the first thing that struck me was the sense of occasion. Everyone was so dressed up. For one muddled moment I thought I'd stumbled upon a wedding. On the other side of the lychgate, a large crowd of people were milling around.

Pillar box hats and feathery fascinators, like corks on water, bobbed about. The hum of chatter was surprisingly convivial. Florid-faced men shook hands while glamorous women air-kissed each other. The only clue of this being a sombre occasion was the colour of outfits. Black suits for the men. Ditto for the women, although a few had opted for dark navy or charcoal grey.

There was a shift in the buzzy vibe when the cortege appeared.

'He's coming,' announced an onlooker. There was instant hush.

Seconds later came the clip-clop of hooves. My eyes widened at the sight of six black horses tossing their heads, slightly skittish under their matching plumes and drapes. Immaculate coachmen were seated on the raised platform of a glass Victorian hearse. The carriage, with its large pumpkin-type wheels could have been straight out of a fairy tale. And then I gasped at the sight of the coffin. It was black and shiny, just like the horses' coats. The lid's middle section bore a large arrangement of roses with a trail of miniature buds, just like a bride's bouquet.

I stared at the casket in horror and momentarily felt faint. Felix was in there. My fiancé. He really was dead. And suddenly the last couple of weeks, dreamlike and surreal, were stripped away. Reality kicked in and it was like being knifed in the solar plexus. My body hunched over, as if in pain, and I was aware of someone starting to cry. Great heart wrenching sobs. Oh God, it was me. I desperately tried to contain the noise, but it was too late – like trying to stop a shaken bottle of champagne from fizzing everywhere. And then, like a Mexican Wave, the rest of the women joined in.

A bell began to mournfully toll. Ushers politely directed everyone into the church. Turning, I caught sight of Henny in the crowd. She was dabbing a tissue at the corner of one eye. A moment later and she'd spotted me. She gave a discreet wave and I nodded by way of acknowledgment. Tara and Freddie were nearby, heads bowed. Arabella was standing with them. She followed Henny's gaze and her eyes snagged on mine. They were hard and cold. Also accusing. I was the first to look away.

Inside the church, vast arrangements of roses and lilies were everywhere. Their heady scent mingled with the smell of incense and candlewax. An empty seat remained by Henny's side. She'd kept her word. I kept mine and slipped into the back row with my parents. So far nobody had recognised me, and I intended to keep it that way.

From this distance I discreetly watched everything going on at the front. Arabella was sitting next to Tara, who was on the left of Freddie. To Freddie's right sat Henny. Her proximity to the immediate family signalled to everyone in the congregation that she was a key person. I wondered how many knew of her affair with Felix. Probably most. And for those who hadn't known, they didn't have long to find out.

One of Felix's uncles went to the lectern to read the eulogy. He waxed lyrical about his fine upstanding nephew who had not only left behind a heartbroken family, but also a devastated girlfriend, Henrietta Cavendish.

Upon hearing Henny's name, a few murmurs had rippled around the congregation accompanied by one or two raised eyebrows. No doubt these were the people who had forked out on wedding gifts delivered to the family home, addressed to Felix and *Sadie*. However, now wasn't the moment for them to get to the bottom of this mystery.

An hour later, emotionally wrung out, I'd looked on at the small group – immediate family and the closest of friends – attending the interment. Along with a few other curious guests, I'd stood at a discreet distance, watching the minister read from the bible.

Mum and Dad, also not wishing to draw attention to themselves, had elected to wait in the car for me.

And suddenly it was all over. Tara, weeping openly, leant on an ashen-faced Freddie. The pair of them looked broken as they moved away from the new grave and its covering of fresh brown soil. Tara's heels momentarily pegged, and Freddie steadied her, before heading back to the waiting funeral limousine. Henny and Arabella, arms linked, followed behind.

A sudden gust of wind whipped at hemlines and threatened to rip off Henny's hat. She put up a hand, ramming it down on her head before pausing. Her head swivelled this way and that. And then she saw me. For a moment we gazed at each other. A silent exchange. Both of us blaming ourselves for the loss of the man we'd loved.

Chapter Fifty-Two

Eleven days had passed since Gaynor had turned up at Jack's house – over a week of wondering what was going on between the pair of them. She was still there. Under his roof. I knew that for sure because I'd now received a text from Jack.

Hey, Sadie. I know you told me not to get in touch until Gaynor had left, but I'm missing you so much (as is William!) *smiley face emoji*. Unfortunately, Gaynor is still here. I've spent the duration of this time gently reasoning with her via guidance from a mate who is a counsellor. She is still threatening to "do something" and playing the emotional blackmail card. My mate is organising a therapist and I'm trying to discreetly trace Gaynor's parents. It seems they have moved since I last saw them. Meanwhile, my efforts to progress this situation have been hampered by not being well. I've been bedridden with some sort of bug. Gaynor is trying to ingratiate herself by looking after me, although I could do without it. Please let me know how you are. Love Jack xx

'My goodness,' said Charlotte, handing me back my phone. We were sitting companionably together in my kitchen on this Saturday morning in a brand-new month.

Outside, April showers were in full flow. Charlotte looked pensive as she sipped her coffee. 'And to echo Jack, how are you?' she asked gently.

'You really want to know?' I said, taking a savage bite of the chocolate cake she'd brought over with her.

'I wouldn't ask if I weren't interested,' she tutted. 'I'd hazard a guess that you're a tad peed off. Would that be a fair assumption?'

'Spot on,' I answered, spraying crumbs everywhere.

'Look' – she pulled a face – 'try and have a little sympathy with Gaynor, eh? After all, you've kind of been in this situation yourself.' She made a seesaw motion with a sticky hand, before licking chocolate icing from her fingers.

'*I've* been in this situation?'

'You know what I mean,' Charlotte muttered. 'Behaving like an unhinged sobbing female.'

My mouth fell open and I instantly put down the cake. 'You mean over Felix?'

'Well, obviously,' she said, looking uncomfortable at me saying my ex's name out loud.

'It's okay,' I assured. 'I'm not about to have the vapours because I've mentioned his name.'

'You have in the past,' she pointed out.

'Sobbing, yes. Unhinged… certainly I had a few moments. But there is one major difference between Gaynor and me. She's clearly a bunny boiler, whereas I am not. At no point did I dognap – or catnap – any of Felix's family's pets, or calmly pick up the Sunday roast's carving knife and

290

threaten to plunge it into my chest before nose-diving into the trifle.'

'Okay, you never threatened to do anything silly, but you were clinically depressed.'

'Charlotte, there is no comparison. I wasn't just depressed; I was also grieving. Gaynor's relationship with Jack ended because he wanted her to move out. Hell, he maintains he never even asked her to move in! He referred to it as the *stealth factor*. A few books here. Some clothes there. And suddenly, like the furniture, she was a permanent fixture. Whereas my relationship with Felix ended because he died. And even if he hadn't, I certainly wouldn't have hung around to graffiti his loft apartment's walls, like Gaynor did to Jack.'

'Yes, she does sound a bit of a nutter.'

'Thank you,' I said, folding my arms across my chest. A defensive gesture.

'Okay, okay. Sorry to ruffle your feathers.'

'Apology accepted,' I said huffily.

'No it isn't.' Charlotte put down her own cake. 'I've offended you. And I really am sorry. You're right. Just because you spent months sleeping a lot and crying buckets and then sleeping some more doesn't mean you were off your rocker. It was just your way of emotionally healing. You did give us all a bit of a scare though, Sadie.'

I sighed. 'I know. And I'm sorry about that too. Grief is a bitch. And I suppose it doesn't matter whether it's the shock of infidelity, or dealing with bereavement, or simply coming to terms with the fact that your fiancé's mother disliked you enough to want to sever all ties, it can send the sanest person a bit... you know...'

'Bonkers?'

I nodded. 'Yes. I can forgive Gaynor because I know she's in a dark place, and hopefully she'll soon come out of it. But the hardest part for me right now is–'

'Missing Jack?'

I sighed again. 'Well, yes, but to be honest the whole thing with him is so new that it seems ridiculous to be missing him. The crazy thing is, I feel like I've known him forever.'

'Oooh, that's soulmate talk,' Charlotte grinned.

'Never mind that,' I tutted. 'I was also going to say that the hardest thing for me is not seeing William.'

Charlotte gave me a sympathetic look. 'Why don't you pop round and take William for a walk? I'm sure Jack won't mind.'

'He wouldn't,' I nodded. 'But someone else might.'

'Ah. Gaynor.'

I shrugged. 'Anyway, enough of my problems. How are things going with Aran?'

'Swallow that bit of cake before I tell you,' Charlotte smirked. 'I wouldn't want you to experience a crumb going down the wrong way.'

Chapter Fifty-Three

I was pleased for Charlotte that her new relationship with Aran was going from strength to strength, but as the days passed, I felt like everything that had happened between me and Jack – the nought to sixty chemistry and the pair of us thundering up the stairs to his bedroom – had simply been a dream.

He sent a few more texts and I did reply, but whereas his texts were full of warmth and saying that he hoped to see me soon, mine were guarded and much shorter. Polite but distant. I had a heart to protect. It had been smashed once before and I wasn't prepared to risk it getting battered again. I wanted to be sure that Gaynor was off the scene.

My inner voice kept taunting me with the usual "what ifs". What if Gaynor did such an amazing job nursing Jack that he thought, "Hell, this woman is incredible. What was I *thinking* of when I told her to leave?" I had recurrent dreams where she was leaning over Jack and mopping his fevered brow – a low-cut top revealing everything – and Jack saying, "Darling, I'd feel so much better if you slipped into bed alongside me."

Meanwhile, I kept myself busy. Charlotte and I booked a

joint stand at a local exhibition and sales went well. The days in between were spent dealing with online stuff and some local bespoke orders.

Rosemary and Thyme had, by now, completely settled in and were a joy to have around. The pair of them occasionally liked to explore the garden and have a nosey around the studio, but overall preferred to stay inside the cottage, for which I was grateful. The last thing I wanted was worries about either of them getting knocked over by a tractor or locked in one of the farm outbuildings beyond Clover Cottage's fence boundary.

Despite loving the pair of them dearly, I still longed to see William. More days passed. Jack messaged to say that he was still poorly, which puzzled me. How long did a bug go on for?

Over the next three weeks Jack continued to text but, as Gaynor was still living under his roof, I wasn't exactly Miss Chatty when replying to his messages. There's only so many times you can wish someone better. It was the same regarding William. It seemed the little beagle was in the same mood every day.

He howls. A lot. I haven't seen much of the dogs to be honest. Gaynor keeps them out of my bedroom saying I need to rest.

Apparently Gaynor was being the perfect nurse. Well, okay, that's my description, not Jack's. But he made mention of the fact that she was looking after him so diligently that there was no time for her to walk Sylvie and William.

One day I dared to ask the obvious.

Have you not been in touch with your GP?

Jack went on to say that Gaynor had apparently telephoned the surgery but she'd been told that "due to the latest variant" the doctor was only prepared to do telephone appointments and currently there was a fortnight's waiting list. The advice was that if Jack's condition worsened, he should go to Accident & Emergency or ring 999.

I don't think stomach flu warrants me adding to an already overburdened NHS.

I sighed as I read Jack's message. It was all very noble not wanting to trouble overworked medics, but that's what a hospital was there for. To help you get better. I tapped out a reply:

This has been going on for some time. What if it's something serious? Like appendicitis?

But Jack immediately dismissed the idea.

Had my appendix out as a kid. Never mind me. How are you?

Yes, how was I? Beyond fed up, was the honest answer. What I really wanted to do was jump into Grace and roar over to West Malling. I wanted to see Jack for myself. There was a tiny part of me, you see, that was starting to doubt his narrative. I felt ashamed even admitting that to myself. But nonetheless the hesitation was there. Was Jack really telling me the truth? Wasn't it rather convenient spinning a story about being unwell when you had an ex-girlfriend under the same roof who was refusing to go away? Also, what if he was giving Gaynor a "sort of" second chance? A "sort of" trial period? Maybe Jack had decided that he quite liked seeing her pert little bottom as she vacuumed the house. Or the endearing way she tucked a strand of blonde hair behind one ear. Or the way her big blue eyes widened so prettily whenever he said her name. Perhaps the whole sickness story was a fabrication to keep me at arm's length. "I have an idea, Gaynor. Let's see how we get along together for, say, a month. What do you think? And if, after four weeks, everything is rosy, I'll let things peter out with Sadie?"

I dithered about going over there. Okay, so there was a new variant causing "stomach flu" symptoms, but I was fairly sure Jack couldn't be *that* contagious otherwise Nurse Gaynor would have likely succumbed to this lurgy too. As far as I could tell – reading between the lines of his messages – Gaynor was in the rudest of health.

'Oh for goodness' sake,' snapped Charlotte, a few days later. 'Stop being so flipping moody.' She was helping me bubble-wrap a couple of pots that Daisy, our local florist, had bought. 'Of *course* Jack's telling the truth about being poorly. He's not seen the rest of the band since going down with this bug. Aran told me so, and my boyfriend has no reason to lie, any more than Jack does.'

'Sorry,' I sighed.

'Go round to Jack's house,' she urged.

I shook my head. 'I don't think that's a good idea.'

'Why not?'

I pursed my lips and shrugged. I was too proud to tell

her that in the last few days Jack's messages had become more sporadic. It was almost like he was deliberately letting contact fizzle out.

'Do you want me to come with you?' Charlotte persisted. 'Are you worried about Gaynor shooing you away with a flea in your ear?'

'Maybe,' I said lamely.

But then the situation was taken out of my hands. Because Jack stopped texting all together.

Chapter Fifty-Four

In the last week of April, things came to a head in a way that I could never have anticipated.

The day started off like any other. Me eating my breakfast at the kitchen table, sipping coffee, and sighing a lot. I kept reflecting on "things" and felt cross with myself for lowering my guard to a man – the first since Felix – only to have him subsequently disappear over the horizon, possibly never to be seen again.

Okay, Jack and I had only had the one date. It was hardly comparable to the full-blown relationship I'd had with Felix. But I kept hearing Jack's words going round and round in my head. "I like you, Sadie... you're very beautiful... can I kiss you?"

He was just spouting rubbish to get you into the bedroom, taunted my inner voice.

On the surface, that made sense. But it didn't resonate with a deeper part of me. Jack had seemed so, well, *nice.* And whilst there were some men who did play the flattery card to achieve a means to an end, I still had a deeper belief that Jack wasn't one of them.

My thoughts fragmented as Thyme jumped up on the

kitchen table.

'Hey, you,' I admonished. 'That's not allowed. It's unhygienic.' He curled his tail over his front paws and regarded me through half-closed eyes. 'Yes, I know. You're the king of the castle and my table is your throne.' I drained my coffee cup. 'Where's your sister?' Thyme lifted one paw, gave it a few licks, then swiped it around one ear. 'Washing herself on my bed, right? In which case I guess she's going to miss out on having some Dreamies.' At the mention of his favourite snack, Thyme let out a yowl of delight and jumped off the table. Alerted by her brother's meow, Rosemary came pitter-pattering down the staircase and trotted into the kitchen. 'Ha! Cupboard love the pair of you,' I grinned, reaching into a Tupperware that contained cat treats. 'Here you go, my darlings.' I scattered a few of the cheesy biscuits across the kitchen floor and the cats instantly pounced upon them. 'Right.' I popped the lid on the container and put it away. 'It's a lovely spring day and I'm going to take myself off for a walk. Hopefully it will get some endorphins going and chase off the doldrums. I'll see you both later.'

Lacing up my hiking boots and reaching for a warm hoodie – one could never tell if a stiff breeze might suddenly come along – I threaded my arms through the straps of a rucksack filled with a few necessities and let myself out of Clover Cottage. I was determined to exhaust myself, but in a nice way.

An hour later and I was rambling across a particularly bucolic part of the hilly North Downs, taking footpaths through fields that had already been treated with fertiliser and muckspreading, stopping every now and again to smile in delight at tiny lambs hugging the flanks of their grazing mothers. The young had had their tails cut to stop flies laying eggs in the wool and causing maggots. They'd also been ear-tagged for identity.

Further footpaths criss-crossed through orchards and fields full of grazing horses before exiting on to meandering lanes. It was a joy to see all the flowers on show. Many of the neat cottage gardens were loaded with tulips, peonies, and lilacs all jostling for space.

Dipping into woodland, I strode on, listening to twigs snapping underfoot. Occasionally another hiker would pass me by, exchanging greetings along the way. I felt my mood finally lifting.

Coming out on the other side of the woods, I stopped for a breather and rummaged in my rucksack for some water. To my left was a large swathe of land full of grazing cows and calves. The little ones were curious and regarded me with huge eyes, while their mothers mooed for them to stay close.

'Don't worry,' I said to one anxious looking mother. 'I'm not about to venture into your field.'

There was a public footpath that snaked through the herd, but it wouldn't have been sensible to have used it at the current time. It was one thing to stroll past a couple of curious ponies, but it wasn't advisable to go into a field full of cows with their offspring.

Another hour passed. I stopped at a quaint pub and

treated myself to a shandy. The weather was holding up nicely, so I sat down at one of the outside trestle tables to enjoy it. I checked a map app to get my bearings and realised that West Malling was only half a mile away. As I sipped, a thought occurred. How easy would it be to stroll past Jack's place? Okay, his development was gated so I wouldn't be able to peer in through his living room window, but I might be able to see if his truck was there. Maybe I should drop him a message?

Heyyy! Long time no hear. How's the tummy bug? Still playing Doctors and Nurses with Gaynor?

My lip curled at the thought of that woman still under Jack's roof. Were they a couple again? Suddenly I had a burning desire to know, and there was only one way to find out – pay a visit. Maybe I could nip into Jack's local shop beforehand and buy some flowers, then ring the buzzer on the squawk box and say they were a friendly gift. Although... did women buy men flowers? I wasn't sure. Okay, I'd buy him a pack of beers instead. Good idea, Sadie.

Feeling encouraged by this new plan, I nipped back into the pub to return the glass and quickly use their loo, then set off in the direction of West Malling with a renewed spring in my step.

However, as I entered St Leonards Street, it transpired that I didn't need to buy beers as an excuse to visit Jack. I now had a totally legitimate reason to buzz his intercom because there, in the middle of the road and causing chaos, were two familiar dogs. They were happily trotting along the central white lines, oblivious to the horns of frustrated drivers and cars attempting to meander around them. I stared in horror at Sylvie and William. What the heck were they doing in the middle of a main road? And where the hell was Jack?

Chapter Fifty-Five

Horns tooted as impatient drivers tried to manoeuvre past the golden retriever calmly trotting after the jaunty little beagle who, tail wagging, was clearly delighted to be taking himself off for an unsupervised walk.

I was astonished that no motorist had pulled over and attempted to catch either of them, but sometimes folks were like that. Some didn't want to get involved. Others were possibly worried about being bitten. But this was no time to ponder upon it.

Aghast, I came to my senses and shrieked, 'WILLIAM!'

His tri-coloured head shot up and for a moment he paused, one paw raised, assessing the woman several yards ahead. Then, a split second later, William gave a yelp of delight and catapulted towards me, just as a car was skirting around him. My eyes widened with horror as its front bumper missed William by a hair's breadth. There was a screech of tyres as the motorist braked sharply, and then a horrible crunching sound of metal upon metal as the car behind ploughed into the driver's rear.

More beeping followed and Sylvie, unnerved, began to bark. Galloping towards me, William took a flying leap and landed in my arms. I hugged him tightly to me, immediately noticing that his collar was missing. Keeping my arms firmly around William's torso, I whistled Sylvie to heel. She bounded over and I realised her collar was missing too. Before I could wonder why, the driver of the pranged car leapt out of his vehicle and began yelling abuse at me.

'You stupid cow, what the heck are you playing at?' he ranted. He was about eighty years old, had the turned-down mouth of a person who was permanently disgruntled, and bore a striking resemblance to Alf Garnett. On his head was a wine-coloured flat cap which currently matched his furious face. 'Fancy walking your dogs off the lead on a main road. Are you thick?'

'They're not–' I started to say but got no further.

A man was emerging from the second car. His grim expression indicated he was also intent on having a few words.

'Excuse me, mate,' he growled at Alf Garnett. 'Don't try and pin any insurance claim on me for hitting your car's rear, because it's *your* fault for braking without warning.'

Alf swung round. 'I beg your pardon?' he roared. 'I braked because this silly tart's dogs were in the road, and I nearly hit one of them.'

'That's not my problem.'

'Well it's not *my* problem either.' Alf jabbed an accusing finger in my direction. 'It's HER problem for not being in control of those bloody animals and–'

'They're not mine!' I protested.

'Well you would say that, wouldn't you,' he argued. 'Because you don't want to find yourself coughing up to repair my vehicle, not to mention' – he rubbed the back of his neck – 'compensation for whiplash due to this neanderthal shunting my car.'

'Who are you calling a neanderthal?' shouted the second driver.

'You! You should have been properly reading the road. You could see there were two loose dogs on the main thoroughfare.'

'No I couldn't, because your car blocked sight of them.'

'I say, excuse me.' A third driver was emerging from his vehicle. A vicar, no less. 'Could you both move your vehicles to the side of the road,' he said, somewhat sanctimoniously. 'You're causing a major traffic jam. The pair of you should show consideration to other motorists when exchanging insurance details.'

'Oh fuck off,' said Alf.

'Well *really!*' said the vicar. 'There's no need to be unpleasant.'

'Isn't there?' sneered Alf, as a line of stationary vehicles began to toot their horns. 'This has just about put the lid on my day. This morning my wife left me for another man. What's there to get excited about at our age, other than new hearing aids?'

'Well I say jolly good luck to her,' quipped the vicar.

'How DARE you!' said Alf, whipping off his flat cap and throwing it down on the ground. 'Stick 'em up.'

'Stick what up?' said the vicar incredulously, his Adam's apple visibly yo-yoing up and down his windpipe.

'Your fists. C'mon. We'll slog it out between us.' Alf began dancing on the spot, jabbing his knuckles like a boxer. 'I've been in the mood for a punch up ever since my Maureen packed her suitcase right after eating her cornflakes.'

This was the perfect moment to make my escape. Not daring to put William down, I jerked my head at Sylvie. She knew exactly what I meant and, plumy tail wagging, followed me around Alf's vehicle and up on to the pavement. Moments later, we were smartly heading off in the direction of Jack's house just as other drivers were getting out of their cars to see why an octogenarian was emulating Rocky in the middle of St Leonards Street.

'I've had enough of this madness.' The vicar's words floated back to me. 'I'm calling the police.'

Chapter Fifty-Six

I was aware that if the police were going to get involved, they'd likely want to talk to me as a witness. However, it would take them a few minutes to get to the scene and I could always return and talk to them when I heard their siren approaching. For now, it was more important to get William and Sylvie safely home.

Jogging now and panting hard – William might be a small dog, but he was no lightweight – I headed towards Jack's place with questions going round and round in my head. Like… where were William and Sylvie's collars? And how on earth had they managed to escape from Jack's garden? The fence was six feet high, and the bottom panels were concrete. Okay, William was a digger. But Jack had previously told me he'd pre-empted the little beagle's tunnelling tricks by placing hard core under the fence. William would've had to have dug down at least three feet to get out of the garden, and no way could Sylvie have used the same escape route – she was four times the size of William.

Reaching Jack's development, I pressed the buzzer on the squawk box. I was panting hard now and the muscles in my arms were screaming. Come *on*, Jack. Answer the intercom. I buzzed again. Perhaps he was on the loo. Or in the shower with the radio playing, oblivious to the summons of the entry phone.

I left it for a couple of minutes, then tried again, this time leaning heavily on the button. If Jack was home, he couldn't fail to hear *that*. I dithered about whether to ring him instead. However, my mobile was in my rucksack, which meant letting go of William. No way was I entertaining that idea on a road like this one, not without a collar to hang on to. I'd have to sit it out. Wait for Jack to get home. And then a small miracle happened.

A woman and her young daughter were coming out of another house. The little girl, fizzy with energy, skipped off towards one of the private car parking spaces.

'Hold my hand, Sophie,' chided the woman. 'You never know if someone is in their car and about to reverse.'

'I looked, Mummy,' said the child. 'Like you taught me.'

'Excuse me,' I called, leaning up against the heavy wrought-iron gate. 'Hellooo!' Sophie stopped skipping and ran back to her mother's side. The woman regarded me suspiciously.

'Yes?'

'Sorry to trouble you, but I have my friend's dogs here and I can't raise him. His name is Jack Farrell. He lives over there.' I pointed to the far side of the development.

The woman hesitated, clearly unsure whether to let a stranger into the complex.

'I recognise them,' she said, coming over and peering

through the railings at William and Sylvie. 'But I haven't seen the gentleman for a while. I presumed he was away, perhaps on holiday. Are you looking after these two?'

'No.' I shook my head. 'I just happened to be passing by and they were wandering in the road. They've caused a minor traffic accident, and someone was talking about calling the police. I have a horrible feeling Jack might find himself in hot water with the law.'

'Oh dear.' The woman dithered, not sure what to do.

'Would you let me in? If there's no one home, I'll leave the dogs in the garden and make sure they're safe and secure before leaving. I'll also ring Jack when my hands aren't so full' – I nodded at William – 'to let him know what's happened.'

'Okay' – the woman was still looking unsure about me – 'but if you don't mind, I'll come along with you. There's been a spate of burglaries in the village recently and' – she gave me an apologetic look – 'one can't be too careful. You see, the residents aren't meant to open the gate to strangers.'

'I quite understand,' I smiled. 'I'm Sadie, by the way.'

'Vanessa,' she replied.

I was more than happy for Vanessa to accompany me because I had started to feel a little anxious. I glanced across at Jack's house. Something felt off. Having Vanessa shadow me was sensible – just in case a burglar *had* visited. I gulped. Perhaps he was still prowling around? Maybe he'd broken in through the French doors at the rear of Jack's house, then shooed the dogs outside so he could get on with collecting his ill-gotten gains without William and Sylvie's barking drawing attention to his presence. Although how two dogs had got out the main gate was a mystery. I had a sudden vision of William jumping on Sylvie's back and slapping a paw against the entry button, but then the picture swiftly dissolved. This wasn't a scene from the movie *Cats and Dogs*.

'I can't think how the pair of them got out in the first place,' I said, as William began to frantically wriggle. He was bored now and desperate to run around.

'Let's get you inside,' said Vanessa.

She punched a code into a pedestrian gate. The mechanism instantly released and I stepped through. A second later and it clanged shut.

'Phew,' I said, putting William down and flexing my tired arm muscles. 'Right, let's get these two inside Jack's garden and out the way.'

'Maybe see if you can raise him first?' she suggested.

'Fair enough.'

I made towards Jack's house with William trotting ahead and Sylvie walking obediently to heel. Vanessa kept pace with me, all the while firmly holding Sophie's hand.

As we moved further into the development, I glanced to my right scanning the parking area that curved away from the main gate. Spotting Jack's Ford Ranger I felt a frisson of surprise. All the indications were that he was home. So why hadn't he responded to me buzzing on the intercom? My scalp began to prickle.

My eyes swivelled back to the house. For one fleeting

moment I thought I caught a glimpse of movement in the lounge. I stared hard at the window just as a bird flew down from the roof. It landed on the sill, tweeting at its reflection in the glass. I exhaled, unaware that I'd even been holding my breath. My eyes were playing tricks.

Walking up the three stone steps, I rang the doorbell, then lifted the shiny brass knocker for good measure and pounded hard. William, disinterested, sniffed a dandelion growing out of a crack in the first step, then lifted his leg and watered it. Nobody came to the door.

'There's no one home,' said Vanessa.

I glanced at Jack's vehicle. Even from this distance I could see it was mucky. Copious amounts of bird poo pebble-dashed the windscreen and fallen leaves filled the gap around the wipers. I was no detective, but this told me the car hadn't been driven for some time. Feeling frustrated, I turned to Vanessa.

'Are you sure you haven't seen anyone here recently?'

'Quite sure. But to be honest I only moved in at the start of the year. Aside from my immediate neighbours, I'm still getting to know the other residents. I'm familiar with the gentleman you're talking about because I've previously clocked him with his dogs. But that was ages ago. I haven't seen anyone going in or out of the house since.'

'I have,' piped up Sophie.

'What?' said her mother in surprise. 'Why didn't you say something earlier?'

'You didn't ask,' she said indignantly.

I crouched down and gave Sophie an encouraging smile. 'Have you seen the man who owns these doggies?'

'No.' She shook her head. 'But I saw her.'

'Her?' I said carefully.

'Yes. The lady with hair like mine.' She pointed to her blonde ponytail.

My heart picked up speed. Gaynor. 'When did you last see her.'

'Today. I was in the lounge playing with my Barbie doll by the window. I have a Ken doll too.'

'That's lovely, sweetheart,' I breathed. 'And what was the lady doing while you were with Barbie and Ken?'

'Letting the dogs out.' She pointed to the pedestrian gate. 'But first she took off their collars. Then she threw them in the hedge. Over there,' she pointed again.

'Did she indeed,' I said softly. 'You are a very clever girl for noticing.'

I straightened up and exchanged a look with Sophie's astonished mother.

'Time to do some snooping,' I said to Vanessa under my breath.

'I don't think I like the sound of this,' she replied, looking anxious.

I didn't answer, and instead shrugged off my rucksack and delved into its depths for my phone. Moments later, Jack's number was ringing. It went to voicemail. I shoved the phone in the back pocket of my jeans, then bent down and peered through the letterbox. Another flash of movement.

This time I hadn't imagined it. It had come from straight ahead. The kitchen. 'Jack?' I called through the gap. 'JACK! CAN YOU HEAR ME?'

And then a hoarse reply. Faint but unmistakeable.

'Help me.'

Chapter Fifty-Seven

I felt as if the world was suddenly tipping on its axis.

'Oh my God.' I leapt away from the letterbox as if it had given me an electric shock. The lid clattered shut as I turned to Vanessa and her small daughter. 'Did you hear that?' I realised I was trembling.

'What?' Vanessa whispered, as Sophie regarded me with huge eyes.

'Jack. He's in there. His voice was very weak, but he was calling for help.'

Vanessa paled. 'Perhaps he's fallen and can't get to the door. What if he's broken his legs, or something?' She began fishing in her bag for her phone. 'We'd better call for an ambulance. I'll ring the Emergency Serv–'

She didn't finish her sentence because the front door suddenly flew open. The three of us shrank back and stared at the blonde woman standing before us. Gaynor.

'Oh *there* you are,' she said to William and Sylvie, giving them both a crocodile smile. 'You naughty dogs!' She turned her attention to me. 'I was just about to put on my shoes and start looking for them.'

The dogs made no attempt to go inside the house. In

fact, Sylvie appeared to be hugging Sophie's legs, and William had repositioned himself so that he was now sitting on my feet. He was also growling.

'Thank you for bringing these two pickles back,' Gaynor prattled. 'I must've accidentally left the garden gate open when I was doing the bins. If you'll excuse me, I must get back to my partner. He's poorly and needs me.'

'My mummy says it's really bad to tell fibs' – Sophie's face had contorted with rage – 'and you are A BIG FAT FIBBER!'

'Excuse me?' said Gaynor, giving a tinkle of embarrassed laughter.

'I saw you earlier,' said Sophie, chin jutting. 'You let these doggies out through the big gate.' She pointed to the pedestrian access. 'Barbie and Ken saw you too.'

'So that's three witnesses,' I said smoothly, giving Gaynor a thin smile.

'Do I know you?' she scowled, dropping all pretence at politeness.

'No,' I said firmly. I wasn't about to refresh her memory. Not in front of this neighbour and her young child. 'Where's Jack?'

'If you don't mind' – she dodged the question – 'I'm very busy and need to get on.' Gaynor lunged forward to grab Sylvie, but there was no collar. 'Damn,' she muttered.

'Their collars are where you dumped them,' I said helpfully. 'In the hedge.'

'Mind your own business,' she snapped, darting towards

Sylvie. She grabbed the retriever by the ears and tried to pull her into the hallway.

'Stop that,' said Sophie, her cheeks pink with fury.

'Clear off,' said Gaynor, giving the child a shove.

'Don't you DARE touch my daughter,' cried Vanessa, scooping Sophie into her side.

Gaynor was starting to look like she was chewing a wasp. Ignoring the three of us, she turned her attention to William.

'GET IN NOW!' she roared. But as she reached out to grab him, he nipped her finger. 'Ouch! You little—'

'Help,' came a rasping cry from upstairs.

'JACK!' I screamed, barging past Gaynor. I ran into the hallway and dashed up the stairs, William hot on my heels.

'In here,' came the faint reply. His voice sounded so weak.

I flew along the landing to his bedroom and shouldered the door open. The sour air within immediately hit me. The room smelt horribly stale, and a whiff of vomit shot up my nose almost making me gag. I stared in shock at the man in bed.

'My God,' I whispered. 'What the hell has been going on?'

Jack was almost unrecognisable. His eyes were sunken, and he was sporting an unkempt beard.

'I'm not well, Sadie,' he slurred. He sounded drunk.

'I can see that,' I said, stepping right into the room and heroically managing not to heave. God, let me get some air into the place. I flung the window wide open and greedily

316

inhaled fresh air before turning round to face him. 'You need to go to hospital.' In the distance came the wail of a police car siren. A moment later and a blue light flashed past the development. Ah. The long arm of the law was about to sort out Rocky. Now wasn't the time to trouble Jack with the details of his dogs causing a road rumpus. I moved closer to the bed and took Jack's hand in mind. It felt dry and papery. 'You need an ambulance.'

'Need... police,' he whispered. 'Gaynor... sacked my cleaning lady... and has been poisoning me.'

My mouth dropped open. 'What?'

'She told me... this morning... said... antifreeze... in my food... a punishment.'

I shook my head slowly from side to side, horrified. But then again, if this woman was unconscionable enough to turn out two dogs in the street and hope the traffic would take care of them, why not also kill a man?

'All because you wouldn't get back together with her?'

He nodded. 'Has given me... twenty-four hours to reconsider... said she'll fake my suicide.' He sounded so feeble, and the effort of talking seemed to be making him weaker. 'Get duvet off... untie me.'

'Untie you?' I said stupidly.

I lifted back the covers and was appalled to find his ankles tightly bound with string. Likewise his wrists, which were resting on his stomach.

'She did this... when I was asleep... when I came to... was trussed up like a chicken... no energy to fight her.'

317

'Dear God,' I muttered, bending over Jack's ankles to look at Gaynor's handiwork. 'I need scissors to undo these knots.'

A shadow fell across the room. I looked up to see Gaynor standing in the doorway. She gave me a twisted smile.

'I don't think Jack has any scissors,' she said carefully. She lifted one hand and a flash of silver glinted wickedly. 'Will a knife do?'

Chapter Fifty-Eight

My mouth was suddenly devoid of saliva.

My eyes flicked from Gaynor's face to the knife, and then back to her face again. Her expression was blank, but there was a messianic light in her eyes that left me in no doubt she was crazy.

My antagonist was squarely blocking the room's only exit. Seeing the knife had flagged up a red alert to my brain, and my body was reacting accordingly. It was now primed for fight or flight. The question was, which option should I take? Stay and fight? Or try and shove past Gaynor and run like the clappers? My thoughts, like a hamster on a wheel, were going round and round – looking at possibilities but not necessarily finding solutions. William had crawled into the small space under Jack's bed. Ominous growling rent the air, but it was obvious he was terrified. There was no sign of Sylvie.

Fresh air was streaming into the room, lifting the curtains. I shivered, which was nothing to do with the breeze ruffling my hair. The window was open enough to hurl my body through, but I didn't fancy the chances of a safe landing on the cobbles below. That said, it might be better to break a leg than receive a fatal stab wound. I wondered where Vanessa and Sophie had gone.

'Let me see,' Gaynor mused, looking at me. 'Where shall I start? With you? Or' – she jerked her head at the bed – 'him?'

Maybe I should try reasoning with her. 'Er, Gaynor, why don't you–?'

'Oh!' Her eyes widened with fake surprise. 'You know my name. That's strange because I don't know yours.' She inclined her head on one side, as if considering. 'Let me see.' She screwed up her face in apparent concentration. I realised it was all theatrics. She was like a cat, playing with a trapped mouse, and thoroughly enjoying herself. 'Yes, it's all coming back to me,' she nodded. 'I remember you now. You're the bitch who's come between me and Jack.'

'Gaynor, please–' whispered Jack.

'SHUT UP!' she screamed.

The sudden swing from pussycat smile to full-blown madwoman made me physically jump backwards, and I banged my lower back painfully against the windowsill's overhang. Automatically, I flung out a hand to steady myself and, in so doing, half turned, catching sight of something that filled me with hope.

Vanessa and Sophie were slipping through the pedestrian side gate. Sylvie was following them. Now they were running in the direction of where the car accident had taken place. The police must still be there sorting things out with Alf Garnett. In which case, all I had to do for now was – I gulped – try and stay alive. On the plus side, reversing into the windowsill meant I'd put some extra distance between me and my tormentor.

'Now then,' Gaynor pondered. 'Where was I? Ah, yes.' She glared at me. 'We were discussing you. You're like a thorn in my side. A nasty spiky thing. Do you know what that means?'

'What?' I muttered. Out of my peripheral vision, I could see a tea tray on Jack's bedside table. I marked it as a potential object to snatch up and use as a shield.

'Thorns need removing,' she said softly, caressing the handle of the knife.

'Yes,' I agreed. 'So, er, would you like me to go now? I can just, you know, toddle off' – I edged closer to the bedside cabinet – 'and leave you two lovebirds to kiss and make up.' I flashed her a bright smile, although it possibly came out as a grimace. My heart was fluttering about like a trapped bird although my legs, thankfully, hadn't yet turned to rubber. Adrenalin was whooshing around my body, ready to give wings to my heels and an extra bit of slamming power to my fists.

'Bit late for that,' she said ruefully. 'You see, Jack no longer loves me.'

'Well he doesn't love me either,' I assured. 'We've only known each other five minutes and, anyway, we're just friends. We've been walking the dogs together.'

'Yes, I discovered that earlier today. That's why I let them loose and removed their collars, hoping they'd get run over. To punish Jack.'

Jack let out a low moan and Gaynor shot him a warning look.

'Surely you risked hurting the dogs more than Jack?' I ventured.

She shrugged. 'Never mind that. I'm more interested in the fact that you were in Jack's bed.' She began to move slowly into the room. 'The night I turned up, you were both interrupted, right?'

I gulped. Terrific.

'Not really,' I gabbled. 'We hadn't actually done anything.' I gave a nervous laugh. 'Just, you know, a little peck on the cheek and a quick cuddle. And anyway' – I bluffed – 'I've since met someone else. My neighbour, would you believe.' Jack shot me an incredulous look as a mental picture of Fred Plaistow possibly flashed through his mind. 'We're nuts about each other.' I had a feeling that Mabel might join ranks with Gaynor if she heard me declaring a sudden passion for her ancient hubby. 'In fact, he's going to move in with me.'

'Congratulations,' said Gaynor, taking another tentative step forward. 'Unfortunately, this doesn't change my situation.'

'O-Oh?' I enquired.

'Even though Jack has now heard all about your new romance, he still won't want me.'

'H–His loss.'

'Yes,' she said, taking another step. Gaynor was now at

the bottom of the bed, holding the knife out in front of her. It wasn't very big. Not much larger than a vegetable knife, but still sharp enough to do some serious damage. She was currently side-on to me, which meant I had a tiny chance of leaping over the bed and through the door if she tried to attack me, although I'd have to really shift to accomplish this. 'How does it feel' – she taunted – 'to know you're going to die?'

I gave a shaky laugh. 'You don't want to kill me.'

'Oh yes I do.'

'Oh no you don't,' I warbled, realising this probably wasn't the moment for panto humour. 'I mean, what would it achieve?' I gestured, palms up, before letting them drop down again, my left hand coming to rest on the bedside table. My fingers curled around the rim of the tray, ready to snatch it up – china tumbling in the process – and have both a shield and a weapon. I wondered if it were possible to wallop the living daylights out of her.

'It wouldn't change things,' she acknowledged. 'But it would make me feel a whole heap better.'

Jack began writhing with agitation. 'Gaynor... begging you–'

'I SAID SHUT UP!' she screamed. Her voice dropped to a threatening whisper. 'One more word out of you and I promise I'll kill you first and make her watch. Is that what you want? For this tart's last memory on earth to be filled with the sight of your blood spraying across the bedroom walls?'

For a moment nobody said anything and there was a highly charged silence. Even William stopped growling. And then Gaynor's concentration seemed to fragment. Something through the window had caught her eye. Her expression changed from the self-assured sneering of someone in control, to that of suffering a major loss of confidence.

'Shit,' she muttered.

'What?' I breathed.

Gaynor didn't reply. Suddenly she was a whirl of activity. The knife flew through the air. As a reflex, I ducked, but the blade pierced the skirting board in the far corner of the room. Now she was spinning on her heel. A second later and she'd legged it out of the bedroom and was thundering across the landing. As she pounded down the stairs, I risked glancing through the window. Relief washed over me in waves. Like a soap bubble popping, my body's unspent adrenalin instantly vanished, and my legs buckled. Shaking violently, I collapsed down on the bed.

'What's happening?' croaked Jack.

I shook my head, momentarily unable to speak. Vanessa and Sophie had returned – with back up. A policeman had hopped through the side gate and was now hotfooting this way, while Sophie importantly pressed the main entrance button to let a panda car into the complex. Sylvie was barking joyfully and wagging her tail. William emerged from under the bed, dust all over his head. A moment later and he'd jumped up on the windowsill and was boisterously barking a reply to Sylvie. From downstairs came the sound of the back door slamming.

'Sadie?' Jack prompted.

'Sorry,' I said, trying to get my vibrating body under control. 'The police are here.'

Thank you, God. Thankyouthankyouthankyou.

'Quick,' he rasped. 'Tell them… she's gone out the back.'

A high pitched scream suddenly rent the air.

'Looks like that isn't necessary.'

Testing my rubbery legs, I cautiously stood up and lifted William out of the way so I could see what was going on. The policeman had intercepted a struggling Gaynor. Sophie was skipping about, looking triumphant.

'I helped catch a baddie,' she was chanting.

'Gedd*off* me,' Gaynor yelled. 'Officer, you're making a massive mistake. The person you want is up there, looking out the window.' She jerked her head in my direction. 'She tried to kill me, but I managed to snatch the knife off her and flung it down before escaping. You need to let me go. My solicitor will make mincemeat out of you. Do you hear? I'm innocent.'

Sophie immediately stopped bouncing about and wagged a small finger at Gaynor.

'Your mummy should really tell you off because you are such a BIG FAT FIBBER!'

Chapter Fifty-Nine

Everything that followed was, to say the least, chaotic.

Somebody retrieved William and Sylvie's collars and a policewoman held on to the dogs while more officers went inside the house.

Neighbours came out to openly gawp as Gaynor was handcuffed. She kept up a steady stream of screeched profanities until she was driven away at speed like a scene straight out of *The Sweeney*. A second panda car idled, blue light flashing, ready to take Vanessa and little Sophie to the station to make a formal statement. I was told I could give mine later, after accompanying Jack to hospital.

'We caught a baddie,' Sophie trilled repeatedly, playing to her audience. 'Before we go' – she turned to the female police officer – 'can I bring Barbie and Ken? After all, they saw what happened too.'

Vanessa wasn't in such high spirits. The enormity of what we'd intercepted had hit her like the proverbial ton of bricks, and she was now white-faced and weepy.

'I should have been a better neighbour,' she kept saying. 'I hadn't seen his dogs. He always walked past my house with them. Every day. I should have known something was wrong. He could have died. And I did nothing about it.'

'Yes you did, love,' assured another policeman with a broad Yorkshire accent. 'You've done chumpion. Bin a flippin' star. We'll make you a nice cup o' tea down the station.'

The wail of an ambulance was getting louder. It stormed through the gates, scattering the chuntering onlookers.

'My goodness,' a matronly looking woman was saying to an old lady holding a porky peke. 'I saw that woman many a time. I even said hello to her once.' She ramped up her sizeable bosom, all set for a good gossip. 'She looked so *normal*.'

'That's the trouble, Betty,' said the old lady. 'The dodgy ones always do. And of course, women always make a better job of it than men. That's why there's more male murderers in jail than females.'

Betty nodded sagely. 'You're right. My Norman would be useless at it, and so would your Bill, whereas us women know how to get the blood off things.'

The idle chit-chat hushed when Jack was stretchered into the ambulance. A policeman briefly hopped into the rear with him, assuring Jack that he would take care of contacting his parents.

'Wait for me,' I called. 'Let me quickly put the dogs away.'

'Forensics need to get in there before you do that,' said the female police officer, coming over with William and Sylvie. 'We'll have to kennel them in the interim.'

My face fell. Not cages. William couldn't cope with it. He'd be having déjà vu about the rehoming centre all over again. The poor boy had had enough disruption in his short little life, especially after this second episode with the ghastly Gaynor.

'I'll look after them for you,' volunteered the matronly Betty, stepping forward. 'They can stay the night with me if you like. I expect you'll be a while at the hospital and then the police station, so you don't want to stress yourself further. Not after what you've gone through here. And you don't need to worry about them. I've had dogs in the past and love them. They'll be safe with me, I promise.'

'That's so kind of you,' I said gratefully.

'Hurry up,' shouted a paramedic. 'We need to get this guy to hospital.'

Moments later and we were impersonating the exit of the first police car, swinging out the gates and setting off at a pace that had the blood pumping round the body. I could hear the siren wailing and, through the rear windows, observed traffic on the road parting like the Red Sea for Moses, as the ambulance roared along, jumping red lights.

Once at the hospital, everything continued to happen at lightning speed. For Jack, there was no five-hour wait in A&E.

'Antifreeze poisoning is serious,' said a harassed doctor, taking me to one side.

'Is he going to be all right?' I quavered.

'Jack is showing classic symptoms. Loss of co-ordination.

Slurred speech. Dizziness. Headache. On the plus side, he says he hasn't vomited for a while and as far as I'm aware he hasn't had a seizure. But we need to run some tests. A build-up of calcium oxalate crystals can lead to kidney failure. We need to be sure there's no organ damage or long-term health complications.' I gulped. Having rescued Jack, I'd naively assumed that the poison would wear off and he'd soon be well again. 'Antifreeze contains toxic chemicals' – the doctor continued – 'and can consequently be life-threatening. The symptoms take time to develop and can be like alcohol intoxication. That's why Jack's speech is slurred. However, try not to worry. Easier said than done, I know, but he's in the best place.'

Telling me not to worry after giving me all the facts was a bit like saying I shouldn't panic about a burning house because the fire brigade was on its way.

'When will you know that he's out of trouble?' I asked, but I was speaking to myself. The doctor's bleeper was going off.

'We'll let you know,' said a nurse, overhearing. She was checking the drip that was now attached to Jack. 'Oh, hang on a minute.' She bent over Jack, putting her ear close to his mouth, then nodded. As he was whisked out of sight behind a curtain, she came over and patted my hand reassuringly. 'Well at least he hasn't lost his sense of humour, which is a good sign. Jack asked me to tell you that his folks are on their way' – she smiled – 'and he added that this wasn't quite the way he'd planned for you to "meet the parents."'

'Oh,' I laughed, as my eyes instantly brimmed.

'He also asked me to tell you' – her face softened – 'that he loves you and could you possibly ditch Fred Plaistow for him?'

I laughed again as the tears now went into freefall down my cheeks. 'Please let him know it's a deal.'

Chapter Sixty

It was easy to spot Jack's parents when they arrived at the hospital. His father was almost a carbon-copy, except for the grey hair and heavy laughter lines that fanned around his eyes. Right now those eyes were devoid of any merriment, as was the case with the worried looking woman clutching his arm.

'Hello,' I said, getting up from the hard plastic chair in the waiting area. 'I'm' – I hesitated, not sure whether to say *girlfriend*, despite Jack's unexpected declaration of love via the nurse – 'Sadie,' I said instead. 'I'm Jack's friend.'

'Are you the girl who rescued my son?' said Jack's mum.

'One of them, Mrs Farrell,' I smiled. 'A neighbour and her little girl also played a massive part. Indeed, they were the ones who raised help.'

'We're so grateful,' said Jack's dad, sticking out his hand. 'I'm Sidney, and this is my wife, Jane.'

We shook hands. 'It's so lovely to meet you both, although I wish it were under happier circumstances.'

'Me too,' Jane agreed fervently. 'And sorry to love you and leave you, Sadie, but we were told to go straight to the nurses' station upon arrival.'

'Of course, but, er, just quickly…' I hesitated.

'Is there something you want us to do?' said Sidney.

'If it's not too much trouble, would you be kind enough to text me an update when you've seen Jack? He has my number.'

'Of course we will,' said Jane.

'Thank you,' I said gratefully. 'Now that you're both here I feel happier about leaving and heading off to police station to give my statement.'

They both flashed me tense smiles, then hastened towards the heavy swing doors that led to Jack's ward. I stared after them, wishing I was following in their footsteps. Instead, I reached for my phone and called a taxi. Best to get the next bit out of the way, and then hurry home to Rosemary and Thyme. They must be wondering where I'd got to and were no doubt waiting for their dinner. At the thought of food, my stomach let out an almighty rumble.

I nipped into the hospital's mini M&S while waiting for the cab and hungrily hoovered up a tuna sandwich. I also rang Charlotte.

'*What?*' she screeched, after I'd given her a condensed update.

'I'm heading over to the police station to give the full version just as soon as – ah, hang on, my taxi is here.'

'Flaming Nora, Sadie,' Charlotte spluttered. 'What time do you think you'll be done?'

'No idea,' I said, waving to the taxi driver.

'Do you want me to do anything?' she asked. 'I could

use your spare house key and feed the cats.'

'Would you?' I said gratefully. 'They'll be disowning me at this rate. Oh, hold the line a sec.'

The cabbie buzzed down his window. 'Are you the fare wanting to go to the police station?'

'Yes, please.'

'Hop in.'

'Thanks.' I buckled up and returned to the conversation with Charlotte. 'And listen, when you feed them, make sure you stay and watch, otherwise Thyme will bop his sister out the way and steal her food. He's more like a dog when it comes to his grub.'

'Okay. And actually' – I sensed Charlotte doing some quick plotting and planning – 'why don't you give me a call when you're done, and I'll pick you up. Tell you what, let's make an evening of it. A bit of a Girls' Night In. I expect you'll be ready for a glass of wine by the time you've finished with the boys in blue. Shall we have a takeout too? I quite fancy a curry.'

'Oooh that sounds like just what the doctor ordered,' I agreed.

'And speaking of doctors, hopefully you'll have then had an update from Jack's parents.'

'With a bit of luck.'

'Okie dokie, see you later.'

We ended the call and I leant back against the headrest and briefly closed my eyes. What a flipping day.

'That was one heck of a sigh,' said the cabbie

conversationally.

'Was it? Sorry. It's just that today has been' – I struggled to find the right word – 'unusual.'

'You can say that again,' he said. 'Earlier on, I was stuck in a long tailback to West Malling. Apparently, the traffic jam was caused by an old boy inviting motorists to have a punch-up. The police were called and, when they tried to calm him down, he told them to stop wasting taxpayers' money and to arrest two dogs – except there weren't any dogs in the vicinity. Poor chap. He'd obviously lost the plot.'

Chapter Sixty-One

The days that followed were one of waiting, so I kept myself busy.

Jack's parents were true to their word and gave me regular progress reports. He was coping well. The hospital had given him antidotes of fomepizole and ethanol to prevent his body from metabolizing the toxic chemicals and to limit kidney damage. They were also closely monitoring his blood pressure, body temperature, breathing and heart rate, and were doing regular blood and urine tests. A chest X-ray had been carried out and – at the last update – the consultant was waiting for the results of a CT scan and electrocardiogram to get images of Jack's brain and measure the electrical activity in his heart. It all sounded horribly scary and frightening, but Jane and Sidney assured me that Jack was looking much better.

Forensics had finished at the house, so Jane and I had been in and scrubbed the place from top to bottom. Sidney had left us to it, preferring to attack the overgrown garden. Huge weeds had been cleared along with the cutting back of shrubs, all of which had gone berserk in a spate of late April showers.

Meanwhile, there was news from the police. Gaynor had been denied bail. Apparently, in the case of an attempted murder, bail is denied when the evidence is both overwhelming and damning.

'I should think so too,' Charlotte had said indignantly.

Jane's reaction to Gaynor had been one of immense anger.

'I can't wait for that woman to go to trial,' she'd fumed as, together, we'd made up Jack's freshly laundered bed. 'I'll be right there in that courtroom when the verdict of guilty is delivered and it will be my greatest pleasure to watch her go down.'

'I'll be with you,' I'd echoed.

In fact, it was fair to say that most of West Malling were closely following the story of the pretty blonde who liked adding something extra to her cooking. The local newspaper had subsequently swooped and splashed Gaynor's picture all over its front page.

LOCAL LAD'S LETHAL LOVER

I'd winced at the word 'lover'. It had made her sound so current, but I'd told my ego to shut up and get over itself. After all, Jack and I weren't in a relationship. Yet. But I knew it was going to happen. It was just a case of when.

The press had also got hold of several other photographs including one of Jack hugging Sylvie, and a badly cropped headshot of William so that he looked like a total doggy delinquent and a menace to society.

Meanwhile, Jack's co-ordination had returned, and he

could now focus properly. Consequently, I was receiving some heart-warming and downright romantic texts that, in the last couple of days, had definitely developed a saucy overtone.

Jane and Sidney were aware that things between Jack and me went beyond the label of "friends", but also understood that whatever was brewing was still in its infancy and very much shiny and brand new.

Due to another global variant hitting the headlines – albeit thankfully mild – I wasn't allowed to visit Jack because of the hospital's precautionary rules kicking in. Thankfully, Jane and Sidney, as next of kin, had managed to see their son a couple of times before this happened, so didn't fret too much. They'd witnessed with their own eyes that their boy was improving and were therefore reassured.

I'd also since been to Betty's house – Jack's kind neighbour – and collected William and Sylvie, taking them back to Clover Cottage. I'd thanked Betty profusely and promised to give her updates on Jack as and when I received them.

'What a bad business,' she'd said, before I took my leave. 'Makes you wonder what goes on in the walls of some homes.' She'd looked heavenwards and tutted. 'Mind you, Gaynor and Jack never seemed lovey-dovey. A bit like me and my Norman I suppose, but then again, we've been together forty odd years. In fact' – she'd been revving up for a good gossip – 'we did one of those garage sales not so long ago. I found a painting covered in cobwebs leaning up against the wall. On the back Norman had written, "To my beautiful wife on our third anniversary. I love you." I came over all nostalgic for a moment and wondered whether to rehang it, but then common sense prevailed.'

'What did you do with it?' I'd prompted, knowing she was waiting for me to ask.

'I got a black marker pen to cover his message, then sold it for two hundred quid,' she'd cackled.

'That's not very romantic, Betty,' I'd giggled.

'Well I was cross with him, wasn't I,' she'd said, giving me an indignant look. 'I'd made a comment about how him at number 22 always kisses his wife good-bye and I said to Norman, "Why don't you do that?". And the silly fool said he was more than happy to kiss the woman at number 22, but he didn't think I'd like it.'

'Oh Betty!' I'd chuckled, taking William and Sylvie's leads from her. 'Go and give your poor Norman a big kiss right now.'

'Not likely, dearie.' She'd pulled her cardigan together over her ample chest. 'It might give him ideas and I have neither the time nor the inclination for all that malarkey.'

On the drive home, I'd chatted to William and Sylvie as if they'd been human. Anyone overhearing might have thought me bonkers.

'Now then, you two,' I'd said sternly, looking at the pair of them in the rear-view mirror. 'You're coming home with me. And woe betide either of you if you upset my moggies. Yes, I'm mainly speaking to you, William Beagle.'

I'd watched him looking back at me in the mirror. He'd listened intently, head comically on one side as if understanding what I'd been jabbering about.

Surprisingly Rosemary and Thyme hadn't seemed particularly fazed by two dogs invading their habitat, although they'd been cautious for the first hour or two. Sylvie had been a particularly gentle sweetheart with both cats, wagging her tail before quietly flopping down in her basket. Moments later, both cats had climbed in with her.

William had earnt a few reprimands from Rosemary for being overly boisterous but, after a muzzle slap, had taken on board his place in the pecking order – last – and settled down too. Suddenly my furry family had expanded from two to four.

But – in the first week of May – everything changed. I hadn't long since returned from a glorious walk with William and Sylvie and was all set to do some work in the studio, when the doorbell rang. Thinking it might be the Ted, the postie, I prepared myself for some cheeky innuendo about the size of his parcel not fitting through my letterbox, but upon opening the door my hands flew up to my face and I gasped aloud.

It was Jack.

Chapter Sixty-Two

'It's you!' I gawped, not quite able to believe my eyes.

'Indeed,' Jack said, giving me a playful grin. 'I do believe we have some unfinished business.' His eyes twinkled mischievously. 'Aren't you going to invite me in for coffee?'

I hastily tried to compose myself. 'Oh my God, yes, yes, come in and–'

'Oomph!' he exclaimed as a tri-coloured hairy bullet came from nowhere and launched himself at Jack, walloping him in the privates. 'William,' he wheezed, kicking the door shut behind him. 'Good to see you too, buddy.'

Sylvie plodded over and gently goosed Jack. Then Rosemary and Thyme decided to check out this visitor and receive some fuss, and then finally, *finally*, I was in Jack's arms and being very thoroughly kissed.

'I've missed you so much,' he whispered, as we came up for air. I could feel his heart beating against mine and I knew that he meant every word. 'I owe my life to you.'

'And Vanessa and Sophie,' I said, hugging him back hard and trying to lighten the suddenly sombre mood. 'Let's not think about the what ifs, buts and maybes. Let's just know that everything is now okay. You're alive. All is well. *You're* well.' I hugged him tighter. Thank God there had been no lasting damage to his health. 'And we're finally together,' I smiled.

He pulled back a little to properly look at me. 'I know we've only known each other a couple of months, Sadie, but so much has happened in that time, I feel like I've known you forever. It's such a weird paradox.'

'I know,' I nodded, completely understanding what he meant. 'It seems absurd that, if I rewind my life to February, I hadn't even met you, and yet here we are in the month of May, and I can't even imagine how you were never in my world.'

For a moment we simply gazed at one another, not saying anything, just greedily drinking in the lovelight in each other's eyes.

'So,' I whispered, at length. 'Where were we?'

'I do believe there was the mention of' – he waggled his eyebrows – 'coffee?'

'Yes,' I breathed, eyes shining. 'But the pair of us still seem to be stuck in the hallway.'

'Not an appropriate location,' Jack observed.

'No,' I giggled. 'Would you like to' – I gave him a come-hither look – 'follow me?'

'Most definitely,' he said huskily. 'And where, exactly, are you taking me?'

'Don't tell anyone' – I looked up at him under my eyelashes – 'but I rather thought the kitchen.'

'You brazen hussy,' he tutted, as I took him by the hand

and led him into the tiny room.

'Sit,' I instructed, pushing him down on one of the chairs at the table.

'That's it, talk dirty to me,' he fake-moaned, rolling his eyes.

'Idiot,' I laughed, opening the larder and reaching for the coffee jar. 'Oh no,' I said, twisting off the lid and peering within. 'It's empty. Will tea do instead?'

'Tea!' Jack clutched his heart. 'I am but putty in your hands. Give me your finest builders' brew and I'll die a happy man.'

'No talk of dying, please,' I retorted, flashing him a look. 'Tea it is.' I grabbed a couple of teabags from the box but, as I separated them, one tore, and the dark leaf within scattered across the worktop. 'Bugger,' I swore, reaching for a cloth to mop it up.

'Nooo,' Jack protested, getting to his feet. 'Don't clean it up.'

'Why ever not?' I asked, cloth suspended mid-air.

'I'll give you a reading.'

'Reading?' I frowned. 'Oh, wait. I remember now. That's right. Your granny taught you. She even has her own newspaper column. *Tessa's Teabags.*'

He gave a snort of laughter. 'You mean *Tessa's Tasseography.*'

Suddenly I was curious. 'Go on then. Tell me my future.'

'Okay, but to get the best result I'm going to have to rip

open a second teabag.'

'Go for it,' I grinned, handing one to him.

'Right, first things first, I need a decent cup. Not something with a slogan on it.' He peered at the mug I'd been about to use and read aloud. '*Keep calm and carry on. What's this on the other side? Oh, I see. I can't keep calm because I have a beagle.* Ha! Very good.'

'I bought it when I *did* have a beagle,' I said.

'Hm.' Jack raised his eyebrows. 'It seems to me that you have not only a beagle, but a retriever too.'

I giggled. 'You're right.'

'Dear oh dear. Those poor dogs. They must be so confused. Anyway, let's leave them out of this for the moment.' Jack rummaged in the overhead cupboard and withdrew a William Morris all-in-one teapot and china cup set, a Christmas gift from Charlotte. 'Perfect!' He set them down on the worktop, swept in the spilt leaves and then added those from the second opened teabag. 'Okay, we're ready to make the drink.' He reached for the kettle and stuck it under the tap. 'Now, then.' He flicked the switch. 'While we're waiting for the water to come to the boil, I'd like you to formulate a clear and concise question – no, don't tell me!' He put up a hand to stop me talking, then returned to the tea making and poured water into the tiny teapot. 'Okay' – he sat down opposite me – 'you can now pour, add some milk, give it a good stir, all the while keeping your question crystal clear in your head. That's it. And take a sip.'

Gingerly, I picked up the delicate china cup and tried

not to slurp. 'Not a bad brew, Mr Farrell,' I said with approval.

He gave me a modest look. 'I have many skills.'

'Have you now,' I murmured, taking a few more sips.

'But I never boast about it,' he bantered. He leant forward. 'Let me check.' He considered for a moment. 'Okay. One more sip. Good. Now swirl what's left three times, from left to right.' Jack watched me. 'Fab. Next, invert the cup over its saucer. That's it. Okay, now we leave it for a minute or so. What shall we talk about while we're waiting?' His eyes bored into mine. 'Oooh, good heavens, Sadie. That's a hot subject going through your head!'

'Do you read minds as well as tealeaves,' I teased.

'Ah, such secrets are mine and mine alone, but I might now know one or two of yours,' he joked, before nodding at the upside-down cup on its saucer. 'Please rotate it three times. That's it. Now put the cup upright again, finishing with the handle positioned south. Excellent. Okie dokie! Time for the fun to begin.' He peered within at the various clumps and clusters. 'Interesting.'

'What?' I said, leaning in too.

'It says here that you're going to have a man come into your life who loves dogs and cats, embraces the great outdoors and is particularly passionate about a woman with flowing red hair.'

'Is that so?' I murmured.

'Yup. The leaves also show a small tri-coloured dog who is keen for the man and woman to properly get together so

he no longer feels like the victim of a broken home. In fact' –
Jack scrutinized the patterns – 'it shows this man and the red-
haired woman living together.'

'Oh,' I said, my tummy fizzing with surprise and
excitement. 'And, er, does the red-haired lady look happy?'

'She does. Deliriously so. Especially when the man goes
down on one knee. In fact' – Jack rolled the cup one way
and then the other – 'I'm seeing confetti and church bells and
a bride – good heavens, it's you – and you're laughing your
head off and looking overjoyed.'

'So this man' – I said, suddenly feeling shy – 'is he going
to ask me to marry him?'

'It seems like it,' said Jack, looking up at me. His face
was suddenly serious. Carefully, he put down the teacup and
stood up. 'In which case' – he murmured, pulling me
towards him – 'the man had better get a wiggle on with
wooing the beautiful lady with the flowing red hair.'

I let Jack enfold me in his arms and, as his mouth came
down on mine, allowed myself to get lost in the moment as
one glorious kiss unfolded into another and yet another.
There was a sudden thump to my right, and a wet tongue
landed in my ear.

'Just a moment,' I said, pulling away. I turned to see
William sitting on the kitchen table. 'Unhygienic!' I said
sternly, scooping the little beagle up and shutting him out of
the kitchen.

Jack shook his head in bemusement. 'Where was I?' he
murmured, his arms encircling my waist.

'You were either washing my ear or kissing me,' I whispered.

'Definitely the latter,' he said, once again lowering his mouth to mine.

THE END

Enjoyed *Sadie's Spring Surprise?*
Then you might also like *The Perfect Marriage.*
Check out the first three chapters on the next page!

Chapter One

Rosie was having a sensational dream. She was in bed with an utterly gorgeous guy. In sleep, she smiled. Fingers were trailing across her hip. Now they were circling her left buttock. Stroking. Ahhh, nice! Arousing. In Rosie's dream, her hand burrowed under the duvet and crossed the short distance between bodies. She touched a toned chest and soft hair. Sexy! Dave, her husband, had a hairless chest. Like his head. Her brow furrowed. She didn't want to think of Dave. Not yet. She wanted her thoughts to be of nothing but this Adonis. But...nooo! A part of her was swimming to the surface of wakefulness. Desperately, Rosie tried to hold the dream. Her mind back-peddled frantically. Oh, thank goodness! Sighing contentedly, she sank back to groggy depths. Lovely feelings were returning. Her hand moved across the hunk's body. It felt so good. Greedily, she began to explore. Down. Down a bit more. Rosie paused. Something wasn't right. Why would she dream about a man having a piercing? And there of all places? Rosie's eyes pinged open. Grey gloom. The early hours were always like that. Rosie blinked rapidly and tried to focus on the features of the silhouette by her side.

'Why have you stopped?' asked an unfamiliar voice.

Rosie instantly released the piercing and the body part it was attached to.

'Dave?' she quavered.

There was a pause followed by the clicking of a bedside switch. The room flooded with lamplight. Rosie stared, bug-eyed, at the stranger beside her. He had hazel eyes and his tousled hair was the colour of dark chocolate. He looked exactly like the guy in her dream.

'I'm not Dave,' he said.

'Christ Almighty!' Rosie sat up, snatching the duvet to her chest.

'I'm not Him either.' The man sounded amused. He propped himself up on one elbow.

'Who the hell are you?' Rosie squeaked. Her heart was pounding. Head hammering. How had she ended up in bed with somebody she didn't know? She thought she might vomit.

'My name's Matt. Matt Palmer. And you?'

'Never mind who I am,' Rosie spluttered. 'Get out of my bed. Go on. Clear off.'

'Well I would,' Matt scratched his head thoughtfully, 'except you're actually in my bed.'

Rosie stared around the room. Her jaw dropped as she took in stark white walls and chic, minimalist furniture. The bed was vast. About an acre of tan leather headboard reared up to the ceiling, and the expensively understated duvet clutched to her thumping heart was definitely not from Primark. This place screamed Sexy Bachelor Pad. It was everything Rosie's bedroom wasn't. No dressing table covered in messy female stuff. No chair propped against the wall bearing a tottering pagoda of Dave's clothes. No untidy piles of shoes due to Dave still not assembling the flat pack cupboard to shove everything into. Her eyes scanned the varnished floorboards. Not a festering pair of underpants in sight. Tell a lie. Her eye snagged on a scrap of lace languishing by the door. Female pants. Dear God. Surely they weren't hers? Carefully, she inched some duvet away from her body and peeked downwards. She was totally starkers. Clasping the duvet back to her, she freed up a hand to clutch her throbbing head. A hangover. Possibly from hell. Or perhaps she'd died and gone to Hell? And suddenly memory began to flood back.

She'd been out with the girls. Lucy's hen night. Lucy, who Rosie had known forever, was getting married next month. And Lucy had been determined to have a hen night they'd all remember. Or not quite remember, in Rosie's case. Her last recollection had been dancing with the girls. Lucy had been shrieking with laughter. Egging everybody on. They'd all worn flashing pink Stetsons and been behaving outrageously. Rosie had shipped enough champagne to christen several cruise ships. Booze anaesthetised you. Made you forget about being trapped in a loveless marriage with a surly unemployed husband and exhausting toddler. And watching Lucy recently – excited, happy, apparently so-inlurve – had reminded Rosie that her own marriage was a sham. But she had only herself to blame. And her widowed mother.

'You're the wrong side of thirty, my girl,' Hester had exhorted. That had been true. At the time Rosie had been thirty-three. She'd also been nursing a shattered heart. Her previous long-term boyfriend, who she'd been crazy about, had cheated on her with an ex-friend. 'Dave is a man with prospects,' Hester's voice had been relentless, like a dripping tap. 'You could do a lot worse. He has an engineering degree! And he's loyal.'

Loyal. That was the word that had finally persuaded Rosie to walk up the aisle four months later and stand before a congregation of two hundred guests to marry Dave Perfect. It was only when she was signing the register that she questioned whether she was truly in love.

Two years later, she definitely wasn't in love. Dave had changed from a kind but boring bridegroom to a bad-tempered out-of-work husband who drank the housekeeping.

'Drink up, Rosie!' Lucy had roared over the music. Glittering lights had glanced off the champagne glasses as they'd toasted the future bride. Rosie had welcomed the high jinks and hilarity. Hell, it had been fun – something she'd not had for such a long time. Certainly not since marrying Dave and drowning in a sea of domestic drudgery, child rearing and financial hardship.

Rosie's mind stumbled back to the present situation.

Where were her clothes?

'Er,' Rosie gulped, 'Mr Palmer. Could I trouble you to lean out of bed please and,' Rosie put a hand on the mattress to steady herself, 'pass me those pants. Over there.' She pointed at the scrap of lace.

'Sure,' said Matt. He tossed his bit of duvet to one side and stood up.

'No!' Rosie screeched.

'No?' Matt swung round. Rosie instantly averted her eyes. She stared at the overhead light fitting. 'I thought you wanted your pants?'

'I do.' There was a small cobweb on the light's shade. Rosie concentrated hard on the silvery thread. 'I just didn't want to see you—'

'Ah. Naked.' Matt bent down and retrieved a hidden pair of boxers. 'You can look now. I'm decent.' He gathered up Rosie's pants and chucked them at her.

'Thank you.' She snatched them up. A quick inspection of the floor didn't reveal any further garments. 'Where are the rest of my clothes?'

'In the hallway,' said Matt.

'In the hall—?'

'Yep. You couldn't wait to get them off,' Matt informed her. 'Insisted on stripping as soon as your feet touched my Welcome mat.'

Rosie clapped a hand over her mouth. Please God don't let her be sick. Not yet. Let her get out of here, wherever here was, and get home. Preferably with a damn good excuse for Dave. He'd not been happy about her going out, or being left with the son and heir.

'Isn't your mother looking after Luke?' he'd asked, aghast.

Her mother? Hardly! Hester had made it very plain that she didn't 'do' babies. On the one occasion Rosie had asked her mother to babysit so she could visit the hairdressers, Hester had vehemently shaken her head.

'Oh no, Rosie. Been there, done that. And never again.' Which was why Rosie had no siblings. 'I look forward to bonding with Luke when he's ready to go to school.' Hester did occasionally visit her grandson, but always on an arm's length basis. She would descend without warning – usually with several blue-rinsed cronies in tow – and expect Rosie to scamper about providing endless cups of tea and cake for them all.

Something landed on Rosie's head.

'Yours I think.' Matt Palmer had retrieved her Little Black Dress. Little being the word. It barely covered her backside. The dress belonged to Lucy. Rosie couldn't afford dresses like this one. These days she shopped at Oxfam or jumble sales, although she made sure she and Luke were always well turned out. Their clothes were always freshly laundered and pressed. Lucy worked in Media and earned a fortune. The contents of her wardrobe were expensive and, like their owner, spent a lot of time in the fast lane.

'Could you–?' Rosie gestured to the bedroom door.

'Sure. I'll leave you to get dressed. I'll put some coffee

on.'

Rosie had no intention of getting cosy with Matt Palmer over coffee. The moment he'd left the room, she rocketed out of bed. Shimmying into the dress, Rosie retrieved Lucy's clutch bag from the bedside table, jammed her feet into Lucy's six inch stilettos (how had she danced the night away in these?) and tottered into the hallway. A clock on the wall displayed the time of a little after six in the morning. Dave would go into orbit.

Stealthily, Rosie crept past an open door. The kitchen. Matt Palmer was peering into a vast American fridge. Reaching the front door, Rosie carefully eased back the bolts. So far, so good. The door cracked open. Instantly a cacophony of noise erupted. Rosie shrieked and clutched her heart. Matt Palmer shot into the hallway. He punched some numbers into a wall panel and the noise instantly ceased. Rosie's hearing continued to ring like a tinnitus victim.

'Off already?' asked Matt.

'Well, yes. Obviously.' Rosie leant weakly against the wall, waiting for her heart rate to steady.

'How are you getting home?'

'Tube.'

'This is Penshurst. There are no tubes.'

Rosie rubbed her eyes wearily. Another missing piece of memory slotted into place. Lucy's hen 'do' had been at The Cavendish Club. This was a hot nightclub out in the sticks and frequented by footballers, rock stars, playboys and City millionaires. Thanks to Lucy's contacts in the media industry, there had been VIP passes. The after-party plan had been to bed down at Goldhill Grange, a sumptuous luxury hotel and spa. However, Rosie had made it quite clear to Lucy that at midnight her pre-booked limo would be collecting her. In reality the limo was a battered Mondeo driven by Karen, Rosie's kind neighbour. Karen had agreed to be taxi in exchange for Rosie doing some cleaning for her. Rosie was going to have a lot of apologising to do for wasting Karen's time and petrol.

'Okay, I'll catch a bus,' said Rosie.

'The bus stop is over a mile away. It's pretty rural here.'

'Then I'll walk,' Rosie said in exasperation. She edged the door open. A bucolic scene of endless fields interspersed with formal gardens greeted her eyes. This apartment was some place. It appeared to be part of a vast country house conversion and set in private grounds that stretched as far as the eye could see. Despite briefly admiring the scenery, Rosie's tired mind registered April showers in full pelt. She had no coat, nor sensible footwear. Stupid, stupid woman. She was meant to be a responsible person. She was a wife…a mother no less. She should have made her excuses to Lucy and stayed at home with Luke. A sudden vision of her infant son crying for Mummy brought hot tears to her eyes.

'Look,' said Matt, 'you're clearly in a pickle. Let me get some caffeine into my veins and then I'll drive you home.'

'I live in North London,' Rosie sniffed. 'It's not exactly around the corner.'

'It's not the other end of the country either,' said Matt.

'Okay.' Rosie nodded. She was aware she didn't sound very grateful. 'Thanks,' she added. 'Um, do you have a bathroom I could use?'

'To your left,' said Matt, 'or there's an en-suite in my bedroom. Take your pick. I'll go and pour the coffee.'

Rosie pushed her way into the main bathroom and gasped. What she'd give for a bathroom like this. It was the size of her lounge. A vast tub was centrepiece. To her right was a double shower. To her left a low fitting toilet jutted out of the stonework. The loo was so contemporary it looked more like a giant fishbowl than a toilet. Everything was marble, porcelain and chrome. A bank of fluffy towels lay in fat rolls on an overhead shelf. The colours were cool and understated. The entirety of one wall was mirrored. For a moment Rosie failed to recognise the stricken blonde that stared back at her. Chalk white face. Black shadows under troubled grey eyes. She had a feeling those eyes would look a good deal more troubled before the day was done.

Chapter Two

Dave was awoken by two things. His ears heard Luke's wails a split second before his nose registered the smell of Luke's nappy. Dave rubbed his eyes and groaned. Crikey, what had happened to the mattress? It felt as hard as a floor. His sat up and blinked. Instead of an expanse of duvet, he was greeted by brown Axminster. Good heavens. He really was lying on the floor, and in Luke's bedroom of all places! He sat up stiffly. Immediately his head began to thump. A wine bottle rolled away from him. Empty of course. He'd have to dispose of that before Rosie saw it. The wine had been a very robust red. Rocket fuel. He shouldn't have drunk it all. Especially after drinking an entire bottle of rosé beforehand. These days he seemed to be drinking more and more. How many times did he open a bottle and tell himself, 'Just the one glass, David. It's good for the digestion.' A mental picture of his protesting liver flashed before him. Irritably, Dave pushed the thought away. Luke, seeing his Daddy awake, stepped up the racket.

'There, there. Hush, hush,' Dave mumbled.

It was possibly the longest sentence he'd ever spoken to his son. Dave didn't understand babies. Certainly he'd never planned to become a father. Luke had been an accident. A honeymoon baby. This was quite a feat considering he'd spent more time in the bar than in bed with his new wife. There wouldn't be any more babies. Dave couldn't remember the last time he'd felt passionate about Rosie. These days his love affair was booze. Not that Rosie complained about the lack of sex, which was just as well because Dave's todger wasn't up for it. In every sense. He'd read about alcohol affecting libido. He was absolutely determined to stop drinking – just as soon as he found another job. As yet, he wasn't sure when that would be. Getting a glowing reference from his last employer wasn't on the cards. Especially after that bit of trouble involving Health and Safety, and an awful lot of cider consumed in the lunch hour.

Dave hauled himself to his feet. The room briefly spun. He stumbled forward and crashed into Luke's cot. The relentless grizzling instantly became ear-splitting howls.

'Sorry! There, there, hush!' Dave attempted to placate his baby son. The stench of Luke's nappy made him heave. Sour wine hit the back of his throat. He couldn't cope with this. 'ROSIE!' he bawled. As his headache revved up, he immediately regretted yelling. Where was his wife? And then Dave remembered Rosie had gone out last night. She'd promised to be home by half past midnight. Luke had been crying for her at that point, which was why Dave had given up drinking his wine in the lounge and taken both bottle and glass upstairs to Luke's nursery. Luke had been so surprised to see a man-person leaning against the Peter Rabbit wallpaper, he'd shut up. Thinking that Luke might just want company, Dave had sat down on the carpet, poured himself another glass and waited for his wife. At some point he'd finished the wine, curled into the foetal position and gone to that safe dark place. The place where money didn't matter, unemployment was irrelevant and you could drink as much as you liked without a wife nagging.

'ROSIE!' Dave yelled again. Luke was now so upset his breath was coming in great chuggy gasps, and his face had gone blotchy. And that wasn't the only thing that was blotchy. Dave's eyes widened in horror as he stared at Luke's white romper suit. Brown patches were evident. The nappy was leaking, which was hardly surprising as it hadn't been changed since Rosie had left the previous evening. But Dave absolutely could not, would not, change it. Just the thought of tackling the nappy's shitty contents made his guts twist. The wine hit the back of his throat again. Clamping a hand over his mouth he fled to the bathroom.

Chapter Three

Matt accelerated along the A21 towards London. This stretch didn't have speed cameras. He floored the BMW X5 M. In seconds the speedo hit ninety. One of the pleasures of driving a motor like this was the effortless ride – it felt as though the occupants were cruising at a mere forty. He gave a sideways glance at his passenger. He knew her name now. Rosie Perfect.

'Feeling okay?' he asked. She looked like death warmed up, and certainly nothing like the gorgeous, exuberant woman in Cavendish's last night. She'd made a beeline for him, and tugged at his sleeve. Licking her lips lasciviously, she had sworn undying sex to him. Right there in front of his client.

'I've felt better,' Rosie whispered.

Matt overtook an Audi. He hadn't had a Sunday morning like this one before. Typically he slept in. Then he'd doss about in front of the Sports channel, burnt out from the working week's activities. Saturdays were better. He usually hit the gym or played five-a-side football with his buddies – hectic schedule permitting. And hectic it was. For Matt was 'a fixer'. Somebody who streamlined companies. Sometimes the companies got sold off, usually for a filthy profit. When Matt was around, a proportion of people were always made redundant. Last night's client was a rich industrialist originally from Yorkshire. Due to the recession, business was suffering. Gregory Tibor owned pet food factories. Tibor's Tasty Titbits was right up there with the other top brands. However, pet owners were switching to cheaper varieties. Tibor shares had dropped alarmingly and right now the pet food chain's industrial belt needed tightening. Matt had been assigned to sort the wheat from the chaff. During their business meeting, Gregory had asked to see the sights. When a client said those two words, he didn't mean Buckingham Palace. Matt had more receipts from Spearmint Rhinos than Sainsbury's. But last night Spearmint Rhinos had been a no-goer. Matt had been nearer to his own stomping ground visiting Gregory Tibor's Kent-based factory, although the setting was Erith rather than Penshurst. Afterwards, it had been easier to whisk his client off to a good Italian restaurant followed by The Cavendish Club. The latter was known for its often famous clients. Gregory was agog at the possibility of bumping into Lewis Hamilton or Nicole Scherzinger. Matt wasn't quite sure how Rosie and her gaggle of tanked-up friends had clinched their entrance wearing flashing pink Stetsons.

The BMW zipped along, merging onto the M25 and, a little while later, the A2. As the vehicle shot through the Blackwall Tunnel, Matt glanced at Rosie. 'Not far to go now. You'll soon be home and then you can sleep off your hangover.'

'I don't think so,' Rosie rubbed her eyes. 'My little boy will be needing me.'

'You're a mum?' Matt couldn't help being surprised. 'You don't look like one.'

'Maybe not right now,' Rosie pulled at the hem of her too-short dress. 'But I will later. When I'm dressed in baggy joggers and covered in regurgitated spaghetti hoops.' She gave the ghost of a smile.

Last night, when Rosie had lurched across the dance floor to him, her smile had been full on and seductive. Gregory Tibor's ego had been mildly dented that Rosie had accosted Matt instead of him, but within seconds the hen in Rosie's party had staggered over too. She'd linked arms with Gregory, who was badly out of sorts with chat up lines. Not knowing what to talk about he'd launched into business spiel about Tibor's Tasty Titbits, whereupon the woman had laughed throatily and said she'd rather hear about Tibor's Tasty Todger. Gregory's eyes had glazed as the woman suggested Gregory join her and her friends at some swanky hotel. Gregory's expression had been an open book – him and half a dozen naked women...Hugh Heffner eat your heart out. As Gregory was between marriages, he had been only too happy to put up a hand in farewell to Matt.

At that point Matt should have left The Cavendish Club and gone, belatedly, to a mate's stag do. But the night had not been so young. Plus he had a seriously drunk woman to prop up – a woman whose friends had abandoned her. By this point Rosie had lapsed into incoherence. Rather than abandon her too, he'd taken her back to his place.

'Take a left here,' Rosie said.

Matt was soon negotiating residential roads lined with Victorian terraces. Some of the properties had upped and come. Others hadn't. Like this one. Matt stared at Rosie's house. Geez. It looked like it needed demolishing. Masonry was crumbling, and paintwork peeling. An ornamental stone cat by the front door stared balefully at him.

'Do you want me to see you in?'

'I'll be fine.' Rosie unclipped her seat belt and swung the door open. She paused for a moment. 'I'm very sorry about last night. Thank you so much for the lift, Mr Palmer.'

'Please, it's Matt. And you really don't have to apologise. It was fun.'

Rosie flinched slightly. She hadn't dared question Matt Palmer about what had happened in his bed. She didn't want to know. If she didn't know, then she wasn't guilty. Rosie slid out from the BMW. She walked up the path, aware that Matt Palmer was watching her. She had noted his incredulous look when she'd pointed out her house – and how the incredulity had turned to horror. Last night Rosie had been in such a hurry to embrace freedom for a few hours, she'd left without her house key. Berating herself, she rapped her knuckles loudly on the front door. It was pointless ringing the bell. It didn't work. Like Dave. Funny he should have so much in common with a doorbell. She rapped again. She could hear Luke wailing. Rosie tried to peer through the frosted panes of glass. She could make out the shape of the hall table and coats hanging on pegs. A minute ticked by. Then two. Tension began to knot in her stomach. Where was Dave? Luke's cries were really distressing. Behind her a car door clunked. Footsteps were coming up the path.

'Is nobody in?' asked Matt.

Rosie turned. 'Yes, yes. My husband is home.' Rosie suddenly felt gripped by panic. What if Dave hadn't been able to cope after all? What if Rosie's plans to force Dave to interact with their son had seriously back-fired? Mental pictures flashed through her mind. Scary images. Dave so appalled at having to pick up Luke, the shock had given him a heart attack. He might be prostrate on the floor – alive but unable to respond. Rosie knelt down and peered through the letterbox.

'Dave?' Her voice was shrill. No response. What if Dave's heart attack had actually been fatal? And he couldn't respond because he was dead? 'DAVE! CAN YOU HEAR ME?' Rosie bawled. Evidently Luke could because his cries redoubled. The letterbox clattered shut as Rosie stood up. She looked at Matt with fearful eyes. 'S-something bad must have happened,' she stammered. 'I need to get inside – now.'

'You want me to break in?'

Rosie looked stricken. 'Yes. Yes, just get me inside. I need to get to my baby. Hurry. Please hurry.'

Matt didn't hesitate. He picked up the stone cat and smashed it hard against one of the glass panes. The noise was awful. Carefully, he stuck his hand through the gaping hole and released the catch. The door swung open. Leaping over broken glass, Rosie flew up the stairs. Matt pounded up behind her. The baby's cries were pitiful. As they crossed the landing, the stench of puke and shit hit their nostrils. Rosie was filled with foreboding. She raced into Luke's bedroom. One moment she was rushing towards the cot, her arms outstretched, and the next she was flying through the air. She slammed into the Peter Rabbit wallpaper. Concussion stars and orange carrots exploded in her vision. An empty wine bottle clunked to a standstill against Luke's cot. Matt watched, horrified, as Rosie slumped to the floor. Dear God. He wanted to rush to Rosie, but instead his feet propelled him over to the cot. Reaching down, he scooped up the distraught infant. The poor little chap was covered in crap and snot.

'Okay, little fella, I've got you. Now let's sort Mummy out.'

'I don't think so,' said a voice. Matt spun round. A wild-eyed woman stood in the bedroom doorway. She was holding aloft the stone cat. 'Put the baby back in the cot. One false move and I'll bludgeon you to death.'

'Who the hell are you?' Matt asked.

'Rosie's neighbour. And I'm making a Citizen's arrest, you murdering pervert.'

There was a groan from the far corner. Gingerly, Rosie put her hands to her temples. Her poor head. It wasn't having a great day. First a hangover, now concussion.

'Karen?' Rosie hauled herself to her feet.

'Get behind me, Rosie. Quick! I've got you covered.'

'But Karen, you don't understand. This is—'

'JUST DO IT!' Karen screeched. Rosie scuttled over to Karen. 'You stay right there, arsehole,' she waggled the cat at Matt. Luke immediately broke into a fresh round of wailing. 'Now for the second time, put the baby down.'

'Okay!' Matt edged nervously round the cot, lowering Luke onto the mattress and making sure the whole thing was wedged firmly between him and the madwoman. 'I meant no harm. I'm just somebody who has given Rosie a lift home.'

Karen paled. Her raised hand wavered. 'You're a taxi driver?'

'He's somebody I met last night,' Rosie muttered. 'I'm so sorry I failed to show up last night, Karen. Did you wait long for me?'

'Geez, Rosie,' Karen lowered her arm. 'I didn't wait at all. Your friend, Lucy, called me half way through the evening. She said she was dragging you off to Goldhill Grange whether you liked it or not.' She put the stone cat down, relieved not to be splattering someone's brains out on a Sunday morning. 'So why did you break in? Did you forget your key?'

'Yes.' Rosie went to the cot, rubbing her forehead. Right now she could really use some painkillers and an ice-pack. 'That and also the fact that Dave wasn't answering the door. I was worried sick about Luke being on his own.' She picked up her son, holding him tight. 'Hush, darling. Mummy's home. Let's get you cleaned up and fed.'

'Rosie, can you show me the bathroom please.' Matt held out his hands. 'I'd quite like to get cleaned up myself.'

'Of course. It's the door at the end of the landing.'

Karen sucked her stomach in as Matt went past. He was quite a looker. Not that she should be noticing, being a happily married woman twenty-three days of the month. For the remaining five days of the month she turned into a screaming banshee and told her husband, Mike, she was leaving him. Mike took no notice of Karen's PMT and merely spent the time keeping a low profile. After Matt had disappeared to the bathroom, Karen felt faintly embarrassed at calling the guy a pervert. But then again, she was due on.

'What's the deal with him?' she hissed as Rosie set about cleaning up Luke.

'Oh, Karen, I'm so ashamed. But now isn't the time,' Rosie nodded her head meaningfully in the direction of the bathroom as she applied Sudocrem to Luke's bottom. 'I'm more concerned where Dave is. What sort of father leaves a baby unattended?'

'A bloody useless one,' Karen muttered. 'It's about time you got shot of him.'

'I can't leave him because I've nowhere else to go.'

'So turf him out instead.'

'I can't do that either. This is his house. Dave's parents left it to him in their Will.'

Karen made a sound of exasperation. 'So where do you think Dave has got to?'

'Ladies?' Matt's voice floated down the landing.

'I'll go,' said Karen. 'You have your hands full.'

Rosie nodded. Expertly she smoothed the tapes down on Luke's clean nappy and snapped him into a fresh romper suit. Swinging Luke onto her hip, she went to see what Matt and Karen were doing. She pushed the bathroom door open. And froze.

Want to carry on reading?

Head over to Amazon to buy a copy.

Also by Debbie Viggiano

Annie's Autumn Escape
Daisy's Dilemma
The Watchful Neighbour (debut psychological thriller)
Cappuccino and Chick-Chat (memoir)
Willow's Wedding Vows
Lucy's Last Straw
What Holly's Husband Did
Stockings and Cellulite
Lipstick and Lies
Flings and Arrows
The Perfect Marriage
Secrets
The Corner Shop of Whispers
The Woman Who Knew Everything
Mixed Emotions (short stories)
The Ex Factor (a family drama)
Lily's Pink Cloud ~ a child's fairytale
100 ~ the Author's experience of Chronic Myeloid Leukaemia

A Letter from Debbie

This is my sixteenth novel and sees a return to the fictional village of Little Waterlow, which was the setting for my last two romcoms, *Annie's Autumn Escape* and *Daisy's Dilemma*. Little Waterlow is a small Kent village not dissimilar to my own stomping ground.

The inspiration for this novel plopped into my head seemingly from nowhere. My inner voice simply piped up, 'What about writing a romance where a rescue dog in turn rescues two newly-single people?' and I didn't even hesitate to mull the idea over. What's not to like? Unless you're not an animal lover, of course! William Beagle is based on my long departed old girl, Trudy Beagle who was a crazy rescue dog with high energy and an obsession for food. She regarded our three (at the time) young children as "her pack" and we have many happy memories of the kids at Greenwich Park, always with a tri-coloured bundle of energy in hot pursuit. Occasionally Trudy Beagle would peel away to steal a sandwich from an unsuspecting picnicker – at which point we would instantly pretend she wasn't ours in order to dodge verbal abuse. Needs must etc.

Rosemary and Thyme are loosely based on my son's beautiful Cretan rescue cats, Zeus and Atlas, whereas Sylvie is completely fictitious. She's based on a dog I would *like* to own – in other words, obedient, wise, and calm. So far, such a dog has evaded me!

I love to write books that make a reader occasionally giggle and provide pure escapism. After intermittent lockdowns and the seemingly ongoing saga with Covid, I hope this story raises one or two smiles.

There are several people involved in getting a book "out there" and I want to thank them from the bottom of my heart.

Firstly, the brilliant Rebecca Emin of *Gingersnap Books*, who knows exactly what to do with machine code and is a formatting genius.

Secondly, the fabulous Cathy Helms of *Avalon Graphics* for working her magic in transforming a rough sketch to a gorgeous book cover. Cathy always delivers exactly what I want and is a joy to work with.

Thirdly, the amazing Rachel Gilbey of *Rachel's Random Resources*, blog tour organiser extraordinaire. Immense gratitude also goes to each of the fantastic bloggers who took the time to read and review *Sadie's Spring Surprise*. They are:

Splashes Into Books; Ginger Book Geek; Kirsty Reviews Books; Chicks, Rogues and Scandals; Lucysbooks26; Ceri's Little Blog; Little Miss Book Lover 87; Eatwell2015; School_librarian_loves_books; Insta - @duckfacekim09; The Bookworm Blog; Snowphiethebookworm; Ravenz Reviewz; My Reading Getaway; Books, Life and Everything; sharon beyond the books; Kim's Reading

Adventure; jay.rae.reads; Tizi's Book Review; Satisfaction for Insatiable Readers; Stacey Hammond; B for bookreview; ChickLitOutEm; Captured on Film; Jazzy Book Reviews; @enjoyingbooksagain; Lilac Mills; The Eclectic Review; and A Part of Your Book World.

Fourthly, my lovely daughter, Eleanor, for assisting with proof-reading.

Finally, I want to thank you, my reader. Without you, there is no book. If you enjoyed reading *Sadie's Spring Surprise* I'd be over the moon if you wrote a review – just a quick one liner – on Amazon. It makes such a difference helping new readers discover one of my books for the first time.

Love Debbie xx

Printed in Great Britain
by Amazon

78525781R00217